A LITTLE INTRIGUE

"Sir Steven, you can't possibly see the action from back there. Come here! Stand between Aunt Clarissa and me."

Eugenia turned to watch the ring below, uncertain whether he would heed her request. But after a moment he stood beside her at the window, his shoulder brushing hers. Eugenia's heart lurched as Steven leaned forward, peering out over the crowd, his body pressed against her side. Suddenly, the little wager she had made with Jane, to make Sir Steven smile, seemed incredibly foolish.

Her gaze should have been riveted to the ring. But Eugenia couldn't resist staring at Steven's profile, mentally tracing the shape of his nose, the fullness of his lips. He had such intelligent eyes, she noted, though his countenance was cold and mysterious. As he watched the fighters, his forehead creased and his lips quirked. The lines etched in his face bespoke years of hard experience. But there was something in his expression, some haunting vulnerability, that intrigued Eugenia. Why did Sir Steven wish not to smile? What had made the man so serious and somber that he could never bring himself to show a moment's joy?

BOOK YOUR PLACE ON OUR WEBSITE AND MAKE THE READING CONNECTION!

We've created a customized website just for our very special readers, where you can get the inside scoop on everything that's going on with Zebra, Pinnacle and Kensington books.

When you come online, you'll have the exciting opportunity to:

- View covers of upcoming books

- Read sample chapters

- Learn about our future publishing schedule (listed by publication month *and author*)

- Find out when your favorite authors will be visiting a city near you

- Search for and order backlist books from our online catalog

- Check out author bios and background information

- Send e-mail to your favorite authors

- Meet the Kensington staff online

- Join us in weekly chats with authors, readers and other guests

- Get writing guidelines

- AND MUCH MORE!

Visit our website at
http://www.zebrabooks.com

A SCANDALOUS WAGER

BESS WILLINGHAM

ZEBRA BOOKS
Kensington Publishing Corp.
http://www.zebrabooks.com

13023627

This book is entirely, completely and solely for Hugh P. Taylor, my best friend, always and forever.

PROLOGUE

London, 1812
The Height of the Season

"Would I lie to you?" asked the starry-eyed, middle-aged and uniformly dimpled wife of a well-placed senior military officer in Cairo.

With a huff, the Prince Regent rolled off her. "I should hope not. I could have that husband of yours brought home, you know."

A gasp accompanied the indignant rustle of bedclothes as the woman strategically draped her nakedness. "It's true, I tell you. My Herbert said as much in his latest missive."

"Posting letters from Egypt, is he?" Prinny struggled to his elbows, reached for a bottle on the nightstand, and tipped it to his lips. After a long drink, he sighed, hiccupped, and said, "Discreet fellow, that Herbert of yours. Undercover in that godforsaken desert, pretending he's a disillusioned double-crossing undercover agent turned Bonapartist, and meanwhile he's posting letters full of French military secrets to his better half in London. Has he sent you any authentic Egyptian artifacts yet, perhaps a mummy to be unrolled in the parlor at your next *salon,* or a stone tablet carved with hieroglyphics that spell out a secret French code? What, no? Well, I'm certain he will. Anything to blow his cover!"

The woman got out of bed and stood staring at the Prince Regent, a counterpane rucked beneath her arms. "How very cruel of you, Your Highness! Herbert is risking his life for this country. Why at this very moment, the French forces in Cairo—however diminished they might be—are probably torturing him for information about you . . . or about Wellesley!"

"I've always said the best spies were the thickest. Those nasty Frogs can pull all of Herbert's toenails out, can't they? Dangle him over a pool of snapping crocodiles! And he won't be able to tell old Boney a blooming thing! Damme, your Herbert wouldn't recognize Wellesley if the two men collided into one another in Watier's. Much less would Herbert Smythfield be in possession of any sensitive intelligence concerning the other's stratagems. Do you think I should make Arthur a duke? Bless me, there's another secret out of the bag! Now, I suppose Bonaparte will know of Wellington's dukedom before he does! Do you think you could keep that little *on-dit* out of your newsletters to Cairo, dear?"

"That isn't funny, Your Highness." The spy's wife gave the Prince Regent a long-suffering look.

His head fell to the pillow, eyes closed. "How many times must I tell you, dear, I do not wish to discuss politics or war with women. Or for that matter, anything of a serious nature. If I did, I would invite Madame de Stael to bed with me."

"Sorry, darling, she's in Cairo, too, just now."

"No doubt diddling old Herbert. Don't mean to alarm you, dear, but I think he is poking his iron in a few too many fires."

"Are you suggesting—"

"I'm not suggesting anything. I'm telling you that Herbert knows nothing because he can't be trusted. And because he can't be trusted, any silly gossip he might have passed on to you is hardly the most trustworthy of intelligence reports."

"But, I assure you, he was most adamant about this. Lord Bowlingbroke, according to Herbert, is practically revered in Bonaparte's inner circle. It is said that Bowlingbroke wears a cockade pinned to his shirt beneath his waistcoat."

"Well, why don't you seduce him then, and have a little look-see at the man's *cockade?* You can report back to me on your findings. I'd be very interested, dear. Consider it a spy mission for your country."

"Oh, George! Do you know what your are? You're a rogue and a scoundrel and . . ." At the lifting of Prinny's brow, the woman's voice took on a distinct purring sound. "And an absolutely incorrigible rakehell."

"Thank you."

"I thought I was performing a patriotic duty by telling you of Lord Bowlingbroke's duplicity."

"You were performing a better duty by pleasuring your Prince Regent."

She chuckled. "My Herbert put himself at great risk to pass on this information, Your Highness. If his letters were intercepted, he'd be executed on the spot. He should get some sort of commendation for exposing Bowlingbroke."

"Ah, a good Tory soldier, a true English hero. It will be said of Herbert that he laid down his wife for his country!" Prinny laughed at his own joke. "Yes, dear, I will see to it that your husband is amply rewarded. Perhaps I shall send him to the Far East next. I hear there is a small democratic uprising fomenting in Burma. Your Herbert is just the sort of man who could ferret out a rebellious monk. I do so hope the rebels will wear a white cockade on their robes. Otherwise, it will be so tricky attempting to tell the Buddhists from the Jacobins!"

Mrs. Smythfield made as if to leave. But as she looked coquettishly over her shoulder, Prinny opened one eye. His gaze raked her half-naked figure, and he crooked his forefinger, bidding her to return.

"Oh, well, just once more," the lady murmured, allowing the counterpane she'd wrapped around herself to fall to the floor.

Prinny closed his eyes again, indulging in the lush softness of Herbert's wife's embrace. But even as the woman pressed her lips to his, he made a mental note to discuss the question of Lord Bowlingbroke's allegiance with Sir Nigel Pennyworthy.

Pennyworthy, one of the Prince Regent's most discreet advisors, kept tabs on the political affiliations of the fickle aristocracy. Valuable chiefly for his social connections and indefatigable carousing, Pennyworthy knew the net worth, sexual predilections and political sympathies of every nabob in Mayfair. He would tell Prinny what this Bowlingbroke was about. Yes, if anyone knew whether Herbert was full of gammon about Bowlingbroke, it would be Pennyworthy.

Opening his eyes, Prinny gave the spy's wife a warm, grateful smile. She'd given him more this morning than she knew she had. She'd piqued his interest as well as his ardor, and for a man as jaded and dyspeptic as he, that was a precious gift indeed. Herbert was a lucky man, Prinny thought.

And the Prince was lucky, too, to have found in Lord Bowlingbroke a new object of interest. Brummel was, after all, becoming a ferocious bore.

ONE

"Good heavens, he's naked as a jaybird!" At Sir Steven's bedside, the deep male voice dropped to a whisper. "Does he always sleep in the nude? That's indecent, I tell you. In his case, especially. Never seen a man built so . . ."

Trevor Sparrow, Sir Steven's valet, put in, "Quite a popular fellow with the ladies, he is."

"I had thought the rumors were pure fustian."

"Plenty of them rumors about Sir Steven is just that, pure lies. But not the one about his, er, attributes. Built like a horse, me master is."

"Well, cover him up, for God's sake!"

Sir Steven St. Charles, only half asleep now that the sun was streaming through his bedroom window, growled his displeasure. The voices at his bedside stubbornly persisted, further nudging him toward wakefulness. As Trevor tossed a counterpane over Steven's lower body, Steven peeked from beneath the arm he'd thrown over his eyes. The sight he beheld caused his stomach to lurch.

"Pennyworthy," he croaked, his mouth as dry as cotton, "what the hell are you doing in my bedchamber at this ungodly hour? Can't you see I'm trying to get some sleep?"

"It's half past eleven, Steve." Pennyworthy was a tall

man with a face that looked like a rockslide. Dismissing Trevor with an imperious nod, he pulled a chair next to Sir Steven's bedside, sat down, and crossed his long reedy legs. "We've got important business to discuss, I'm afraid."

"Would you bring me some coffee, Trevor?" Sir Steven said as his valet exited the room. Then he sighed, ran his hand through his hair, and pushed himself into a half-sitting position against a bank of pillows. "We have no business to discuss, Pennyworthy. I'm finished in the spy business, all washed up, don't you remember?"

"I'm giving you a second chance."

"I don't want a second chance. I'm perfectly happy now."

"What man wouldn't be? Staying out all night, playing cards till dawn. Going to the opera with a different demirep on your arm every evening. Diddling every widow in Mayfair."

"Widows need love, too, you know."

Pennyworthy allowed himself a grudging chuckle. "I suppose they do. You always were a quick wit, Steven, always ready to make a joke of any situation."

"Well, I made a joke of myself. And you got the last laugh, Pennyworthy, so why don't you just get out of my bedchamber, hustle on back to the Home Office, and explain to your superiors that I'm not interested in spying on any more Englishmen suspected of being disloyal to good old Britannia. Why should I be? You didn't believe me when I told you that the Earl of Fitzhaven—"

"All that's behind us, Steven. And besides, I'm no longer in the Home Office. I work for the Prince Regent now. In an unofficial capacity, of course."

It took a moment for that news to filter into Steven's alcohol-numbed brain. "Of course," he said, at length.

"Well, then, all the more reason for you to get out of my house."

Pennyworthy seemed not to hear him. He fell silent when Trevor reappeared, and waited patiently while the valet served Steven a cup of steaming, fragrant coffee. When Trevor had gone again, Pennyworthy said, "It's Lord Douglas Pomroy, the Earl of Bowlingbroke. The King has reason to believe that he's a French sympathizer. But this isn't old Paris, you know, we can't just round him up and send him to the guillotine."

"Too bad. Makes you appreciate Robespierre, doesn't it?"

"He's a well-respected man, this Bowlingbroke, absolutely beyond reproach. He's blissfully married, a rarity these days, and his daughter is all the crack this Season. This is a sensitive assignment, Steve. Bowlingbroke has lately insinuated himself into the Prince's closest circle of friends. We can't have the *ton* thinking Prinny's on a foxhunt for Bonapartists."

"The House of Lords wouldn't like that."

"That's where you come in. Bowlingbroke's a regular social butterfly. And, as I mentioned, his lovely daughter is presently enjoying her first London Season, so when he's not cavorting at country house parties, he's doing the pretty in every Mayfair drawing room he can get himself and his family into. Which is a considerable number."

"Where do I fit into this picture?" Steven snorted.

"You're the perfect man for the job. Oh, don't look so innocent, I know what a tomcat you've become. There's not a female over the age of forty in this Town who hasn't cast her eye on you."

"I am *not* adept at doing the pretty, as you say."

"But you're just as welcome in as many drawing rooms as Bowlingbroke, if you will go. *And you are a bachelor.* In need of a wife."

"The last thing I need is a wife."

"No one will think it a bit odd when you show some interest in Bowlingbroke's daughter—"

"Get someone else to do your dirty work, Pennyworthy." With a sturdy frown, Steven gulped his coffee. "I'm retired."

"You're out of retirement as of this moment."

"Not for a million pounds, old man."

"No, I knew you wouldn't do it for money." Pennyworthy smiled unctuously. "You're not that sort of man, are you? I've something else to offer you."

Something about Pennyworthy's voice made the hair on Steven's neck bristle. He locked gazes with the man, instantly aware that his future had quite suddenly and unexpectedly arrived at a crossroads.

"It's the Earl of Fitzhaven you want, isn't it, Steve?"

Steven's fingers clutched the coffee cup so tightly that the fragile china cracked. Luckily, the cup was empty, and Steven had only to fling the broken pieces onto the floor.

"Yes, I thought so," Pennyworthy whispered, leaning forward. "Bring down Bowlingbroke and I'll give you Fitzhaven. How's that for a deal?"

Steven said nothing. And he said nothing as Pennyworthy slowly stood and slid the chair he'd been sitting in back to its original spot. He said nothing more as Pennyworthy left the room and closed the door behind him. *Bowlingbroke for Fitzhaven.* It was a bargain made in Hell.

And it was a bargain that Sir Steven St. Charles was powerless to resist.

Less than forty-eight hours later, a hothouse crush raged in Sir Nigel Pennyworthy's Watershed Lane town house. On the dance floor, eligible bachelors spun young women wearing fashionable gowns so flimsy that the outline of their figures showed clearly. Crowded around the punch table were anxious mamas, watching and judging every move their daughters made, and every move that was made toward their daughters. And swimming through into this sea of social ambition were the dandies, fops, and Corinthians, all the men of marriageable age, sufficient wealth, and acceptable social standing, who made up the pool of candidates from which tonight's debutantes fished for a husband.

"There he is again, that dashing Lord Delaroux," Lady Jane Bowlingbroke, a lithesome blonde of near perfect proportions, whispered to her best friend and confidante.

The other young lady, a swan-necked brunette with big brown eyes and chestnut hair piled high on top of her head, followed Jane's gaze. "Good heavens, his waist is smaller than mine!"

"He's probably wearing a girdle, Genie. He's just the sort who would." Jane snickered.

But Lady Eugenia Terrebonne wasn't the least cowed or adversely influenced by Jane's condescending tone. Perhaps that was the reason the young women had hit it off so famously when they'd met a few years earlier while on holiday in Bombay, Jane with her parents, and Eugenia with her globe-trotting mother. For while Jane, whose doting parents had thoroughly convinced her of her self-importance, intimidated nearly everyone she met into simpering sycophants, Eugenia seemed immune to others' opinions—including Jane's.

At times, Eugenia's independent way of thinking isolated her from others, causing her to be labeled a bluestocking. But the truth of it was, she'd grown up in a sort of tug-of-war between her parents, two entirely incompatible people who'd had the misfortune to marry one another, and who, in their constant feuding—which often involved one or the other of them traveling to some far corner of the earth simply to avoid an argument, or to win one—had managed to convince Eugenia that she was responsible for her own happiness. And that marriage was a prison.

Her smile was the shield behind which she hid. Looking now across the crowded dance floor at the handsome Lord Robert Delaroux, Eugenia's practiced and very pleasant expression remained fixed. "No matter what you say, Jane, he *is* handsome."

"You don't mean to tell me . . ." Jane giggled. "Oh, come now, Genie, you can't be serious. He's a silly fop, a mannequin, for heaven's sake! No one in London takes him seriously."

"I think you should arrange for him to be invited to your father's annual masquerade party. It's short notice, but there's still time."

"You can't mean it! Father would never invite such a paperscull!"

"How do you know he's a paperscull, Jane? Do you know him? I mean, really know him? I don't give a fig what everybody else says. Perhaps there's more to Lord Delaroux than meets the eye."

"Well, we're about to find out, aren't we? You've drawn him over with that pretty smile of yours. He's coming straight toward us."

Half bemused by her friend's heightened color, Eugenia sipped her punch. She greeted Lord Delaroux's arrival with a friendly nod, then allowed him to take her gloved hand and brush his lips along her fingers.

After an awkward pause, he shook Jane's hand, a bit too firmly perhaps, his lips tightening as he said hello.

"Hello, Lord Delaroux." Jane's retroussé nose seemed to tilt a little higher. "What a *colorful* jacket. What color *is* that, did your tailor say?"

"He called it lime green." A glint of fear showed in Lord Delaroux's eyes.

"Ah." Jane narrowed her gaze. "And when, pray tell, did you decide to grow whiskers?"

"It's a goatee." Delaroux stroked it self-consciously. "Do you like it?"

Jane said, "Oh, yes," in a deliberately unconvincing tone.

"I like it," put in Eugenia.

Delaroux grinned, showing his perfect, white teeth. "Thank you. Then I shall keep it." His eyes, wide and impossibly green, sparkled. "You look lovely tonight, too, Lady Eugenia. As do you, Lady Jane."

Jane rolled her gaze to the ceiling and sighed. Noting Delaroux's mortification—and what man wouldn't be mortified, for to suffer a cut from the inimitable Lady Jane Bowlingbroke was to be put at risk for complete social annihilation—Eugenia impulsively laid a hand on his arm. She felt the urge to console him, but she could only think to tell Delaroux again how attractive his goatee was.

"Do you *really* like it?" he asked earnestly. "I mean, really? My mother fancies it, you see, but some of the fellows at Brooks's said . . ."

He seemed mollified by her blandishments, but Eugenia's mind wandered as he soliloquized about the virtues of his goatee, and debated whether he should allow his whiskers to grow more thickly beneath his bottom lip.

Jane's cheeks meanwhile turned to scarlet. Delaroux had returned her cut by ignoring her, but Jane, the most charming bully Eugenia had ever met, was not a woman to be ignored. Watching Jane over Delaroux's shoulder, Eugenia held her breath. She thought she might ask Delaroux to dance, if only to get him away from the simmering Jane for a moment. Mercifully, she was spared this diplomatic effort by the materialization of another man, this one considerably older than Delaroux, far more conservatively dressed, and infinitely more serious in aspect, expression, and demeanor.

In point of fact, the newcomer looked as if he'd lost his best friend. "Hello, Delaroux." He greeted the wasp-waisted dandy with an air of weary resignation—or was it contempt?

"Sir Steven St. Charles!" Delaroux's face lit up as he pumped the newcomer's hand. He slapped the man on the back, seeming not to notice the look of irritation that flashed on St. Charles's face. "Didn't know you cared for these sorts of gatherings! Too early for the card tables, is it?"

"The games will wait." A muscle leapt in St. Charles's jaw. "Aren't you going to introduce me to your friends, Robert?"

Delaroux announced Lady Jane and Lady Eugenia, careful to avoid making eye contact with the former while striving mightily to maintain his visual rapport with the latter. Eugenia, however, could not tear her gaze from Sir Steven.

She supposed, in the initial moments of her meeting him, that his most compelling physical feature was his short, thick dark blond hair, trimmed around his ears with military precision and standing up as stiffly as a platoon of soldiers at attention. Unlike Delaroux, he lacked the currently fashionable and unruly male beauty of a Lord Byron. His eyes, a pale blue, were startlingly wolfish. His brow showed the scars of a turbulent adolescence. Deep lines bracketed the corners of his mouth. And though his lips were well shaped and full, even sensual, they appeared permanently fixed in a half sneer.

An unbidden heat suffused Eugenia's cheeks. Belatedly, when the man's gaze bore into hers, she realized she'd been staring at him. Embarrassed, she sipped her punch and looked away. But she couldn't beat back her curiosity about the unsmiling Sir Steven St. Charles.

He took Eugenia's proffered hand, squeezing her fingers gently, bowing politely, performing all the rituals of etiquette that showed his good breeding and manners. But it was Lady Jane upon whom he turned his attention, and for some unfathomable reason, Eugenia was, for the time, a trifle envious of her friend.

Jane gave St. Charles a dazzling smile. "Are you a newcomer to London, sir? Is that why we have never met?"

One corner of the man's mouth lifted. "I don't frequent these sorts of soirees. I'm afraid I lost my taste for warm champagne."

"Oh? When?" Jane teased.

Steven quashed the urge to say, *Yesterday*. "After I returned from Egypt," he replied.

"But, that was over ten years ago," Delaroux said gaily. "It's about time you got back into circulation. You can't spend the rest of your life in gaming houses and broth—well, gaming houses." When he caught sight of St. Charles's quelling look, Delaroux's Adam's apple bobbed convulsively.

"Are we to assume you are a war hero, then?" Jane asked. "Were you a colonel? Or a major?"

"A war veteran, yes." Sir Steven's expression was guarded. "Hardly a hero. I was a colonel, but I've resigned my commission now, and would rather not be addressed by my military rank, if you don't mind."

"Oh, I don't believe it!" Jane tapped him on the shoulder with her ivory fan. "A real, live hero! I'll bet you've killed a hundred Frenchmen. Were you at Trafalgar, sir? Were you there when Nelson took a cannonball in his thigh?"

St. Charles stiffened, Eugenia was quite certain of it. But his gaze fastened on Jane while he leaned conspiratorially toward her. "I'm afraid I prefer not to discuss that topic, my lady. Perhaps we can explore my military background some other time, when we are not surrounded by—" He looked at Delaroux as if he were the enemy. "Well, when we are not surrounded."

Delaroux gave a little huff.

For once, Jane's flirtatiousness annoyed Eugenia. Wishing desperately to get away from it, she said, "Would you care to dance, Lord Delaroux?"

"Oh, call me Robert, and for heaven's sake, yes!" He took Eugenia's hand and swept her onto the dance floor.

As they whirled about, Eugenia watched over his shoulder as Jane batted her eyelashes and smiled coquettishly at Sir Steven.

Lord Delaroux was watching, too. "Well, they seem to have hit it off famously."

"It happens sometimes, love at first glance."

"Do you think him handsome?"

"Handsome?" Eugenia struggled to keep the emotion from her voice. What did she care if her best friend had made an immediate connection with a handsome war veteran? Indeed, she should be happy for Jane. "I hadn't considered it. Now that I study him, though . . ."

Now that she studied him, Eugenia seethed with confusion. Sir Steven had barely noticed she was alive. She asked herself why she cared. Sheer jealousy, that's all it was. It wasn't an emotion she experienced frequently; in fact, Eugenia couldn't recall ever having been envious of Jane for any reason, unless, of course, it was because the girl's parents were so blissfully happy and well married. Perhaps it was Jane's condescension toward Delaroux which, along with Sir Steven's instant attraction, combined to make Eugenia feel inferior or left out. Whatever it was, she just had to get over it and stop acting like a child.

Sir Steven St. Charles wasn't the only eligible man

in London, after all. There were many men in Mayfair, why in this very room, who were just as handsome and just as interesting. There was Lord Robert Delaroux, for instance, a good-looking fashionable man—perhaps a bit too fashionable, but Eugenia had long since given over judging a person by his clothes—who clearly regarded Jane's toplofty attitudes as tedious. She should be happy that she was dancing in his arms. She should be happy that Jane was now dancing with Sir Steven, smiling up at him, looking for all the world as if she might melt into his embrace.

God help her, but the sight of Lady Jane Bowlingbroke and Sir Steven dancing made Eugenia's stomach flip-flop. She met Lord Delaroux's gaze and he smiled down at her, rather wistfully, she thought. Had her attraction to Sir Steven been so obvious that Delaroux felt pity for her?

If that was the case, Eugenia would quickly disabuse Delaroux of that notion. "St. Charles is a handsome man, I suppose," she said, forcing a smile. "But, he's not nearly so handsome as you."

Robert Delaroux's eyes widened. "Do you really think so, my lady?"

"Would I lie to you?" she whispered in his ear as the music ended and Lady Jane Bowlingbroke's silvery laughter wafted from the opposite side of the dance floor. "And by the way, do call me Eugenia. *Robert.*"

Relieved when the music ended, Sir Steven led Lady Jane from the dance floor. Sir Nigel Pennyworthy had pointed out the young lady's father when Steven first arrived, but Steven had yet to be introduced to the older man. Glancing about the room, however, he glimpsed the tall, gray-haired man staring at him. Inwardly, he smiled. His dance with Jane had the desired effect. He'd attracted Bowlingbroke's attention. It was only a matter of time before the target of his investigation wandered into close range.

"I've taken a notion to see a boxing match!" Lord Robert Delaroux announced.

"You'd better be off then," Steven replied.

"Not tonight, St. Charles. Tomorrow night." Delaroux grinned at the ladies. "What do you say, Lady Jane? Are you game to attend a boxing match?"

"I don't think that's the sort of place you should take a lady," Steven objected. "Good heavens, her father will have your head on a platter for exposing his daughter to such a tawdry spectacle."

But Lady Jane warmed quickly to the prospect of an outing, especially one so illicit. "Father needn't know," she said, her face lit with mischief. "As long as I am in the company of Lady Eugenia and Lady Clarissa, he'll be satisfied that I am properly chaperoned. Your Aunt Clarissa won't tattle on us, will she, Genie?"

Eugenia's expression wobbled between a smile and a frown. "Aunt Clarissa is completely trustworthy. But, a boxing match, Jane? I'm afraid I quite agree with Sir Steven. It isn't a proper place for ladies—"

"Pish-posh! Didn't we have this discussion just last night, Genie? When Father forbade us to waltz? Didn't we have this discussion last week as well, when Father told us we were too green to stroll in Vauxhall Gardens, with or without a chaperone, and too young to exercise our cattle in Rotten Row—"

"He's your father, not mine. Those rules were laid down for your edification. Besides, he didn't object to your riding in the park in an open carriage, as long as it was driven at a moderate rate of speed by his groom. He simply put his foot down when you wanted to wear britches and gallop around the track on that wild beast of yours—"

"Pharaoh."

"—like a man."

Delaroux let out a bark of laughter. "Did you really, Lady Jane? How mad!"

Steven didn't think it mad at all, though he wondered how much of Jane's daring was an attempt to get her father's attention. Watching the defiant little minx toss her blond curls, he began to understand the effect she must have on Lord Bowlingbroke, the control she exercised over him. The man might be one of the *ton*'s most powerful political brokers, but in the hands of his beautiful and headstrong daughter, he was likely as firm-minded as a bowl of gruel.

A flash of insight came to Steven. He should be encouraging Jane's misconduct, not inhibiting it. Her value as bait depended on the extent to which she possessed her father's attention.

Aware of a child's tendency to do the opposite of what she was told, he suggested to Jane, "Your father would most likely punish you severely, my lady. 'Twould be an act of sheer disobedience, not to mention *unprecedented courage*, which I do not advise, mind you, were you to attend a boxing match."

"My father is far too protective." Jane did, at least, sound a trifle sympathetic toward him.

"Mayhaps, but at least he takes an interest in you," Eugenia said.

Steven vaguely wondered at the genesis of that remark, but the element of uncertainty and vulnerability in Eugenia's voice superceded his curiosity. He derived that she could be persuaded to attend the boxing match. "I quite agree with Lady Eugenia. 'Tis far too dangerous an outing to even consider. Delaroux is quite negligent even to suggest it."

Delaroux, sensing the ladies' temptation, was suddenly reckless in his enthusiasm toward the scheme.

"Oh, come now, with Aunt Clarissa in tow, we can't be accused of corrupting the young ladies. It isn't as if we will be *alone* with them!"

Eugenia gave a look of mock indignation. "Yes, now that would be sinful, wouldn't it?"

Steven couldn't help but appreciate Lady Eugenia's dry wit. He looked at her more closely; he'd been consumed by thoughts of Lady Jane Bowlingbroke, a pretty chit, but one to whom he gave no more consideration that he would a worm upon a hook. In his preoccupation, he hadn't seen Lady Eugenia clearly.

Indeed, she was the sort of woman who benefitted from a second look. Lady Eugenia Terrebonne was a rather thin young thing, with slender arms and fingers. In her lemon yellow gown, with its high Empress waist and scooped neckline, she seemed all arms and legs at first glance. Coltish, almost.

But when he studied her, really studied her, he saw the delicate jutting of her collarbones and the pulsing hollow at the base of her neck. *A neck worthy of a seventeenth-century portrait painter,* Steven thought. Perhaps a little too long by contemporary standards, but with her large, blinking brown eyes, and straight nose, it gave her the look of a deer.

His mind reeled backward to the previous winter. He'd been on his country estate, hunting for sport, when he encountered a deer, a huge animal with an impressive rack of antlers. His heart leapt at the sight of such a magnificent trophy.

Every instinct in his body told him to raise his gun to his shoulder and shoot. He took dead aim at the creature's beating heart. He wrapped his fingers around the trigger guard and stared down the barrel of his gun.

He'd killed before, many times. In Egypt, he'd killed for his country and he'd killed to defend himself. But he hadn't been able to pull the trigger that day. The buck had turned its head and looked in his direction. A cold thrill had run up Steven's spine as he met the gaze of that animal, so beautiful and full of dignity.

Oh, he knew the deer couldn't see him from that distance. But perhaps the gentle beast had sensed Steven's presence. Staring at the deer, Steven's finger itched and his heart pounded. A terrible silence filled the woodland; for an awful moment, Steven felt the animal was judging him.

When the buck finally bolted and ran, Steven lowered his gun. His muscles ached, his blood roared violently in his ears. He'd lost his courage, he thought. He'd lost his toughness, his sharp edge. Something in him had changed in the years since he'd left the Home Office in disgrace. Steven had begun to drown his sorrows in wine and numb his fears with the comfort of purchased women. He'd taken on the melancholy of a beaten man. He couldn't even bring himself to kill a deer.

She stared at him, wide-eyed and frankly curious. "Are you all right, Sir Steven?" Lady Eugenia's voice seemed to come from inside a tunnel.

At once, Steven realized he'd been gaping at her while his mind flashed on pictures of does and deers and bucks and wobbly kneed fawns. Embarrassed, he felt a familiar heat roil through his body. It was the heat that came from desire and frustration, the heat of a man who has first realized the beauty of an unobtainable woman. It was an unbidden heat that Steven would just as soon quench with a bottle of whiskey as confront.

He looked around. Delaroux had engaged Lady Jane in an animated conversation about London's most popular pugilist.

"Yes, I'm quite all right, Lady Eugenia." Steven didn't intend to sound so harsh, but he was unaccustomed to anyone inquiring as to his welfare. "Too much punch, I suppose."

"Well, here, have a snort of something stronger." Eugenia pulled open the drawstrings of her small beaded reticule and extracted a tiny silver flask. "My Aunt Clarissa gave it to me. It's whiskey. For medicinal purposes, of course."

"Of course." Slightly shocked, Steven accepted the flask. His fingers brushed against Eugenia's gloved ones, sending a streak of warmth through his body that was only intensified by the whiskey as it burned down his throat.

After taking a short swig, he handed the flask back to her. Just a few days earlier, Steven would have downed the entire contents. That was before Pennyworthy had given him this new assignment. Tonight, the need to dull his senses was secondary to his purpose of getting to know Lady Jane Bowlingbroke.

"This Aunt Clarissa of yours must be quite an original. I don't think I know of very many aunts who would agree to chaperone their niece to a boxing match, or allow her to go about Town with a supply of whiskey in her purse."

"She is very much like her brother, my father, I'm afraid." Eugenia sipped delicately, then replaced the flask in her purse. "Aunt Clarissa does what she pleases. In that respect, she is much like my mother, too. My aunt does not allow anyone to tell her where she can go and what she can do. That is likely why she is not married."

"Ah. Does marriage necessarily restrict a woman's license to do as she pleases?"

Eugenia toyed with the strings of her reticule before looping them about her slender wrist. "My observation, sir, has been that marriage is often a prison in which two people, through their joint foolishness, are sentenced to spend their entire lives. Perhaps if Parliament made it simpler to obtain a divorce . . . but, then, that isn't going to happen, is it?"

"You're terribly young to be such a cynic." Steven took a step closer, drawn to her.

"So frequently, a man and woman think they are in love and they impulsively race off to get married, only to discover, some time later, usually after they've created a child, God forbid, that they are quite incompatible, perhaps outrageously so."

"You have some personal knowledge of this sad state of affairs, do you?"

"Indeed. My parents, sir. Ask anyone who knows them. It is common knowledge. They *despise* one another."

The adamance with which Eugenia announced her parents' mutual animosity was sobering. Yet her fingers played nervously with her satin purse strings, and her chin wobbled a bit.

"Don't you know anyone who is happily married?" Steven asked her quietly, grateful that Delaroux continued prattling on about the rules of boxing to a surprisingly attentive Lady Jane.

"Jane's parents appear to be terribly in love." Eugenia glanced sideways at her friend. "Yes, I suppose many couples are happily married. But I know of many more who are not. Were your own parents happily married, Sir Steven?"

He felt a sudden heat beneath his collar. Lady Eugenia's inappropriately personal question stunned him into an instant of silence. Then a flood of memories overwhelmed him. His mind flashed on an image of his parents; their solidarity as a couple had once lent continuity to his life. Now that they were gone, he couldn't honestly remember any real displays of passion between them. Yet, he missed them terribly.

"Yes," he finally croaked. Clearing his throat, he was

embarrassed at the emotion evident in his voice. "My parents, God rest their souls, were very happily married, I think. Unfortunately, they died together a few years back. In a carriage accident. I think about them every single day."

"Oh, forgive me!" Eugenia's hand went to her scarlet cheek. "What an impertinent question . . ." Her voice faded.

"I am not offended, my lady. Saddened, perhaps, but not offended." Steven stepped as near to her as decorum allowed. Her big brown eyes were hypnotic, her vulnerability irresistible. The urge to run his fingers down her pretty neck was painfully strong, but he dared not lay a finger on her.

Breathing deeply, he inhaled her aroma, a tantalizing perfume of soap and lavender. It seemed the room had faded, leaving the two of them alone in the foreground. Eugenia's lashes flickered against her cheeks, and she sighed. Her lips were slightly parted, and Steven ached to kiss them.

"Are you all right?" he whispered.

"I'm so sorry," she whispered back. " 'Twas rude of me to speak so bluntly to a stranger. You are a stranger, aren't you? What I mean to say is, I don't know you at all. I shouldn't have said what I—"

He laid a finger on her lips, then quickly removed it. "Shhh. Say no more. Your question made me nostalgic, that is all."

"I am sorry about your parents."

"Sweetling," he replied, "I am more sorry about yours."

A tear glimmered in her eye, but she quickly dashed it away with her fingers. Then a shaky smile lifted the corners of her lips, a smile that somehow entered Steven's body and curled around his heart. Had he been free to give in to his impulse, he would have wrapped Eugenia in his embrace and never let her go.

He felt he'd shared an intimacy with her, though she couldn't possibly have understood the emotion her question had provoked.

When she looked directly, boldly, into his eyes, his body grew hard with desire.

"Are you in, old man?" Delaroux's voice intruded, vaulting Steven back to reality. "Tomorrow night, then?"

"Tomorrow night?"

"Got a frog in your throat?" Delaroux gave him another annoying slap on the back. "Hope you're not becoming ill, not tonight! We're planning an adventure. We're going to the boxing arena tomorrow evening, the four of us. And Lady Clarissa Terrebonne, of course."

"Are you certain your Aunt Clarissa will chaperone us, Genie?" Lady Jane asked.

"Quite certain," Eugenia answered.

"You appear a trifle pale yourself, dear." Jane linked her arm in her friend's. "Come, we shall make our way to the punch table and fortify ourselves for tomorrow night. We should not spend the entire evening chatting with these two gentlemen anyway, should we, Genie?" She smiled flirtatiously, first at Delaroux, then at Steven.

Laughing, Delaroux made an elaborate show of bowing.

Steven nodded, his gaze fixed on Eugenia's. "Good night, then. Till tomorrow evening."

The ladies turned and crossed the room.

Delaroux, stroking his goatee, stood shoulder to shoulder with Steven. "Quite a fetching little minx, isn't she?"

"Which one?"

After an uncertain hesitation, Delaroux said, "The brunette, of course. *Eugenia*. Oh, Jane's all right, but she's a bit full of herself for my tastes. Rather have a woman who knows when to keep her mouth shut. Like that pretty little Eugenia. Do you think she fancies me? She tried not to show it, but I caught her looking at me. Yes, I'm sure of it. She likes me, but she's too shy to show it. Well, I relish a challenge, really, I do. Tomorrow night is going to be a lark."

Suppressing the urge to plant a fiver in Delaroux's nose, Steven replied coldly, "Tomorrow night, Robert, could well be your undoing. If Lord Bowlingbroke ever finds out we've taken his daughter to a boxing match—"

Delaroux's green eyes widened. "Speak of the devil," he said with a jerk of his head.

Steven turned, chagrined to find himself standing toe to toe with Douglas Pomroy, Earl of Bowlingbroke.

TWO

"You were talking with my daughter." The earl was a tall, broad-shouldered man with thick silver hair combed straight back. He had a peregrine's beak for a nose, and one eye that narrowed slightly as he stared at Sir Steven, appraising and challenging him without apology. Bowlingbroke possessed the bearing of a richly self-entitled individual, and if his demeanor even dimly reflected his character, he held an unshakably high opinion of himself.

"Lady Eugenia is a lovely young woman," replied Sir Steven.

Delaroux, whose head had been nodding reverently ever since the earl materialized, cleared his throat and said sotto voce in Steven's ear, "The earl's daughter is Lady Jane Bowlingbroke."

" 'Twas *my* daughter you danced with, not that rapscallion Terrebonne's, for God's sake!" the earl exclaimed.

"I see." Steven glanced at Delaroux, half expecting to see the man tugging his forelock. Then he met Bowlingbroke's hawkish gaze. "Yes, well, Lady Jane is a pleasant young woman, also. I very much enjoyed meeting her."

"Her mother and I do not allow her to converse with strangers, much less dance with them." The earl's tone made it clear that he did not expect, nor would he tolerate, defiance of his fiats.

"Then, permit me to introduce myself."

Before Steven could say anything, Lord Delaroux blurted, "My stars, where are my manners? Douglas Pomroy, the Earl of Bowlingbroke, I am pleased to introduce one of my *best friends,* Sir Steven St. Charles. Or should I say Colonel? St. Charles was in Egypt, you see—"

"That was a long time ago." *And we are anything but best friends,* Steven thought silently. He extended his hand to Bowlingbroke, who gripped it with as much strength as he could muster. But Steven's right arm was deceptively strong, and the earl's eyes grew large with grudging respect.

"You do not wish to be addressed by your former military title, sir?" Bowlingbroke asked.

"I prefer not." Steven withdrew his hand. "I am a civilian now, retired, and quite happily so. I pray only that the war will soon be over."

Bowlingbroke nodded. "As do we all, sir."

During the tense silence that followed, Delaroux pinched the tip of his nose and shifted his weight nervously. Sir Steven and the earl stared at one another.

At length, the earl said bluntly, "If you have any designs on my daughter, St. Charles, you'd best know from the outset that I will not allow her to be married off to any scoundrel who takes a fancy to her."

Delaroux gulped audibly.

Barely able to conceal his amusement, Steven replied, "I just met your daughter, Your Grace. I do not yet know whether I fancy her."

The earl's nostrils flared. "You do not know—of all the impertinent remarks! Why, there's not a buck in this room wouldn't give his left chestnut to marry my daughter!"

"I'm a trifle older than most of the bucks in this room," Steven said. "Perhaps my notion of what is desirable in a woman is not the same as theirs. Plus I am old enough to know that when a man courts a woman, he must consider whether he is compatible with the rest of her family. And it seems, Your Grace, that you and I are not hitting it off so very famously."

"Indeed not!" The earl's chest puffed out. "I forbid you to speak with my daughter, sir, ever again! If you do, sir, I will—"

Call you out, were the words on the tip of the earl's tongue.

For an instant, Steven thought sickly that he might have to conjure up an apology for the old man. Being called out would do little to further his investigation into Bowlingbroke's alleged French sympathies. Fortunately, however, he was rescued by the appearance of a woman who looked remarkably similar to Lady Jane, only that she was twenty years older.

"Are you threatening to cross swords with another of Jane's potential suitors, dear?" The lady put a restraining hand on the earl's arm and smiled indulgently at him.

Bowlingbroke's angry expression vanished. In its stead bloomed a radish-tinged blush and a look of flustered embarrassment. "But Sally, dear, this confounded upstart made as if he ain't even interested in our Jane—"

The woman laughed easily. And prettily, too, Steven thought. He took her proffered hand as Delaroux babbled an almost incoherent introduction.

"Are you all right, Robert?" she asked.

"My throat's a bit dry, don't mind if I have another punch, would anyone like a drink?" he stammered.

Bowlingbroke eyed Delaroux with a mixture of pity and bewilderment as the young dandy sauntered across the room. "Damme, but that boy is strange," the earl muttered.

Ignoring her husband's vulgarity, Lady Sally Bowlingbroke continued to smile at Sir Steven. "This one hardly looks like an upstart, Douglas."

The earl's focus quickly returned. "Well, then, he's too old for Jane. Not suitable at all. He should leave her alone from now on."

"Does she fancy him?" Lady Bowlingbroke asked her husband.

"How should I know? The child's affections shift daily. Last week, she thought she fancied Lord Turnbull, the week before it was Prinny's younger brother."

"Not that it is any of my business, but I should think you'd want to shoo Prinny's brothers away," Steven said. "I wouldn't want a daughter of mine, if I had any, to fall in love with one of those disreputable characters."

"Quite right," Lady Bowlingbroke said. "We were relieved when Lord Turnbull turned her head, to tell the truth."

"You were relieved, Sally. I wasn't." The earl's bottom lip thrust forward like a pouting child's. "Turnbull's got a bit of a reputation, dear."

"For what, dear?"

The earl shook his head, evidently unwilling to disclose such unsavory information to the sensitive ears of his beloved wife.

She looked at Steven again. "Oh, well, it doesn't signify. Jane doesn't like him anymore. He came to Almack's with a tear in his stocking a few nights ago."

"How dreadful," Steven said. "No man who has a tear in his stocking is worthy of your daughter."

"According to my husband, no man is worthy of Jane, period."

"Poppycock! I only want her to be happily married, Sally. I want her to find the perfect husband. What is wrong with that?"

"Nothing, dear. But I am happily married and I did not find the perfect husband."

"Oh, Sally!" The earl was thoroughly outdone and outwitted. He started to say something, then clamped his lips shut. Staring across the room at nothing, he worked his jaw, apparently quelling a violent outburst. Finally, he turned, pointed a long, thick finger at Steven, and said, "Mark my words, young man, if you are even so much as thinking about courting my daughter, you'd best go about it with as much reverence and respect as if you were courting the Queen herself! For I will not tolerate a bounder chasing her skirts nor will I allow a fortune hunter inveigling himself into her untested heart."

"I assure you, Your Grace, I am neither a bounder nor a fortune hunter."

"Well." Grasping his lapels, the earl stood ramrod straight. "See to it that you behave honorably toward her. Or I will have no alternative but to—"

"Douglas, dear, didn't you say he wasn't even certain whether he liked her?"

"For God's sake, Sally, every man who sees Jane is smitten with her."

Lady Sally Bowlingbroke's smile finally faltered. "Is that so, Douglas? Dear me, I hope she does not share your opinion. For that would make her a very dull girl, wouldn't it?"

Steven, having succeeded in getting Bowlingbroke's attention—for that was, after all, the purpose of his attending Pennyworthy's soiree—abruptly allowed as how he'd been pleased to meet Lord and Lady Bowlingbroke and that he was late for a card game and had to leave. The earl barely said good night, but Lady Bowlingbroke smiled warmly at Steven again and bade him a pleasant evening.

"I hope to see you again, sir," she said as her husband made a rude grunt and turned away.

Eager for a breath of fresh air, Steven made for the

door. He hated these sorts of parties, where people posed in their finest outfits, and where every dance, every conversation, indeed, every unspoken physical gesture that passed between the participants became fodder for drawing room gossips the following day. He couldn't get through the throngs of people quickly enough.

But he was halted in the entrance hall by a birdlike clasp around his arm. Turning, he stared into Delaroux's worried gaze. "What the devil! Take your hands off me, Robert. And what the hell did you mean when you introduced me as one of your best friends? I hardly know you outside Watier's and Tattersall's."

Delaroux looked crestfallen. "I've always liked you, Steven. I thought you liked me, too. Forgive me for exaggerating our acquaintance, but that blasted old Bowlingbroke stares down his nose at me as if I were a . . . nobody! Just wanted the old man to think I had some *substance.*"

"And you think that being known as *my* friend lends you substance?" Steven felt a pang of pity for the poor boy.

"You are held in high regard among the *ton,* St. Charles, you must know that. Even if you have scowled constantly since the day you returned from Egypt. Even if you shun every parlor in Mayfair, and prefer to spend your time prowling the gaming houses and brothels. You're a war hero, after all. And your movements in London have been cloaked in mystery. Some tonguewaggers go so far as to suggest you were once a spy, but that's ridiculous, isn't it? Still, the speculation intrigues the fashionable ladies, especially the widows. You must be very successful with the widows, are you not, old man?"

"Thank you, Robert, for sharing this intelligence with me." St. Charles wanted to slap the younger man. "It is always good to know one's reputation. I am leaving now. I have had enough of this silly party. Christ on a raft, I don't know how even you can stand it!"

"Only he is an overbearing prig, isn't he?" Delaroux took a step toward Steven, who took a step backward. "Bowlingbroke, I mean. Even if I were interested in Jane, which of course I'm not because she's far too high in the instep for my tastes, that father of hers would throw me off."

Recalling his duty to the Home Office, Steven hesitated. "Yes, well, he is a bit—"

"Jane calls him overprotective. I think he is a tyrant."

"Then why on earth do you wish to risk your neck by taking Jane and Eugenia to a boxing match?"

A tentative smile trembled on Delaroux's lips. "Because the ladies want to go! And it will be ever so much fun. And with Aunt Clarissa as chaperone, the old eagle need never know!"

"You're ripping it too close to the seam, Robert. I ought not to be a party to such tomfoolery. We are asking for trouble."

Delaroux's head bobbed gaily. "Perhaps. But I am willing to take the risk, sir. Are you?"

Nodding curtly, Steven sighed. "Pick me up in your carriage at eight o'clock sharp tomorrow night. From there, we will go to the Terrebonne's. I presume you know where this Aunt Clarissa resides. And if this escapade blows up in our faces, Robert, don't say I didn't warn you. We might both find ourselves on the dueling field before this is over."

A sort of fevered intensity lit in Delaroux's eyes. He really was quite mad, Steven thought, but there was something puplike about him, as if he were desperate for affection and would do almost anything to obtain it.

"Tell me something, St. Charles."

"I'm in a hurry, Robert, what is it?"

"What are you planning to wear tomorrow night? And do you think I should carry my white-thorn cane, or would it simply be in the way once we are at the boxing match?"

As Sir Steven departed, Delaroux stood stroking his goatee and admiring his reflection in a looking glass hanging on the wall in the foyer. A casual observer might have thought the man supremely satisfied with the mirror's image. But Steven knew that men who stared at themselves obsessively saw nothing but defects.

"Dashie, settle down, girl!" Lady Clarissa Terrebonne sat on a pink and green chintz-covered sofa in the first-floor drawing room of her Curzon Street town house. Beside her, a fitful old dachshund, with eyes as opaque as milk jugs, trod the cushions and whined. Only after she'd made several circles, did the dog settle down beside her mistress and begin to pant rhythmically. "I declare, this is one of the most daring adventures you girls have embarked on. Why, Jane, dear, if your father ever discovered—"

"If, if, if! But he shall not!" Across from Lady Terrebonne, Lady Jane Bowlingbroke perched on a delicate gilt chair. In a pink-striped gown and cherry-colored pinafore, she looked as much a part of the room's decor as the patterned French wallpaper or the pink-enameled panels of the dadoed walls.

"Do not be so certain, Jane." Standing at the sideboard, Lady Eugenia refilled her tiny silver flask with whiskey.

"Genie, have you emptied your flask so quickly?" Aunt Clarissa frowned. "Dear me, child, I fear that you are drinking too heavily of those spirits. Did I tell you that your mother gave me that little flask? 'Twas a gift to her from some rakish sheik she met while painting watercolors in Persia."

Not wishing to explain how her flask came to be empty, Eugenia asked, "Have you ever seen any evidence of Mother's watercolors, Aunt?"

The question seemed to provoke Lady Clarissa to distraction. "Your mother is a very talented artist. That is why she travels all over the world in search of worthy subjects."

"And never has a single painting to show for all her intrepidness."

Lady Jane said, "I wish my mother were as exciting as yours, Genie. My parents are such dullards."

Eugenia crossed the room and took the gilt chair opposite Jane's. "I only wish that my parents were as dull as yours. And as ordinary. Believe me, Jane, you wouldn't like it if your parents had declared war on one another, then traipsed off to opposite ends of the earth to reconnoiter and plot their attacks."

"Oh, dear, don't let's get started." Lady Clarissa's wattled chin quivered as she patted Dashie's head. Ten years older than her brother Sir Albert Terrebonne, Clarissa looked every bit her age and nothing like Eugenia. Short and round, with ginger-colored hair piled willy-nilly atop her head, she was deceptively matronly in her appearance. The crocheted shawl, stiff lawn dress, and sturdy boots she wore projected an air of Puritanism. But beneath her primness was one of the most unconventional and eccentric souls Eugenia had ever met.

Aside from her fanatical devotion to Dashie, for example, Clarissa collected doorstops, and there were more than a few of her acquaintances who'd noticed that some of theirs were missing subsequent to Lady Clarissa having paid a call.

But not a one of her friends had ever had the courage

to accuse Lady Clarissa of purloining their doorstops. The woman was simply too benign. Not to mention that her brother Sir Albert had a ferocious temper and would undoubtedly hasten to trounce anyone who dared utter a word against his sister.

Eugenia could only wish that Sir Albert felt such loyalty and devotion to his wife, Lady Alexandra.

"Let's talk about something else, then," suggested Eugenia. "What did you think about Lord Delaroux's jacket last night, Janie?"

Flaxen curls bounced as Lady Jane shuddered. "Dreadful!"

"And his goatee?"

"Scandalous!"

"Oh, dear," Lady Clarissa murmured. "He's grown a goatee? Oh, he is a bad boy, that one."

"Very bad," Jane said. "And he drives Father mad with his silly grins and peacock airs!"

"I think he is rather sweet," Eugenia said. "He always dances with us, Janie, no matter who else is present. He brings us punch, he devises mischief, and he drives like a bat out of hell every time he gets us in his barouche. What more could you ask for?"

Jane's cheeks colored. "I could ask for a good deal more, such as a pink who knows how to dress properly and one who could carry on a conversation with Father without swallowing his tongue!"

"That is a great deal to ask for," said Lady Clarissa.

"Someone like Sir Steven, for example." Lady Jane turned an expectant gaze on Eugenia.

Surprised at the little shock that rippled through her body, Eugenia fell silent. She'd met St. Charles only once, the night before, and yet she'd spent nearly the entire day thinking about him. Or rather, his picture had inhabited her mind, like a dream that she couldn't remember the whole of, but couldn't quite forget, either.

She shouldn't have said what she did. Blurting out the fact that her parents despised one another was silly. Sir Steven probably thought her an indiscreet brat, a *child*. Her domestic problems would be a triviality to a man who'd been to war. He had most likely dismissed her as an inconsequential little bit of baggage, a girl who just happened to be standing beside the magnificent Lady Jane Bowlingbroke, whose heart every bachelor in Town seemed determined to win.

Regret burned through her, but Eugenia tamped down her emotions. If Steven preferred Jane, nothing could be done about it. It wouldn't do to let Jane see her envy. And Eugenia had no intention of allowing anyone, even Aunt Clarissa, to know how deeply she'd been attracted to Sir Steven St. Charles. It was a passing infatuation, she assured herself, a little secret pleasure which would dissipate the moment the man committed some egregious faux pas such as picking his teeth with a sliver of match, or wearing the wrong sort of boots.

She almost hoped he *would* do something rude or boorish to ruin her infatuation. It was, after all, so painful to be intrigued by a man who was intrigued by someone else. And it was painful, yes, physically so, to try and remember every angle and shadow of his handsome face, to recreate every nuance of his voice, and to relive every word he had spoken to her. She'd never felt this way before, never experienced this sort of obsession. She hated the feeling of powerlessness that had come over her. And she couldn't wait to see him again.

Mr. Greville, the butler, appeared on the threshold and announced the arrival of Sir Steven St. Charles and Lord Robert Delaroux. As Eugenia and Jane stood, the gentlemen entered, Delaroux in the lead, crossing the room to Lady Clarissa with a glowing smile on his face.

"Lady Clarissa, you look absolutely beautiful!" He took the spinster's hand and lovingly kissed her knuckles.

"Don't forget Dashie, my lord!" Lady Clarissa said.

Without missing a beat, Lord Delaroux bent even lower and gave the dog a kiss on the head. He bowed to Jane and Eugenia, neither of whom regarded it as a slight that he greeted Dashie before them. Then, he introduced Sir Steven to Lady Clarissa. At last, he and Steven stood before the mantelpiece while the young ladies resumed their seats.

He was, Eugenia thought of Sir Steven St. Charles, *not* the most handsome man she'd ever seen. His nose was a trifle prominent; acne had once ravaged his brow. His expression was that of someone permanently bereft, and when he crossed his arms over his chest, he projected haughty detachment, as if he were present in Lady Clarissa's drawing room, not by choice, but by some sort of moral duty. She ought not to have thought him so wildly appealing, but she did.

A wave of heat worked its way up from Eugenia's toes to her face. A swig from her flask would have calmed her nerves, but she didn't dare in front of Aunt Clarissa. Instead, she had to sit and smile and pretend she wasn't in the least interested in the handsome man standing on the hearth, and that she wasn't even remotely aware of his slender hips and muscular legs, legs that were encased in buff breeches so well-fitted they hugged every muscle of his calves and thighs and showed the outline of his masculinity.

Her lashes flickered and she averted her gaze. Good God, but she'd never seen a man built so . . . so much like a man. She looked at her aunt, saw the older woman's gaze sweep over St. Charles's figure, saw the widening of Aunt Clarissa's eyes . . . and Eugenia very nearly released a nervous giggle. Had it not been for Delaroux and Lady Jane chattering away, she would have had to excuse herself to gain privacy, splash cold water on her face, and rid herself of the tingly, prickly feeling that invaded her limbs.

Her very toes tingled. She dared another glance at Sir Steven. This time he caught her gaze and stared back, his blue eyes penetrating. There was not the least hint of a smile on his lips, but his expression was not unpleasant. Rather it was frank and curious, as if he were questioning her interest in him. Incapable of sustaining eye contact with the man, she looked at Jane. The heat in Eugenia's blood soared uncontrollably.

"You've grown terribly quiet," Jane said. "You're not chickening out on us, are you, Genie?"

"On the contrary, I'm looking forward to the boxing matches. Who is on the bill tonight, Lord Delaroux?"

"Call me Robert, if you please, and I don't want to have to remind you again!" Delaroux removed a crumpled broadsheet from his inner vest pocket, and recited the names of the night's competitors. "Gentleman Jack is going at it with Dickson Creevy, the young upstart from Dublin. That's in the third match, but we'd best be on our way if we want to see the start-up rounds!"

Aunt Clarissa stood, upsetting Dashie, who tumbled to the floor in a heap and stayed there, seemingly frozen. Lord Delaroux scooped up the dog, but his quick action failed to invigorate the animal; rather, Dashie lolled on her back in his arms, somewhat like an infant, blinking her clouded eyes and apparently relaxing completely. Delaroux, clearly at a loss as to what to do with the dog, looked entreatingly at Lady Clarissa.

"She is very old, my lord," confided Lady Clarissa.

"And suffers so from anxiety whenever she is separated from me. She seems to like you though, or at least your goatee. Oh, dear, I hope you don't mind that she is licking you in the face. Some men are so prissy about such things."

Delaroux's smile was as feeble as the dog he held. A muscle in his face spasmed as Dashie nibbled on his chin whiskers.

"I wonder, would you hold her there, yes, just like that, until Mr. Greville comes and takes her?" Lady Clarissa reached out, patted Dashie, and gave Delaroux a warm, encouraging smile. "Oh, good Dashie, Mr. Greville will sit with you while I am gone. Wait here, my lords. I shall send him up! Can't have Dashie brought downstairs, you know. Upsets her so to see me leaving out the front door with my cloak on! Come girls, we shall wait for the man in the carriage."

"Oh, for pity's sake," Jane complained as she hurried down the steps. "We will never hear the end of it if Dashie ruins his goatee."

"Dashie could only improve the looks of that goatee," Aunt Clarissa replied.

In the foyer, Lady Jane donned a light woolen pelisse with military epaulets while Eugenia draped a handsome dark gray cape over her simple pale gray muslin gown. The difference in their attire was stunning, and Eugenia noticed, perhaps for the first time, that she appeared somewhat drab beside her best friend.

Inside the dimly lit carriage, squashed in between Aunt Clarissa and Lady Jane so that the gentlemen could sit on the leather bench opposite, Eugenia forced down another surge of restlessness. She wasn't jealous of Jane; no that wasn't it at all, she realized. She wouldn't have been caught dead in that cherry-colored getup of Jane's; the whole ensemble looked to Eugenia like a concoction of froth and sugar, a confection meant to be eaten, not worn.

No, it was her attraction to Steven that was eating her up inside. It was the fact that he wasn't at all interested in her, and there wasn't a thing she could do about it.

Except forget about him, and focus her mind on something else.

"We should have a wager, Jane," Eugenia said, gasping as Aunt Clarissa's girth spread out along the squabs and the girls were squeezed more thoroughly against one another and the side of the carriage compartment. "It will make this outing a good deal more exciting."

Jane replied breathlessly, "What a grand idea! What shall we wager on?"

"I don't know much about boxing."

"Nor do I," Jane managed.

"Wager on something else, then," Aunt Clarissa suggested. "Such as how many times Lord Delaroux will stroke his chin whiskers during the boxing match. I believe he did it three times while standing at the mantelpiece."

"And would have done it more if the mirror hadn't been so inconveniently placed behind him," Eugenia said.

"He fancies you," Jane declared. "Don't you think so?"

"I think he likes every woman under the age of ninety," returned Eugenia.

"He's a fickle rogue, that's what he is!" Jane cried.

Eugenia gave her friend a measured sidelong gaze. "I find myself in the dizzy and curious position of alternately defending and ridiculing the man."

"Well, he is nothing but a light-headed flirt; you said so yourself."

"Oh, delightful!" crowed Aunt Clarissa. "And to think I was flattered by his attentions. Do you mean to say it wasn't my amazing beauty that caused him to linger over the back of my hand like that? Dear me, what a letdown. Well, it doesn't signify. I still think him splendidly entertaining, if you want to know."

Jane sniffed. "I think him silly."

"All right, then, we shall bet on something else," Eugenia said.

"I know." Jane gave a little grunt as Aunt Clarissa's hips oozed wider on the bench. "We shall wager on Sir Steven's behavior."

"What about it?" Eugenia released her breath, well aware that every inch of her own expansion added discomfort to Jane's predicament.

"Ouch! Move over, will you?"

"I can't!" said Eugenia.

Aunt Clarissa said, "I'm very sorry, dears! There doesn't seem to be as much room in these new carriages as there was in the old ones!"

Eugenia glanced out the window. The carriage lamp cast a golden glow on the street outside, and the men could be seen exiting Lady Clarissa's town house and making their way to the street. "Hurry, Jane, we've got to decide. They'll be here in a moment."

"Sir Steven—oomph!" Jane's elbow jabbed Eugenia's ribs. "The man never smiles. Never!"

"So? Would you like to bet that he smiles during the boxing match?"

Aunt Clarissa shifted her weight. Eugenia pressed closer to Jane. Jane gave a tiny shriek and spurted from her seat, landing in the floor on her hands and knees.

"Oh, dear," murmured Aunt Clarissa.

"Hurry, name the bet!" said Eugenia, as boot steps crunched closer.

Jane, her pretty hat tilted precariously to one side, looked over her shoulder, blew a feather out of her mouth, and purred mischievously, "I bet you cannot get Sir Steven to smile, Eugenia."

"Oh, what a jolly bet," Aunt Clarissa warbled.

The door to the carriage opened just as Eugenia met her friend's challenging gaze and said, "All right, Jane. You're on."

THREE

Lord Delaroux, smelling faintly of dog, and crouched in the threshold of the carriage compartment, surveyed the scene in an instant. "Are you injured?" he asked, assisting Lady Jane to her feet. "Here, let me help you onto the squabs."

He took her hands and guided her to the opposite bench. Jane fussed with her hat and her pelisse while Lord Delaroux looked around nervously.

From outside the carriage came Sir Steven's deep voice. "I daresay, Robert, we should consider altering the seating arrangements."

"Yes, yes." Robert was by far the tallest of the group, and aside from Lady Clarissa, the widest hipped. Clearly, he and the older woman should share a bench, with the other three sharing the opposite, but Delaroux hesitated.

Sir Steven's impatience seemed at a breaking point. Climbing into the carriage, he said, "Sit by Lady Clarissa, Robert, and you, Lady Eugenia, you must sit beside Lady Jane. Come now, we are going to be late if we don't hurry!"

Jane sprang up and deposited herself beside Eugenia. Sir Steven settled in beside Eugenia, nearest the door, while Lord Delaroux sat opposite with Lady Clarissa.

The tiger slammed shut the door, and after a moment, the equipage lurched forward.

Packed tightly between Jane and Sir Steven, Eugenia felt every bump in the road and every bounce in the gig's undercarriage. Awareness of Steven's muscular leg, flush against hers, caused her nerves to twist. Grateful that the near darkness concealed her flustered condition, she said little during the drive through the West End, content to listen to Delaroux and Jane discuss the upcoming match.

It occurred to Eugenia that Jane and Delaroux were two of the most garrulous people she'd ever encountered. Not for a moment did they cease their dialogue. Even had Eugenia or Sir Steven or Lady Clarissa wished to interject, it would have been unlikely that the two would have allowed it.

"Where are you taking us, Lord Delaroux?" Jane asked, her cheerful countenance more a testament to her steely resilience than to her forgiving nature.

"To Fives Court in Little St. Martin's Street, and please call me Robert. The sparring ring is all the crack of late, especially since the Pugilistic Club has begun to patronize it."

"Sparring?" Eugenia asked. "Are we not going to see Tom Cribb or Bill Richmond or Gentleman Jack knock a man's head off?"

She thought she heard a muffled chuckle emerge from Sir Steven, but when she turned to look at him, his jaw, in the shadows, was as hard as stone.

"You might get a gander at Bill Richmond, as he is the license holder at the Horse and Dolphin Tavern next door," Delaroux replied. "But no one's head will be knocked off. These exhibitions are done as much for the spectacle as for the gamesmanship."

"No bare-fisted bruisers," added Sir Steven.

"That's right, the men will wear boxing gloves and the match will be stopped before anyone is pounded senseless."

Without voicing her opinion that a boxing match was not a boxing match unless someone at least got his lip split or his nose bent, Eugenia rode the rest of the way in silence. While Lady Jane and Lord Delaroux chattered, clearly oblivious to all but themselves, Eugenia held her elbows as tightly to her sides as she could, and pressed her knees together. Each shift in the coach's movement, each turn in the direction they traveled, pressed her closer against Sir Steven's side. And every time her hip slid into his, or her shoulder rubbed against his, an agonizing streak of heat shot through her.

By the time the carriage rumbled to a stop, Eugenia was exhausted. The gulp of fresh air she got between disembarking the gig and entering the boxing theater fortified her. Mentally, she chided herself for allowing any man, much less the surly, unsmiling Sir Steven, to affect her so radically.

Inside the Fives, she was immediately distracted by a din of laughter and shouts. The masculine ambience was emphasized by bare brick walls, floors strewn with crushed peanut shells, and of course, the main attraction, a raised boxing ring in the center of the room. Smoke and the scent of male perspiration filled her nostrils. A little frisson of excitement spread through Eugenia's body.

A throng of men in black beaver top hats, occupied with the twin tasks of quizzing and wagering with one another, surrounded the ring. In the grandstands lining the walls sat the Fancy, that sect of society, including both high- and low-born, devoted to the sport of boxing. Interspersed among the crowd was a handful of women, some clearly prostitutes, some ostensibly respectable, all of whom appeared to be having great fun. In total, Fives

Court exuded the air of an underworld fraternity, a slightly wicked place that Eugenia was delighted to see.

A hatless, older man in vest and shirtsleeves approached Lord Delaroux. After a hushed exchange, Delaroux withdrew his money purse, and unfolded a wad of paper currency. Only when the hatless man had carefully counted the notes did he stuff them in his pocket and jerk his head toward a rickety wooden staircase that clung to the back wall.

"That's more than any of these other rapscallions paid to be admitted. You've been rooked, Robert," Sir Steven declared, and the ladies nodded in agreement.

Delaroux smiled and made a flourishing gesture. "This way, ladies. Up the stairs, that's right!"

And in a few minutes, the party found itself in a small private room with two large open windows that allowed them to lean out and overlook the entire scene. Against one wall was a table laden with a tray of tiny sandwiches, and beside the table, a cask of beer was at the ready.

"Oh, Lord Dela—I mean, Robert!" Lady Jane cried. "It's just the thing. Now we can see everything that happens in the milling ring and in the audience, too. Without being crammed next to all those gawking men."

Eugenia and Lady Clarissa were equally impressed with Delaroux's ingenuity and thoughtfulness. Sir Steven nodded approvingly, though his lips failed to twitch in anything dimly resembling a smile.

A gong clanged, announcing the first match, and the crowd erupted in a din of cheering and shouting. Eugenia and Aunt Clarissa stood at one window, while Delaroux and Jane stood at the other. Steven remained a few feet behind, sipping from a mug of beer, and—or so it seemed to Eugenia—showing not the least bit of interest in the fight below.

She threw a glance over her shoulder and saw that he

was looking at Jane. A deeply resented flash of disappointment shot through her. Instantly, she buried that emotion; it was foolish to expect a man not to look at Jane, with her perfect figure and cheerful, cherry-colored gown. Sir Steven was like every other man, Eugenia concluded, drawn like a moth to the flame of a pretty blonde.

"What are their names?" Aunt Clarissa asked, staring at the fighters.

Delaroux answered, or rather shouted, above the roar of the spectators. "That's Dancing Dick O'Hannigan, a newcomer from Dublin. Dick's the fellow with the red colors tied round his waist. The other's Ned Sparks—he's the favored winner."

The boxers, naked from the waist up and wearing nothing below but loose cotton breeches, circled and stalked one another like big, wary cats. Sparks, at length, went on the offensive. But Dancing Dick, whose sobriquet was well deserved, leapt and swerved as if he were in a ballet, consistently avoiding the brunt of his opponent's glove.

Eugenia, enthralled, was nevertheless mindful of her wager with Jane. "Sir Steven, you can't possibly see the action from back there. Come here! Stand between Aunt Clarissa and me."

She turned to watch the ring below, uncertain whether he would heed her request. But after a moment he stood beside her at the window, his shoulder brushing hers. His nearness was shocking, necessitated by the fact that he was flanked by Aunt Clarissa on his other side. Eugenia's heart lurched as Steven leaned forward, peering out over the crowd, his body pressed against her side. Suddenly, her little wager with Jane seemed incredibly foolish.

Her gaze should have been riveted to the ring. But Eugenia couldn't resist staring at Steven's profile, mentally tracing the shape of his nose, the fullness of his lips. He had such intelligent eyes, she noted, though his countenance was cold and mysterious. As he watched the fighters, his forehead creased and his lips quirked. The lines etched in his face bespoke years of hard experience. But there was something in his expression, some haunting vulnerability, that intrigued Eugenia. Why did Sir Steven wish not to smile? What had made the man so serious and somber that he could never bring himself to show a moment's joy?

"Are you a member of the newly formed Pugilistic Club, sir?" she asked.

He continued to stare at the scene below. "Watching men pound one another's face to mush is hardly my idea of sport. I have witnessed enough brutality in my day."

They might as well have been alone. Aunt Clarissa was mesmerized by the spectacle below. Delaroux and Jane were engaged in the most competitive conversation Eugenia had ever heard, both talking excitedly at the same time and in increasingly loud volume. Determined to draw out the mercurial Steven, Eugenia plunged forward.

"What sort of things are you interested in, then, sir?"

The fine lines that bracketed his eyes deepened. Without looking at her, Steven said, "I enjoy a good book now and then. I like the opera—if it's done in Italian, that is, not this silly comic opera that is so popular on Haymarket Street. I used to enjoy . . . well, that does not signify, does it? To be honest, I like to be alone."

"You used to enjoy what?"

He drew in a deep breath, crossed his arms over his chest, and frowned. "I suppose there was a time when I enjoyed the company of a lady. There was a time when I enjoyed the art of conversation, but that, dear girl, was a long time ago."

"Before you returned from Egypt?" Eugenia asked quietly.

His eyes closed tightly for an instant, and when they opened, his expression and his profile had hardened to granite. "Sometime thereabouts."

"Did you see terrible things in Egypt?"

"Yes."

"Is that what you think about now . . . when you are alone?" Eugenia stood a little closer to him, her slippers beside his boots, her bosom against his shoulder.

"I try not to," he rasped.

She ached to touch him. She ached for him just to look at her. But he was far away and deeply inside himself.

"Would it not help to talk about the things that trouble you, sir? To a friend, I mean. To someone you trust and perhaps love."

"There is no one like that."

"Don't you have a friend? Someone other than Lord Delaroux, I mean."

"Delaroux is an acquaintance, not a friend."

"Is there no lady in your life, someone you have a fancy for?"

"Good God, no."

"I find that difficult to believe. You are very handsome and intelligent, and, if I may be so bold, very intriguing."

"And you, child, are very naive to think so."

"Haven't you *ever* been in love, sir?"

"I would thank you to cease your interrogation, Lady Eugenia."

"Don't you *want* to be in love?"

"*In love?*" He sneered. "Begging your pardon, but do I look like a man who wants to be in love? You insult me, Lady Eugenia. I do not *want* to be in love, nor do I *need* to be in love, and any man who thinks he does is nothing more than a deluded romantic! Look at Delaroux there, he talks incessantly about love, but he is like a puppy dog, panting after every woman who smiles at him. Why should a man sugarcoat the facts, I say? Why speak of love when it is more often lust or even economics that shackles men and women in unhappy marriages?"

"What a dreadful way of looking at things," Eugenia murmured.

"I should think that you would agree with me, given the present state of your parents' union. Can we not now do what we came here to do, that is, watch the boxing match?" he asked, turning away.

But Eugenia knew that Steven wasn't watching the fighters even though his gaze was directed at the ring. Her chest squeezed; she could have kicked herself for inciting this unpleasant exchange. Good heavens, she was supposed to make Sir Steven smile, not goad him to the edge of a black abyss.

"I am sorry, Sir Steven." She touched his arm, but quickly withdrew her hand, aware that her overture was inappropriate and most likely unwanted. "It was rude of me to ask such impertinent questions. I have made a cake of myself once again. You must think me monstrous rude. Can you forgive me?"

He faced her then, his pale blue eyes penetrating. "Are you always so utterly candid, Eugenia? Do you always ask such incisive questions of people you hardly know? Truly, you are either the most curious person I know, or else . . . well . . ." His voice trailed.

Stunned, Eugenia stared at him. She had never thought of herself as particularly candid, but then she had never contrived to conceal her feelings, opinions, or emotions. "Have I been too honest, sir? Have I over-stepped the boundaries of propriety? If so," she said, a bit archly, for though she knew she'd spoken brazenly, she rankled beneath his imperious scowl, "I am doubly apologetic."

"I must admit you have shocked me twice, first by confiding in me the news of your parents' unhappiness—"

"I assure you, 'twas no confidence. The whole of London knows," Eugenia inserted.

"And second, by questioning my personal life."

"What should two people converse about, then? The weather? Politics? The latest scandal?" Eugenia's contrition over having offended Sir Steven turned quickly to irritation. "Do you consider me some artless green girl lacking in subtlety or discretion? Is that it? Perhaps you think women should keep their mouths shut altogether, or merely speak when spoken to. Or is it that you cannot tolerate someone looking past that hard exterior of yours? Is it that you are afraid to let someone get to know you, sir? Is that it?"

His face paled. In a blink, his expression registered shock, then an anger that was out of proportion to Eugenia's probing questions.

"You do not know what you are talking about," he told her, but the truth was, she'd loosed an arrow that had pierced his heart. "You know nothing of me."

"No. I do not. And it is obvious that I never shall, though whether that it is a good thing, I cannot possibly fathom. You are undoubtedly a man all to yourself." Eugenia drew herself up, her huge dark eyes narrowed, her neck elongated. "How very admirable, sir, that you do not need to be in love."

"I do not. I—I have my work." He pinched the bridge of his nose, realizing too late that the inquisitive Eugenia would most certainly ask him what sort of work he was referring to. "Managing my financial affairs and my country estate, that is. Most men delegate their responsibilities to caretakers and accountants. I prefer a more hands-on approach."

"So you have responsibilities. Like any other important man. But you have time to tour the gaming hells with enough regularity to meet the likes of Lord Delaroux. Any man who is seen in his company cannot be said to be living the life of a monk."

"I never said I lived as a monk. Celibacy has never been an aspiration of mine."

"Oh, so you admit you are in need of female company in order to satisfy your physical urges. But you have no need of any emotional entanglement. Am I stating your case fairly, Sir Steven?"

A roar erupted in the crowd below.

Lady Clarissa shifted her weight and jabbed her elbow in Sir Steven's side. "I hope you have some blunt riding on that Dancing Dick fellow!"

Looking down, grateful for the interruption, Steven saw that Sparks was flat on his back. Delaroux yelled encouragement to the prostrate boxer while Lady Jane clapped her hands and laughed heartily. Eugenia gave her aunt a tepid smile, crossed her arms over her chest, and glowered at Steven.

Her breath was warm on his neck. "You haven't answered my question, sir."

"I have no intention of dignifying such a silly question with a response."

"You are a coward."

Her whispered accusation blistered his composure. Steven grit his teeth, willing himself not to explode. His desire to take Eugenia by the shoulders and shake her was dangerously strong. But he could only injure her, and thereby have his revenge, through hurtful words. "All right then, I will answer you, Lady Eugenia. Yes, I do have physical needs, and, yes, there are any number of women in London willing to allow me into their beds. No, I do not want an emotional entanglement, not now, not ever. I haven't the time for it. Had I the time for it, I still wouldn't want it."

"Why?" She was back to being her purely curious self now, without mockery, without pretense. She looked sincerely perplexed. "Why wouldn't a man want to be in love with a woman? What would make a man shun familiarity, loyalty, and love?"

"A man needs a hard edge to survive in my world," he replied. "Moreover, I like to know that I can go where I want, when I want, and with whom I please. I cannot be distracted by the trivialities of courtship, nor do I wish to undertake the responsibility of being in love. I do not wish for someone to be in love with me, either. It is too suffocating, too circumscribing. The day-to-day minutia of a relationship I find to be incredibly boring."

She stepped back, her lips slightly parted.

"You look as if I have just confessed to murder," he said quietly, a trifle pleased that he had shocked her, though he couldn't have said why.

"Far worse," she said. "I do not believe I have ever met a man so coldhearted, so cruel."

"It is never cruel to be honest. Cruelty would be to mislead a woman, seduce her, allow her to believe I might one day truly love her. No, Lady Eugenia, I do not lie to women. If they come to bed with me, they do so willingly. With no promise of marriage or love or even friendship."

"A very well-rehearsed response, sir," Eugenia said.

"I must admit I am ceaselessly amazed that women refuse to take what I have said at face value. They so often believe they can change a man, rehabilitate him, coax him out of his melancholy with sweet smiles and warm embraces. More often, they wind up humiliated and wishing they had listened more carefully to what was being told them."

She paled a little, and her eyes watered, as if she'd suffered a stinging slap to her cheek. Steven's anger had roiled through him, consuming every decent impulse he might otherwise have had to spare this young woman his debauched, cynical, and jaded views concerning the illusion of love. But now his anger was spent, and he was staring at an innocent lady who had every right to be shocked and repulsed by him. He was repulsed, too, and sickened by his own excess. What small effort would it have been for him to keep his mouth shut? Why did he have to unleash his anger and his vitriol, not to mention his thinly disguised hurt, on her?

Because he liked her, he supposed. And liking a woman led to wanting her, and wanting led to needing. And needing led to being controlled by a woman. And Sir Steven St. Charles was far too old and wise to ever fall into that trap again. Lady Catherine had cured him of his need for love; he would never be controlled by passion again.

He clenched his jaw, imagining Lady Catherine, her long black hair strewn on a pillow, lips bruised from lovemaking, cheeks flushed. Steven's fists knotted tightly. For in the picture that his mind painted, Catherine was not alone. Hovering above her—in the bed she'd once shared with Steven—was the Earl of Fitzhaven, the treasonous devil that Steven would do anything to bring down, even if it meant making himself the bait in a little game of cat and mouse with Lord Bowlingbroke.

"Steven, old man, you look as if you've lost your family fortune," crowed Lord Delaroux when the final bell clanged. O'Hannigan was declared the undisputed winner and a rather limp-limbed Sparks was scraped off the boxing mat.

The tension of the first match having dissipated, the crowd below began to circulate in a steady buzz of visiting, back-slapping, and vigorous wagering. Above stairs, the party abandoned their places at the open windows, opting to stand around a small table laden with trays of sandwiches, wedges of cheese, biscuits, and miniature sausages. A keg of ale had been provided, and Delaroux passed round mugs of dark, yeasty smelling beer to everyone. Eugenia, famished as usual, fell suddenly quiet as she sampled the catered fare and pondered the meaning of Sir Steven's outburst.

It *was* an irrational outburst, she concluded silently. Worthy of a female, if the truth be told, and totally unprovoked. Oh, she'd been too bold, that was true enough. Her questions were far too personal, and pressing Sir Steven even after he requested that she cease interrogating him was beyond all bounds of decency.

But Eugenia wasn't reared in a household where the niceties of decorum were strictly enforced. Her parents, however socially significant they might be, were vociferously passionate people, prone to sturdy disagreement, yelling matches and, on rare occasions, even pitched battles where basalt figurines became projectiles and old family portraits were snatched off the walls and used as shields.

Recalling her parents' last row, the one that resulted in their departing London and taking off for opposite corners of the earth, Eugenia couldn't resist a private chuckle. If Eugenia was the most candid individual Sir Steven had ever met . . . well, then, what would he think if he ever met her parents?

Delaroux made a fist and jabbed Steven's arm. "Lost a handsome amount of blunt, did you?"

"I never wager on boxing matches, Robert. Or anything else that is beyond my control. That is why, when it comes to gambling, I prefer whist over Faro, poker over hazard . . . and horseflesh over women."

Eugenia's throat constricted. A beat passed during which everyone in the tiny room stared at Sir Steven,

Aunt Clarissa with a tiny sausage poking from her lips, Lord Delaroux with an uncertain smile trembling on his lips, for he undoubtedly wished to gauge the others' reactions before he committed to his own, and Lady Jane, her face frozen in a pretty rictus of titillated shock.

It was Jane who broke the silence. Hands propped on her hips, she tossed her head and said, "Sir, that is the most provocative remark I have ever heard a gentleman utter. Surely, you are joking."

"Of course, he is," Delaroux said, his smile guttering like a candle.

"No, I am not." Steven shrugged, glanced at Eugenia, then turned his cold blue gaze on Jane.

"I demand an apology," Jane said.

"You shall not have one."

She gasped. "Sir, my father will hear of this!"

Oddly, Steven seemed not the least bit perturbed by this news. "A man who stakes his fortune on something or someone he cannot control is a fool. A horse can be controlled; a woman cannot."

Jane met Steven's gaze, and as she held it, her color darkened. "You are suggesting that by their very nature, their very *uncontrollability,* as it were, women are inferior to cattle."

"No, that is not what I am suggesting," Steven drawled.

Eugenia looked at Delaroux, whose reddening countenance betrayed his emotion. Bemused, she watched him fidget while Jane and Steven sparred. It was evident that the interplay between the two made Delaroux uncomfortable, but Eugenia couldn't understand why. Was he embarrassed that his "best friend" had committed such an egregious social gaffe? Or was he offended by Jane's readiness to engage with Steven in what Delaroux himself had once referred to as her "too high-in-the-instep" tone of voice?

"You did not listen to me." Steven spoke to Jane as if no one else were as present in the room. "I said that insofar as gambling was concerned, I preferred horse-flesh to women. That is because horses can be trained or beaten into submission, whereas women are to be respected and cherished. Through their conditioning, then, and because of their rightful expectations of men, women are not to be counted on for total obedience or consistency. They are unpredictable creatures, and therein lies their beauty, their charm, their enigmatic allure. But I wouldn't stake my country estate on a woman, and I wouldn't attempt for one moment to force my will or my wishes on her, either."

An involuntary bark of laughter escaped Eugenia's lips. Aunt Clarissa chuckled a bit, too, but seemed too occupied with eating sausages to get worked up over Steven's contrived soliloquy.

"So, you do not believe that women are inferior?" Jane stared at Sir Steven hypnotically.

"On the contrary, Lady Jane," he said quietly, his voice as warm as cashmere, "I believe women are vastly superior to men. You, for example, are an unparalleled beauty and as lightning quick with your wit as any man I have ever conversed with."

His blandishment had a markedly visible effect on Jane. She giggled, touched her throat, nervously sipped her ale.

Beads of sweat dotted Delaroux's upper lip. He looked like a driver who had somehow let the ribbons slip from his fingers, and having lost control of his runaway gig, was on the verge of panic as it careened around a sharp turn.

A wave of nausea replaced Eugenia's laughter. Sir Steven and Lady Jane were locked in a mesmerizing gaze. Was it possible that this man, this stone-cold, unfeeling cad, who a moment ago had confessed that he had no use for friends, much less for love or women, was now flirting outrageously with Lady Jane Bowling-broke, right beneath Eugenia's nose? Was it even re-motely possible?

Eugenia had to allow that it was. Watching them, she thought it seemed as if a gauntlet had been thrown down—by which one of them, Eugenia wasn't certain. At any rate, they appeared to be singularly well matched when it came to stubbornness and high-mindedness.

Perhaps this truly was a love-match. Perhaps that first spark of attraction Eugenia had seen between Jane and Steven when they danced the night before had ignited into full-blown love. Perhaps her best friend was des-tined to marry the unhappy Sir Steven St. Charles. Per-haps she would be Lady Jane's maid of honor at the marriage of the Season when it was all said and done.

She should have been happy for her friend, thrilled to see the fireworks exploding between Jane and the mys-teriously handsome Sir Steven.

Instead, her stomach soured and her chest constricted as she watched their dueling gazes. She loved Lady Jane and wished nothing but the best for her. But the thought of Jane and Steven falling in love and getting mar-ried . . . Eugenia hated to admit it, even to herself, but the thought of Steven's loving Jane caused her heart to ache.

FOUR

"Daddy would have him drawn and quartered," Jane announced gaily.

"The earl would have *us* drawn and quartered if he knew where we were last night," Eugenia answered.

It was a bright, sunny morning and the girls were in the cobbled alley behind the Curzon Street town house, giving a bath to Lady Clarissa's aging dachshund, Dashie. In coarse linen skirts and aprons, they could have been pretty young scullery wenches performing their day's chores. Squatting on either side of a huge tub of soapy water, they alternated the difficult task of holding Dashie still while the other scrubbed and rinsed the tiny dog.

"How did she get this filthy?" Jane asked, wringing her sponge over the dog's back.

Eugenia wrinkled her nose. "You know she can't see a thing, poor darling. Yesterday when Cook opened the kitchen door to pay for the oysters her vendor brought, Dashie made a run for it. Of course, she couldn't tell the mud puddles from the piles of horse—"

"I get the picture!" Sitting on her haunches, Jane turned her face to the sun. "Oh, I don't mind really, I'm in such a happy mood today."

"A happy mood? Last night, you were so put out with Sir Steven, you couldn't sleep. I heard you! You tossed and turned half the night before you fell off."

"Yes, well, that was last night. And I wasn't really angry. Just shocked, that's all, to hear a gentleman speak so crudely."

" 'Twasn't crude," Eugenia said.

"Genie, you defend everyone. 'Sturth, it is a shame that women cannot be barristers. You'd make an excellent criminal defense lawyer."

"Well, he wasn't exactly being crude, Jane. He was just being . . . oh, I don't know." Eugenia allowed Jane to take hold of Dashie. She sat back on her heels, staring hard at her best friend. A myriad of emotions swirled through her, none of them particularly noble or honorable. But it occurred to Eugenia that perhaps Jane wasn't so enamored of Steven, after all. Or, if she was, that she could be persuaded otherwise.

Another more troubling thought occurred to Eugenia. She'd imagined that if Steven shattered her heroic image of him, that if he committed some embarrassing social gaffe, for instance, her infatuation would disappear. But it hadn't. Sir Steven had literally shocked the party into silence the night before with his *risqué* remarks, and still she found him wildly appealing. So appealing, in fact, that she was contemplating turning her friend Jane against him.

To what purpose, Eugenia could not have said, for she'd concluded that Steven cared not a whit for her. Still, the little devil perched on her shoulder refused to settle down. Even before she spoke, she felt a guilty, wicked thrill.

"Do you know, I was never able to make him smile."

"Good heavens, I had forgotten!" Jane laughed as Dashie shook his head, spraying water all over both girls. "I won the bet, you owe me."

"Owe you what?"

Jane bit her lower lip. "We forgot to name the stakes,

didn't we? Well, we're hardly veteran gamblers. Oh dear, I don't know what I shall make you pay!"

Eugenia brushed a strand of damp hair from her face. "I don't think he has ever smiled. He is truly one of the most sour men I have ever encountered!"

"Demonic!" Jane said.

"Hateful!" Eugenia chimed.

"Do you think he has ever killed a man?"

"Surely, in Egypt, he killed a great many," Eugenia said grimly. "I suspect all that killing did something to his mind. The least provocation could cause him to snap, lose control, go on a murderous spree—"

"Genie, that is terrible! Do you truly think he is that depraved?"

"You said yourself, your father would have him drawn and quartered."

"I was exaggerating. Besides, I was referring to Sir Steven's faux pas, not his penchant for killing."

"Still, a man who would say such a thing in the presence of ladies cannot be thought of as civilized. It's his tragic background makes him so barbaric. Poor man."

"He took it back. He amended his statement."

Eugenia scoffed. "He realized he'd frightened us. He's not an imbecile. He danced his way out of the hole he'd dug for himself. He's got a way with words, that's all. It just makes him all the more dangerous."

Jane shuddered. "Blackguard!"

"Murderer!" Eugenia whispered.

A moment of silence ticked by. Eugenia watched Jane's expression closely, awaiting any sign that her friend was thoroughly repulsed by Sir Steven. Jane preoccupied herself with scooping Dashie's bathwater with a cup and pouring it over his back. But her brow was furrowed and her pretty bow-shaped lips pursed. Eugenia gave herself a mental pat on the back; it was clear that her condemnation of Steven had drastically altered Jane's perception of him.

"Well, it is settled then," Jane said at length.

"You mean you will never speak to him again?" Eugenia asked.

"On the contrary. His devilish streak merely makes him infinitely more interesting, Genie, more interesting and more dangerous than all my suitors put together. Especially Lord Delaroux, who wouldn't dare to swat a bumblebee if it landed on his nose! What was it Lady Caroline said about Lord Byron? That he was 'mad, bad and dangerous to know'? Well, that description fits Sir Steven to a tee!"

"Oh." Eugenia's throat constricted. Struggling not to show her disappointment, she rubbed her wet hand over her face.

"I shall see to it that he receives an invitation to Father's party next week. Do you think I should?"

"Indeed no! 'Tis entirely too late to invite anyone else."

"You asked me to invite Lord Delaroux just a few days ago."

"But that was a few days ago, Jane. The party is a masquerade, and Sir Steven has not had sufficient time to obtain a suitable costume. He will be offended!"

"Pish-posh! I do not think we need fret about offending Sir Steven. Not after what he said last night. Dear Genie, I believe the man's skin is thick enough to withstand the sting of being invited to a party at the last minute!"

"You are making a mistake, Jane!"

"Because he is so dangerous?" Eugenia lifted a dripping Dashie out of the tub. "Don't worry, nothing can happen to me as long as Father is in attendance. Besides, don't you think it is very exciting to have a murderer in our midst, Genie?"

"I think it is foolish, and—" Eugenia tossed a large towel over Dashie's head and took the dog into her arms. Beating back tears, she vigorously rubbed the squirming animal dry.

"Oh, come now, Genie! 'Tis unlike you to be afraid. You don't have to talk to him if you don't want to!"

"I'm not afraid of him! It's just that—well, it's just that, he's not a nice man. He is so unlike Lord *Call-Me-Robert* Delaroux. Now there's a nice gentleman, so eager to please and full of frivolity! A bit fussy in his dress, but what man doesn't have a fault or two? We're not perfection ourselves, are we, Jane?"

"There you go again, defending Robert!"

"I'm just saying he's a pleasant gentleman. Wealthy, too. And eligible. A girl could do worse!"

Lady Jane, an inscrutable smile on her face, stood and wiped her hands on her wilted apron front. "As well as I know you, Genie, you never cease to amaze me."

Eugenia stood facing her, the swaddled Dashie held tightly against her bosom. A breeze, made pungent by the stables that lined the alley behind Curzon Street, tickled the girls' noses and ruffled their disheveled hair. With her skirt hem wet and her halfboots drenched, Eugenia felt like a drowned mud-lark. Lady Jane, on the other hand, had somehow managed to keep her bodice dry and her pinned-up blond hair in perfect order.

"I have an idea—" Jane began.

Eugenia groaned. "I need a warm bath and a cup of tea before I can hear anymore of your madcap ideas."

"You lost the first bet because Sir Steven never smiled."

"Just tell me what I owe you!"

"Now there's the rub." Lady Jane propped her hands on her hips. "We should have fixed the stakes before we wagered, dear. The only thing to do now is to make another bet. This time whoever loses has to kiss . . . the man chosen by the winner!"

"Do you mean that if I fail to make Sir Steven laugh, I must kiss any man you name?"

"If you win, I will have to kiss any man *you* name."

Eugenia shifted Dashie to her hip and gaped at Jane. "You are joking, are you not? Oh, Jane, 'tis scandalous!"

"Yes," Jane said, laughing. "It is, isn't it? But to make the game fair, I will grant you until the stroke of midnight at Father's masquerade. If you haven't made Sir Steven laugh by then, Genie, you're done for!"

The girls were still chuckling when Lord Robert Delaroux came round the corner, resplendent in a suit cut from dark blue twill. Beneath his jacket, he wore a pale blue brocade waistcoat, and as accessories he sported a rakish straw hat and a totally useless walking stick.

"Hello, ladies!" He approached jauntily, tipping his hat, squinting against the glare of the late morning sun.

Eugenia quizzed the man from the tip of his boots to the top of his hat. "What in the world are you dressed for, Robert? You're as brightly decorated as an Easter egg!"

Immediately, she regretted having blurted such a teasing remark. Lord Delaroux's smile wobbled and his sparkling emerald eyes watered. She hadn't meant to hurt his feelings, but she did have the most horrible time keeping her mouth shut.

Before she could retract or amend her statement, Lady Jane said rather crisply, "Did we forget an appointment, my lord?"

"No, no! I only meant to leave my calling card, but Lady Clarissa told me you were out here, giving Dashie a bath. Dear me, I did not intend to startle you, or inconvenience you—"

"You didn't! Did he, Jane? Would you like to come in for a cup of tea?"

"Oh, Genie! In these old dresses?"

"Another time, perhaps," Robert said quietly.

The moment grew oddly awkward. Jane all but snatched Dashie from Eugenia's arms, then clutched the shivering dog against her chest and stared at her sodden boots. Eugenia, believing she had insulted or embarrassed Lord Delaroux, felt responsible for the tension.

She was even more confused when Lady Jane threw Lord Robert a haughty look and said, "You and your friend Sir Steven are to be invited to Father's masquerade party next week. The two of you are good friends, are you not?"

"Yes, very good friends!"

"Well then, Father cannot very well invite one of you without the other, then, can he? 'Tis short notice, I know—"

Robert's face brightened. "That's all right. I cannot speak for Steven, but I shall be there."

Lady Jane nodded, mumbled something about being chilled to the bone and bade a quick good-bye to Lord Robert. Eugenia, thoroughly rattled, smiled warmly at the gentleman, said good-bye, then hurried after her friend. Lord Robert Delaroux stood in the alleyway, totally perplexed but thrilled beyond belief to have received an invitation to Bowlingbroke's masquerade.

A wave of subterranean vibrations had just rolled through Curzon Street, leaving Lady Jane discombobulated, Lady Eugenia disappointed, and Lord Delaroux disproportionately gay.

Sir Steven St. Charles sat at a card table, his expression, or lack thereof, schooled in the perfect poker face, albeit the game at present was rummy. The air in the small room was acrid and thick, the atmosphere tense. At three in the morning, he'd ginned too often, and won too much of the other players' money to be assured a safe passage home. The grumblings surrounding him, and the discreet appearance of two pie-faced ousters who now flanked the only door leading to the stairwell, convinced him that his purse was subject to being confiscated at any moment, and his person was liable to be pummeled into obscurity in the bargain.

That's what he deserved for patronizing such disreputable hells. Remorse pricked him, but it was too late to second-guess his decision to play at Mrs. Pommard's. He chose her establishment because he craved the anonymity of the place and the seediness of it, too; after his evening at Fives Court, he had an unnatural urge to punish himself, to deprive himself of any light-hearted amusement. His black heart ached with regret and the only way to exorcize his demons was to fraternize with the underworld.

Of the four men remaining in the game, three had suffered a radical reversal of fortune. The player on Sir Steven's left folded, laying his cards faceup on the table and pushing back in his chair with a disgusted grunt. "I'm out."

The man on Steven's right folded, also.

One player remained, and as Steven's gaze flickered across the green baize, he saw his opponent execute a nearly indiscernible sleight of hand. The man was cheating.

Steven's heart thundered, but his face remained implacable. Accusing a man of cheating was tantamount to issuing a challenge. And Steven didn't want to have to kill another man, not over something as trivial as a game of cards. On the other hand, honor demanded that he expose the knave.

"Gin," the cheater said salaciously, displaying his cards. "I win. Take yer medicine, sir."

"How interesting." But Steven continued to play his turn, taking a card, rearranging his hand, then discarding. "I am afraid it is you, however, who must take his medicine, Mr. Fletcher." He fanned out his cards on the table and exhibited four queens and three jacks.

The cheat squinted. "My hand beats yers. I've got seven straight, all diamonds!"

"Including the queen of diamonds, I see," drawled Steven. "Odd that this pack of cards should have five queens."

Fletcher's face became a purple bruise as he placed both hands on the table and slowly pushed himself to his feet. The air between the two men was charged with tension, and the bouncers beside the door shifted their weight nervously. The other men at the table shoved back their chairs and stood, jaws slack and eyes round, reluctant to intervene but more than willing to witness a fight, a calling-out or a cold-blooded murder.

Silently ticking off his options, Steven rose to his full height. He gestured at the pile of markers, paper currency and vowels piled in the center of the gaming table. "I won, Fletcher. You had best leave now, before it's too late."

Beneath Sir Steven's pale blue gaze, Fletcher hesitated. Moisture appeared on his face, and his eyes narrowed. "You don't scare me none, sir. I know what they say about you, that you killed a legion of Frenchmen in Egypt and that you came home a ruthless man. But I'm not afraid to cross swords with ye—"

"Are you calling me, out, Fletcher? Because if that is the case, I believe I am entitled to choose the weapons, and they will not be swords."

"What, then? Pistols?" The man's tongue darted across his upper lip.

"On the contrary. If you challenge me, I will fight you with my bare hands. And I will kill you, Fletcher, don't doubt it for a second. Do you wish to die?"

Eyes widening slightly, Fletcher took a step backward. Then he halted, his hands hanging loosely by his sides.

Steven's breathing normalized; his pulse slowed. His reputation for being cool, calm, and collected during battle was well deserved. He knew that a nervous opponent was the most dangerous kind. "The money's not worth dying over, is it, Fletcher?"

"Is it to you?"

"No. But honor is. And a man who allows himself to be cheated has no honor."

"Do you expect me to turn tail after you've accused me of cheating?"

"I expect you to realize when you're beaten. Don't be a fool. Walk out of here now, and you'll walk out alive. Challenge me to a bare hands contest and you'll wind up dead."

An elongated instant of silence passed during which the men faced each other down and nothing but the creaking of the floorboards in some distant region of the house was heard.

The flickering lamplight glinted off the brass knob on the door behind Fletcher. Steven saw the doorknob turn. His muscles coiled, ready to spring.

Suddenly, Fletcher's right hand became a blur as he reached inside his jacket. A pistol materialized, a crash sounded behind Fletcher, and a shot cracked the silence.

Lord Robert Delaroux burst into the room. The bouncers guarding the door lunged at him, but he had already thrown himself at Fletcher's back when the pistol shot was fired. The bullet went wild, skimming Steven's shoulder, ripping his jacket and branding a stripe of raw skin on his upper arm.

Ducking, Steven skirted the card table. Delaroux,

locked in an unloving embrace with Fletcher, yelled, "Run, Steven, run!" But that was not even a possibility. Recognizing the danger Delaroux had placed himself in, Steven threw himself between the two men as another shot split the air.

This time, the bullet slammed into a wall, erupting in a spray of plaster shards. The two men who'd folded their cards a moment before now scrambled over one another in an attempt to exit the room. Even the bouncers vanished; Fletcher's weapon had more bullets in it and the man was firing off shots as rapidly as he could.

Another shot, a shattered lamp, and the room faded to shadows. The three men tumbled about the room, legs and arms flailing, fists pounding noses, heads slamming the floor. Fletcher, flat on his back, drew up his knee and gored Steven in the groin. The pain was blinding, and for an instant he was paralyzed. Rolling off Fletcher, he fell to the bare floor, barely able to breathe.

Delaroux managed to get astride Fletcher, and with his superior weight, pinned the man to the floor. But the pistol continued to erupt. A random shot exploded a windowpane; on the street below, a woman screamed. It was only a matter of time before one of those bullets found a body.

Steven's vision returned. He scrambled to his knees, gasping. When he looked over, his blood ran cold. Delaroux had his hands around Fletcher's neck, but the cheat had his pistol pointed straight at Delaroux's nose.

The three men froze. Delaroux's green eyes blinked uncontrollably. Steven feared for Delaroux's life.

"Pull the trigger, Fletcher, and I swear to you that I shall kill you."

"I have two bullets left, sir." Fletcher was on his back and outnumbered, but his weapon made him king of the room. "One for this rambunctious dandy, and one for you."

"If you kill him and not me, you're a dead man. You'll have to kill us both and if you do that, you'll be dancing in the wind within a sennight."

"They'll have to catch me first." The hammer clicked; Fletcher cocked the gun. Delaroux gulped.

Steven said, "Don't be a fool. You win. The money is yours. You won't enjoy it if you're rotting in prison."

Fletcher licked his lips. "I'll take the money, then. But if you try any funny business—"

"Stand up, Robert," Sir Steven said. "That's it, very slowly. Now, drop the gun, Fletcher."

But the cheat refused to give up his weapon. With some effort he regained his feet, then backed away from Delaroux and Steven. Steven stood, dusting off his hands, watching Fletcher, watching Fletcher's pistol.

With one hand, the man stuffed as much paper money into his coat, into his pockets, and beneath the waistband of his trousers as he could. Abandoning the chits and vowels, he edged toward the door, his pistol still held aloft, his expression wary. At the threshold, he turned and pounded down the steps as fast as he could.

Delaroux lunged, but Steven reached out and laid a restraining hand on the man's arm.

"Let him go, Robert."

"But why? He took your winnings! The money was yours, wasn't it?"

"Yes. The money's not important. But Mr. Fletcher is brandishing a gun and I don't feel like getting my head shot off tonight. Don't worry, I will find the cheat and see that justice is done. Next time I meet Fletcher, it will be on *my* turf."

Lord Robert Delaroux exhaled, apparently relieved. He ran his hand through his hair and straightened his necktie. The color returned to his face along with a boyish grin. "Thanks for saving my life, Steven. I'm much in debt."

Steven suppressed the impulse to smile. "Your inter-

ruption was fortuitously well timed, Robert. It is I who
should be thanking you. At any rate, we escaped without
catching a bullet between our ears. Fletcher will have
his comeuppance. What say we go somewhere else and
share a bottle of port?"

Mrs. Simca ran a more serene house of ill repute
where men could also have a game of cards, a bottle of
whiskey, or a quiet conversation. In the drawing room,
Steven and Robert sat on plush red velvet chairs, a table
and a bottle of port between them. Robert withdrew an
elaborately enameled snuffbox and passed it to Steven.

It wasn't his vice of choice, but Steven took a pinch,
held it beneath his nostrils, and vigorously inhaled. Almost immediately, he experienced a buzzing of his
senses and a leap in his heart. Returning the box to
Robert, he thought it wasn't surprising that so many men
were addicted to tobacco. The sensation was pleasurable,
even euphoric.

He considered himself fortunate; even in the days of
his deepest depression, when Steven frequently drank
and caroused all night, he never developed a debilitating
need for drink or drug or sex. Steven's past debaucheries
served only to distract him from his own troubling
thoughts. He was not an addict.

Robert partook, sighed, then tucked his snuffbox inside his vest coat. His gaze followed a pretty young red-
head as she sauntered past. Her hips swished provocatively,
invitingly. Robert looked at Steven, lifted his brows, and
winked.

"I am not interested in bed sport tonight, Robert. Feel
free to indulge yourself, if you must."

The smile slid off Robert's face. "No, of course not.
'Twould be rude of me to abandon you now."

"How in the hell did you come to be at Mrs. Pommard's?" Steven asked at length.

"I came looking for you, of course! I have urgent news to tell you!"

Steven felt a twinge of irritation. He didn't like the idea of anyone looking for him, marking his time, or tracking his whereabouts. "And what made you think I would be there?"

"I went to three other houses before I thought to go to your home and question your valet. Trevor Sparrow gave me a list of your usual haunts."

"Trevor told you where to find me?" Steven's irritation deepened.

Robert took a gulp of port. Wearing a childlike grin, he admitted, "Don't be angry with him, Steven. I fed him quite a clanker, I did. Told him it was a matter of life and death. Unfortunately, he gave me quite a long list of your usual haunts. When I got to Mrs. Pommard's, I dashed inside and asked the first gentleman I saw whether you were there. I would never have found you without the gentleman telling me you were playing cards."

"What gentleman?"

"The gentleman at the Faro table. I'd never met him before. Tall, blond fellow. Handsome bloke." Robert frowned. "Told me his name, but I can't remember it."

A beat passed during which Steven absorbed this bit of intelligence. The Earl of Fitzhaven was a good-looking bloke with blond hair. Was it merely a coincidence that the man below stairs at Mrs. Pommard's fit Fitzhaven's description?

"Can't you remember his name?" Steven asked.

With a shrug, Delaroux shook his head.

Pinching the bridge of his nose, Steven resisted the temptation to wrap his hands around Delaroux's neck and throttle him. "Well, don't keep me in suspense, then. What is this urgent news you have for me?"

"We've been invited to a party, you and I. Well, we are going to be invited, that is."

"A party. And you consider that an urgent matter?"

"In this case, yes. 'Tis a masquerade party, and we haven't much time in which to assemble costumes."

"If you think for one moment that I am going to attend a masquerade—"

"The Earl of Bowlingbroke has an annual masquerade party, you see, and it is one of the most exclusive gatherings of the Season. I know we will be invited because I paid a call on Curzon Street this morning. Jane and Eugenia were giving that silly dog Dashie a bath. You should have seen Lady Jane—"

"Yes, I'm sorry I didn't."

"She looked positively—"

"I'm sure she did." The truth was, Steven could not have cared less if Jane had a Dutch tulip growing out of her head. It was the blasted party he was suddenly interested in. If Bowlingbroke invited him, duty demanded Steven to attend. "When is this spectacle to take place?"

"A week from Friday."

"Christ on a raft! That's not enough time to put together a costume. 'Tis an insult, being invited at this late date!"

"I imagine it was an oversight we hadn't been invited before. Although after your provocative remarks last night, I am surprised Jane didn't tell her father to strike us both from the guest list."

"I do not think Lady Jane was offended." On the contrary, Steven thought, the girl seemed to be completely titillated. Unlike Eugenia. He felt a sharp pang of remorse that he was so rude to someone as sweet as she.

It couldn't be helped; duty compelled him to establish

a friendship with Jane. Eugenia was unimportant in his scheme to learn more about the Earl of Bowlingbroke.

Robert shrugged. "At any rather, Jane says we are to receive our invitations before tomorrow noon. Which is today, noon. By the time we get home, catch a few hours' sleep, and wake in time for nuncheon, we shall have been invited."

"How glorious."

"You do not seem excited. This is the event of the Season."

"I am happy to attend, Robert. Not for the reason you might expect, but I am more than pleased to accept Lord Bowlingbroke's invitation. Have you given any thought as to what you are wearing?"

"I've thought of nothing else. I am going as one of the bard's characters. The world's greatest lover. *Romeo*."

Steven nodded approvingly. But he dreaded exchanging his uniform of breeches and lawn shirt for a ridiculous costume. It wasn't in his nature to draw attention to himself. "I shall have to give this conundrum some serious thought."

"If you don't mind my saying, old man, you give everything too much serious thought."

"Perhaps Trevor Sparrow can be of some assistance. Do you happen to know what Jane and Eugenia are wearing?"

"Haven't a clue. 'Spose we could ask them, though I doubt they'll tell us. They will want their costumes to be a surprise."

"Superstitious, eh? Like a bride who cannot see the groom before the wedding ceremony?"

Lord Delaroux shook his head. "Everyone wears their mask until, at the stroke of midnight, Lord and Lady Bowlingbroke unmask themselves and invite their guests to do the same. We won't know who Jane and Eugenia are until then. Unless we guess, that is. And we will have a high time trying to find them out."

Despite his groan, Steven felt a stab of excitement. A masquerade ball where the participants remained anonymous until midnight offered great potential to probe Lord Bowlingbroke's sympathies. As much as he hated to admit it, getting invited to the costume party was a stroke of luck.

"I guess there's nothing for it, then, but to dash off to Bond Street with Mr. Sparrow. We haven't much time," he said, rising. "I want to thank you, Robert, for intervening on my behalf this evening."

"It was pure chance that I entered just when Fletcher was going to shoot you. I only provided a distraction, nothing more."

"Nevertheless, I am in your debt."

Lord Delaroux seemed inordinately pleased. Standing, he chafed his palms eagerly. "Come on, tell me, what are you thinking of wearing to the ball?"

"You said the masks don't come off until midnight." Slapping Delaroux's shoulder, Steven said, "I intend to be as coy as a virgin bride, Robert."

"But I've done told you!"

"So you have. But you'll learn soon enough that it is always best to keep an air of mystery surrounding you. Until then, Mr. Romeo, I bid you adieu."

FIVE

Bond Street at two o'clock in the afternoon was a bustling shopping district as well as a thoroughfare of social intercourse. In a little shop called Madame Truffaut's, the girls had found an exquisite array of Belgium silks, Irish lace, and Indian madras. With finishing touches yet to be done on their costumes, they gazed at buttons, beads, and ribbons in glass cases, perused fashion plates depicting the latest Continental bonnets and gowns, and stood before full-length mirrors with fabric swatches wrapped around their bodies. As always, they exchanged frank opinions regarding one another's choices. But the one thing they hadn't discussed candidly was Lady Jane's upset earlier that morning.

"Do you want to talk about it?" Eugenia finally asked softly. She ran her fingers over a bolt of fabric, but her gaze was fixed on Jane's pinched expression.

Lady Jane glanced around the shop. "I don't want to discuss it in Mother's presence."

"Lady Bowlingbroke is in the fitting rooms," Eugenia said, skirting the table. She touched her friend's arm and looked directly in her eyes. "Now, look at me. You've been as Friday-faced as Boney's boot maker since Lord Delaroux came around. Did I make you angry by commenting on his florid jacket? La, but I'm completely befogged as to why my uncouth remark would get you going on so."

With a sigh, Lady Jane shook her blond curls. "It was not your fault, Genie. It's just that—oh, it's so difficult to put into words!"

"You've never been reticent with me before. Why start now?"

"It's all about Father and Mother, you see. I dare not contradict them. They are not like your parents, accustomed to a civil war raging inside their very own home at all times."

Eugenia, flashing on a picture of her parents in full battle regalia, muskets and sabers at their sides, cringed. "What is it that you disagree with them about?"

Crumpling a handful of dotted Swiss, Jane hesitated. "I shouldn't tell you. Father said this was a private family matter, not to be discussed with anyone else."

"Then you must decide for yourself whether 'tis wise to confide in me. I cannot imagine what information could possibly be so sensitive that your best friend couldn't be privy to it, but then, I suppose your father is a very wise man."

"Not always!" Jane's face suddenly turned dark pink. Her normally smooth brow was now as wrinkled as the fabric she crushed in her hand; her ordinarily bright and laughing eyes were now blurred with tears. "Oh, Genie, I wish I had your parents! They are so . . . far away!"

"Yes, they do have that to commend them." Lady Eugenia smiled blandly at a passing shopper. Taking Jane's arm, she guided her toward the rear of the store, where a grouping of chairs and a display of satin slippers stood. "Let us sit for a moment while Lady Bowlingbroke is measured for her costume. I'm certain she won't miss us."

"No, she won't," Jane said, sniffing.

For a moment, the girls sat quietly while Jane dabbed at her tears with a linen she'd extracted from her reticule and Eugenia patted her arm consolingly.

At length, Jane lifted her head and offered a feeble smile. "Please don't misunderstand. I do adore my parents. And they are nothing but kind and generous toward me. They only want what is best for me, and for me to be happy."

"That seems to be a common goal of parents, although they frequently confuse what they want for their children with what is in their children's best interest."

"Just so." Lady Jane swallowed hard. "I believe I am in love, Genie. Don't ask me to tell you with whom because it is all too ridiculous and Father has forbidden me to even think of forming an alliance with him!"

Eugenia's throat constricted. Eugenia was in love? "It must be someone I know," she said slowly. "If I guess, will you tell me?"

Jane squeezed her eyes shut and shook her blond ringlets.

"Were we with him at the sparring match?"

A tiny gasp escaped Jane's lips.

"It has to be Lord Delaroux or Sir Steven." Eugenia fell silent for a moment, recalling Eugenia's reactions to both men. "And you did nothing but defend Sir Steven's misconduct this morning, while you literally fled from Lord Delaroux when he appeared in the alleyway."

"You can't hide your emotions from me, Jane. I'm your best friend. Besides, actions speak louder than words. And you said yourself that Lord Delaroux was a silly goose."

"I never said he was a *silly goose!*"

"Or something very nearly like that. And compared to Steven, he is! Although it wouldn't hurt Steven to lighten his mood a little, would it?"

"Do you really think Robert is silly?"

Eugenia inhaled deeply, grimly sympathetic to Jane's predicament. Yes, it seemed entirely sensible to her that Eugenia would fall in love with Sir Steven. After all, he was a paragon of masculine virtue, with his rugged good looks and his mysterious background. That he was determined not to be in love made him all the more wickedly alluring. It also made him a dangerous target of Jane's desire, not just because her father had forbade any courtship between them, but because it was quite likely Sir Steven would refuse to return Jane's affections.

Or would he?

Staring at Jane, Eugenia wondered if any man could resist her delicate pastel charms. She wished, on the one hand, only happiness and contentment for her best friend. On the other hand, Eugenia couldn't bear to think of Steven loving another woman. The mental image of Steven gazing lovingly into Jane's wide adoring eyes made Eugenia's stomach lurch.

With a sigh, she put her arm protectively around Jane's shoulder. "There, there. I quite understand your situation. A woman can't help her feelings, can she?"

Jane slanted Eugenia a quizzical look. "Genie, you cannot possibly understand."

But if Eugenia's parents had imbued one characteristic in her, it was to be a good sport and a loyal friend. "I do understand. I understand what it is to be in love and unable to express one's emotions."

"Do you?" Jane squeezed Eugenia's hands in her own. "Oh, Genie, you are a dear friend!"

"Have you decided what you are going to do?"

"I am so confused! I do so want to please Father and Mother! But . . . I love him, Genie. I cannot help myself. He is all I think about, all I dream about."

"Perhaps you are infatuated—"

"No. He has flaws and I see them. He is not perfect and yet his imperfections make him even more lovable to me. For all his eccentricities, I would not change a thing about him."

There was no question in Eugenia's mind that Jane

was talking about Sir Steven. "I am certain you will do what is right, Jane. You have a good head on your shoulders and your heart is in the right place."

With a delicate sniff, Jane apparently banished her doldrums. A wicked little grin suddenly and unexpectedly played at her lips as she leaned close to Eugenia. "I do so hope you win our bet, dear. For then you must order me to kiss the man of your choice. And you wouldn't want me to kiss a frog now, would you? *Dear, dear, dear Eugenia?"*

A male voice, disturbingly familiar, interjected. "Now that we have established how dear Eugenia is, might I ask what the two of you are in such serious conference about?"

Sir Steven looked from Eugenia to Jane, puzzled by the ladies' shocked expressions. Whatever they were discussing so intently, it apparently had nothing to do with the shoe selection at Madame Truffaut's.

Embarrassed, he took a step backward. "Forgive me for interrupting. In truth, I was out of line."

But it was too late. Lord Robert Delaroux bounded into the slipper section of Miss Truffaut's at precisely the same moment Lady Sally Bowlingbroke emerged from the fitting rooms. Exclamations of surprise went up among the ladies while Delaroux, looking extraordinarily pleased with himself, graced everyone with his brilliant smile. Then, to add to the festivity, Lady Clarissa Terrebonne appeared, wearing a sweet, sly little smile on her lips.

Steven discreetly retreated to the edge of the suddenly crowded shoe department.

"Aunt Clarissa, what are you doing here?" Eugenia sprang to her feet.

"I have important news, Genie. It couldn't wait!"

"And what are *you* doing here, Lord Delaroux?" asked Jane.

"Call me Robert, *please,*" he said. "And I am doing the same thing you are doing, I'm sure. Shopping, that is!"

"My, this establishment is popular." Lady Sally, smiling enigmatically, stood behind her daughter's chair.

Polite greetings were exchanged, with great deference paid by the men to the regal Countess of Bowlingbroke.

Lady Clarissa laughed easily. "Madame Truffaut carries the most exotic things, Sally. I'm hardly surprised everyone has arrived here at the same time to shop."

"Sir Steven and I are here to be fitted for our costumes," Lord Delaroux said. "Although we're sworn to secrecy and cannot reveal whom or what our disguises will be."

"As it should be!" Lady Bowlingbroke looked down her straight, keen-tipped nose. "Secrecy is of the utmost importance, Robert. By the way, Clarissa, I do hope you will attend this year."

"How very kind of you, Sally. But I am afraid that will be impossible. You see, there has been a change in plans. A rather happy one, I venture to say. But it will necessitate my being absent from your party."

Eugenia had met Sir Steven's dark gaze, and her heart thumped painfully as he stared at her. But Aunt Clarissa's cryptic pronouncement drew her attention. "What are you talking about, Aunt?"

"We've had the most wonderful news! That is why I am here. You see it simply couldn't wait—"

Lady Bowlingbroke's interjection was surprisingly gentle. "Please, Clarissa, don't keep us in suspense. What is it?"

"Her letter came in the post today. Minutes after you left, Genie. I don't suppose you'll be wanting to go to the masquerade, either!"

"Not go?" Eugenia's mouth fell open. The idea was preposterous. She'd planned her costume for months.

"Your mother will be arriving in London that very morning, dear!" Aunt Clarissa clapped her hands gleefully. "Isn't that wonderful! We haven't seen Alexandra in ages, Genie. You won't want to go traipsing off to a party with your mother home."

Feeling as if she'd been punched in the stomach, Eugenia's shoulders involuntarily slumped. Aunt Clarissa was correct; of course, Eugenia was happy to hear that her mother would be arriving in London soon. It had been over a year since her parents had waged their last battle and retreated from the battlefield they called their marriage. Eugenia missed them both sorely.

But the idea of sitting at home listening to Alexandra Terrebonne tell wild tales of handsome sheiks, wealthy pashas, and romantic foreigners while the Bowlingbroke masquerade raged without her made Eugenia's hair stand on end.

Managing a weak smile, she said, "That is wonderful news, Aunt."

"I have an idea," said Lady Sally Bowlingbroke. "Bring Alexandra with you, Clarissa. Surely she can throw together a costume in half a day. As widely traveled as she is, I wager she can pull one from her trunk without difficulty."

" 'Pon my reputation! That is an excellent suggestion." Aunt Clarissa bubbled with excitement.

Eugenia looked from Aunt Clarissa to Sir Steven. Arms crossed over his chest, he stood silently, staring back at her. His blue eyes and pained expression filled her with trepidation. Awareness of something unspoken connected them. Steven read Eugenia's thoughts—she saw them reflected in his gaze—and embarrassment flooded her because her thoughts weren't particularly nice.

Lady Alexandra Terrebonne at the Bowlingbroke

masquerade? What would have been a jolly party now sounded as festive as a beheading. Eugenia loved her mother. But Alexandra was sure to create some sort of scene; she always did. She was as outrageous a woman as she was beautiful. Which was the very reason Albert Terrebonne had married his wife in the first place. *And* which was the reason he hadn't been able to live peacefully with her once he had married her.

Eugenia took a quick, jagged breath and said shakily, "Oh, yes, that is a fine idea. Mother shall be thrilled to attend the masquerade, I'm sure."

"Genie, it will be such fun!" Jane cried. "Your mother is always the life of the party!"

Jane didn't understand; she couldn't. Jane's parents were as ordinary as oatmeal. Jane's parents, no matter how misguided they were in warning her off Sir Steven, were at the very least united in their efforts to raise their daughter. Jane's parents were above reproach, never the target of gossip or the subject of scandal.

Jane's parents were happily married.

A wall of hot tears threatened to burst behind Eugenia's eyes. Her gaze flickered down, then up again. Sir Steven still stared at her, his gaze questioning, intense. In the background, Lady Bowlingbroke and Aunt Clarissa rattled on about what a grand surprise it would be when Lady Alexandra Terrebonne unmasked herself at midnight. But Eugenia wasn't listening.

She looked at Steven and saw nothing else but him. His expression, unsmiling and serious, somehow conveyed an intimacy, a warmth, a private understanding. She thought he knew what she was feeling. She thought he was the only man who could possibly know what she was feeling. And it pained her deeply to know that he saw through her so easily and yet he was as remote to her as a desert island.

Her chest ached with frustration. Her limbs tingled

with dread. But Lady Eugenia Terrebonne, ever her parents' daughter, had been taught never to whine or feel sorry for herself. Steeling her composure, she tore her gaze from Sir Steven and forced a serene smile to her lips. If her mother was attending the Bowlingbroke masquerade, she had no alternative but to grin and bear it. Besides, she told herself, she should be thrilled by the fact that Alexandra was returning to London after nearly a year's hiatus.

The physical act of smiling actually made her feel better. Eventually, Eugenia always told herself, the smile she pasted on her face would be genuine. Unlike Sir Steven, she believed that smiling was beneficial to one's health. She would never allow the world to know how unhappy she was that her Mother would be attending the Bowlingbroke's party. More importantly, she would never allow anyone to know how saddened she was to learn that Lady Jane Bowlingbroke was in love with Sir Steven St. Charles.

God, but she was transparent—to him at least!

Emotion flashed on her face and glimmered in her pretty brown eyes. Staring at her, Steven was reminded of the deer he'd encountered in the forest just a few months earlier. She looked so vulnerable, so perfect.

The jumble of people in Madame Truffaut's slipper department disappeared from Steven's vision. All he saw was Eugenia; all he felt was her sadness.

She loved her mother, that was plain enough. He'd seen the little candle burst of pleasure that lit her eyes when she heard Lady Alexandra Terrebonne was returning to London. But almost immediately, that light had faded and she'd exhaled, appearing exhausted and pale.

Her parents, he surmised, were a difficult couple. From what Eugenia told him, he deduced she was in the middle of a tug-of-war. The Terrebonnes got along about as well as the Plantagenets and the Lancasters. Perhaps they loved one another; perhaps they didn't. Whatever they felt, it wasn't apathy. Clearly, they gained some pleasure from engaging one another in warfare. Otherwise, they wouldn't participate in such spirited battles.

Her anguish was palpable. Steven watched Eugenia's features as she struggled to suppress her emotions. When she turned her limpid eyes on him, a streak of emotion ran through him. He didn't like that. He didn't want to sympathize with Eugenia; he didn't want to feel anything for her. He had a mission to accomplish, and caring for Eugenia would only interfere with that.

Yet, he did feel something for her. Her sweetness and her vulnerability touched him. He wished he could protect her, wrap her in his arms and shield her from the pain her family's warfare had caused her. He had the sudden, inexplicable, and absurdly inappropriate urge to hug her tightly to his chest and spirit her away, take her to some safe haven where he could be alone with her, pet her and soothe her. Good God, he had lost his mind!

Half aware that his name was being bandied about in the conversation surrounding him, Sir Steven stood at the edge of the slipper area, pretending to scan the tiny shop, feigning interest in the dazzling array of fabrics and notions. Surreptitiously, however, he studied Lady Eugenia, that enigmatic little creature whose upset had moved him so. What was it about her that appealed to him? Was it her beauty? Or was it her frankness, her guileless honesty, her courage in openly showing her emotions?

She might as well have pinned her emotions to her sleeve, Steven thought, so readily apparent were they. How unlike him! How novel a concept to the likes of Sir Steven St. Charles, a man who prided himself in keeping all his feelings bottled up inside, never troubling anyone else with them, never daring to show them to the world.

But that was what he'd been taught to do. His own parents, though happily married, had never openly argued or fought. Thinking back, he couldn't recall a single lively debate between them. Indeed, his parents had never discussed their feelings, their emotions, their hopes and dreams. Steven's mother had been a paragon of feminine virtue, all duty and sacrifice. His father was a stalwart individual who'd have died rather than shed a tear in public. No, now that he thought about, Steven realized his parents' marriage had been a rather colorless one. Solid, but colorless. Nothing like the rollicking marriage the Terrebonnes shared.

We are, after all, our parents' children, Steven thought. He gazed absently at a row of fashion plates gracing a long refectory table. Then he moved farther away from the congregation in the shoe department. His mind was too full of confusion to participate in Lord Delaroux's animated conversation. Whatever the dandified lordling was talking about evidently was of great interest to the ladies. *Let Delaroux entertain them.* Steven was far too overwhelmed with his private musings to join in that frivolous exchange.

Beneath a glass counter, elaborately embroidered ribbands wavered and blurred. In their stead, he saw Lady Catherine's face, her expression years ago as she turned her head on the pillow and stared at him. Her gaze, once so warm and loving, held nothing but coldness and accusation that fine spring morning. She looked at Steven as if she despised him.

Lord Fitzhaven, the man Steven believed to be a French sympathizer, leapt from Catherine's bed and hurriedly threw on his clothes. "I suppose you'll want to call me out, Steven," he shouted, snatching his coat.

She didn't even bother to cover her nakedness. She

rolled to her side, propped her head on her hand, and watched the men with feline detachment.

"Get out," Steven had said quietly, menacingly. He had no interest in dueling with Lord Fitzhaven. Oh, he'd like to see the man swing from the end of a rope, that was true enough. But as a spy, not as an unscrupulous bounder.

The Earl of Fitzhaven fled, never to be seen in London again.

"Why so glum, sweetling?" Catherine had said, her voice as icy as her heart. "It isn't as if the two of us are in love."

"Not in love?" He took a step forward, but halted, terrified of his own emotion, the anger that boiled in his blood. Catherine's slightly amused smile filled him with rage. "Good God, you have betrayed me! How could you do such a thing?"

She pulled the counterpane over her breasts then, covering herself as her smile faded. A look of bewildered pain clouded her dark eyes. "How could I—*Merde!* What sort of man are you, Steven? For years, I have tried to get close to you, to break through that brick wall you have built around your heart. But you never let me in!"

"What the devil do you mean?"

"You keep secrets, you nurse grudges, you harbor feelings inside your soul that will never see the light of day! You never confide in me, you never tell me what you are feeling. Oh, you know how to pleasure me in bed, yes! In bed, you are an expert lover. But out of bed, you are a stranger to me."

Steven, blind with pain and anger, stood mute, his hands fisted at his sides. "Don't do this to me," he whispered.

"Didn't you notice, Steven? In the last year, didn't you even notice that I had changed?"

He had not. He didn't have time. He'd been busy working, performing his duties for the Home Office. He couldn't be distracted; he couldn't afford to waste his time worrying about his lover's feelings.

She sat up, her eyes snapping, her features hard. "Get out, Steven. Get out, and don't ever come back. It's too painful loving someone who can't return an ounce of affection. I cannot stand it any longer!"

Slowly, he turned. Leaving Lady Catherine's bed-chamber, Steven sensed that deep within him, something had died. Everything Catherine said was true. Her actions were understandable. He'd neglected her, driven her out of his life. She was, after all, a woman, a flesh and blood creature who needed love . . . just like everyone else . . . everyone else except Sir Steven St. Charles.

Steven didn't need love. Steven didn't need anyone.

Steven didn't need that pretty little girl named Lady Eugenia Terrebonne, whose gaze had fastened on him, whose imploring eyes had filled with tears, then dried in an instant of courage and feistiness. No, he didn't need her or anyone else. He needed only to fulfill his mission for Sir Nigel Pennyworthy. He needed only to find Lord Fitzhaven once again.

This time Steven wouldn't allow the wretched spy to escape justice. This time he would see to it that Fitzhaven was exposed. This time, Steven would get his revenge.

Lord Robert Delaroux's voice finally penetrated Steven's thoughts. "What do you think about that, old man?"

"I'm sorry." Steven hadn't the foggiest idea what Steven was referring to. Shrugging one shoulder, he glanced at Eugenia. A smile trembled on her lips. Whatever Delaroux had suggested apparently made her happy.

"I said what do you think about an outing to the opera? My favorite soprano is performing in Orange Street tomorrow night. It's not the King's Theater, granted, but Mrs. Partridge sings in English—"

"English?" Steven started to blurt that opera was meant to be sung in Italian, but the quick widening of Eugenia's eyes stifled his impulse. "Yes, well that does make the opera more accessible, doesn't it? Of course, I will go."

"Splendid! It is settled, then." Delaroux turned to the ladies. "At seven o'clock sharp Steven and I shall swing by Cuzon Street and pick up Lady Jane, Lady Clarissa, and Lady Eugenia."

His enthusiasm was infectious, Steven had to credit him there. Even Lady Bowlingbroke laughed merrily. And though the prospect of another evening spent pretending he was Delaroux's close *friend* chafed his very last nerve, Steven could hardly decline this latest invitation. Not if he wanted to continue his investigation.

Even as he graciously bowed to the departing Lady Bowlingbroke and her entourage, however, Steven realized he wasn't making much headway in getting closer to the Earl of Bowlingbroke. His plan had been to insinuate himself into the earl's life by befriending—perhaps even courting—his daughter, Lady Jane. But every time he was in Jane's presence, Steven was distracted by her friend Eugenia. Eugenia was far more interesting than Jane. Eugenia, in fact, was bewitchingly attractive.

Determined not to be distracted by her, Steven scowled at Eugenia as she glided past him. It simply wouldn't do for him to reveal his attraction for her. He had a duty to fulfill, a mission to accomplish. He couldn't afford to be distracted by tender, romantic impulses toward Lady Jane Bowlingbroke's best friend. His feelings for Eugenia were of no moment; he should and he would ignore them.

But when she met his gaze, his heart leapt and his body stiffened. Desire and longing streaked through his bloodstream like hundred-proof whiskey. Lady Eugenia Terrebonne did something to him that no other woman had ever done.

It was as if she'd taken a hammer and chisel, and cracked a fissure in the rampart surrounding his heart.

Her ability to see straight through him amazed Sir Steven. And he deeply resented the intrusion.

The ladies, excluding Aunt Clarissa, who returned to Curzon Street in her own carriage, spent the afternoon scouring every bazaar and boutique in West End. Lady Sally Bowlingbroke was indefatigable in her effort to find the most sumptuous gold braid to adorn her costume and the perfect wig to complete her disguise.

When, late in the afternoon, the countess declared she was going to make one last foray to Burlington Arcade, the young ladies Jane and Eugenia begged to be released from their servitude. It took some persuasive talk to convince Lady Bowlingbroke of their need to confer and conspire in connection with their own costumes, but at last she relented, and allowed them both to be driven to Aunt Clarissa's in a hackney cab.

In the hour before supper, they lay exhausted on Eugenia's bed, bolsters propped beneath their knees, stockinged feet elevated.

"Have you seen Dashie?"

Eugenia opened her eyes to see Aunt Clarissa standing in the center of the bedchamber, wringing a linen kerchief in her hands. "Perhaps she is under your bed."

Certain that Dashie was not in her room, Eugenia nevertheless rolled off the four poster, dropped to the carpet on her hands and knees, and peered beneath the bed. "I see a few dustballs and a pair of slippers I thought I'd lost, Aunt. But I do not see Dashie."

"Oh dear! She has been missing now for over an hour.

I do so fear that she has slipped out the back door again
and gone to visit that monstrous little mongrel that lives
two houses down."

Jane peeked out from beneath the damp washrag that
covered her eyes. "Isn't Dashie too old to be interested
in the opposite sex?"

"You're never too old, dearie," Aunt Clarissa replied.

Jane giggled and replaced the washrag.

"Have you looked in the drawing room, Aunt?"
Eugenia asked, crawling back into bed. "And in your
water closet? Perhaps she slipped down the stairs into
the wine cellar when Cook wasn't paying attention."

"Cook swears the basement door has been closed all
day—"

Footsteps in the corridor caused Lady Clarissa to fall
silent. She turned as a gentle rapping sounded at the
door.

Eugenia called, "Come in," the door swung open, and
there stood Mr. Greville with a rather sheepish-looking
Dashie cradled in his arms.

Aunt Clarissa exclaimed, "Oh, Dashie, thank God,
where were you?"

Reluctantly, Mr. Greville said, "She was in the street,
my lady. Rescued by a gentleman who said he had seen
you walking Dashie and knew where the little dog lived.
He brought her home, none the worse for wear, it appears."

"Dashie, you bad girl, you!" Taking the dog from
Greville, Aunt Clarissa hugged it tightly against her
chest—so tightly, in fact, the little animal whimpered
with discomfort. "And when I find out who left the front
door ajar, I shall punish that individual severely!"

A bemused-looking Greville lingered in the doorway.

At last, after nearly smothering Dashie with kisses
and admonishments never to frighten her like that again,

Aunt Clarissa said, "Is there anything else, Mr. Greville?"

"This, my lady." He handed her a thick vellum envelope. "The gentleman handed it to me as he handed over the dog. Thought it was a bit odd, I did."

With a puzzled look, Aunt Clarissa crossed the floor and handed the envelope to Eugenia. "It has your name on it, dear. Why don't you open it?"

Sitting up, Eugenia took the proffered missive. Turning it over, she noted that the expensive paper was sealed with a thick glob of red wax. Her fingers ripped open the envelope and she extracted a folded piece of parchment. At first glance, the letters sprawled across the page in wild, almost illegible abandon.

"Whoever sent it has terrible penmanship," Jane said around a yawn.

Glancing behind her, Eugenia saw that Jane was peeking from beneath her damp towel again. "Quite right." Eugenia focused intently on the words. As she discerned their meaning, a frown tugged at her lips.

"What is it, dear?" Aunt Clarissa asked.

"Read it out loud, for pity's sake!" Jane said.

" 'Dear Lady Eugenia Terrebonne, I am happy that I was able to be of some assistance to your aunt . . .' "

Sitting upright, Jane peered over Eugenia's shoulder. "How very odd that the gentleman should pen you a note before returning Dashie."

Aunt Clarissa, clutching Dashie to her bosom, appeared to be in need of a vial of hartshorn. "Extremely odd. Oh, Dashie, if anything had happened to you—"

Eugenia faced Jane. "This letter is sealed, which means he wrote it *before* he found Dashie in the street. Unless of course he wanders around town with a bowl of hot wax and a seal on his person. Or in his carriage."

Pulling the bell cord, Aunt Clarissa murmured,

"Highly unlikely. At any rate, Dashie and I are going to take a nap."

Within minutes, a young serving woman entered the room. Instantly recognizing Lady Clarissa's state of distraction, the maid helped the older woman from Eugenia's bedchamber. Only when Eugenia heard her aunt's door click shut, did she dare voice her suspicion.

"Do you know the author of the letter?" Jane asked, pointing at the name scrawled on the bottom of the page.

Biting her lip, Eugenia stared hard at the name. "No. In truth, I have never even heard of a Lord Fitzhaven."

SIX

"Blast it to hell, Robert, why can't we simply send round a porter with a message?" It was late in the afternoon, and Sir Steven's patience with Delaroux was wearing thin.

Delaroux sprawled languidly on the squabs opposite Sir Steven. "Because we cannot. We told the ladies we would pick them up at seven o'clock. That was before we learned the opera is sold out for the first performance tomorrow night. We have no choice but to attend the later one."

" 'Tis rude to pay a visit at this time of the day. If you are bound and determined to pay a call, you should wait until tomorrow. Besides, I want to go home." Truth be told, Steven craved a drink. And as his nerves grew more frazzled, the more his thirst intensified.

When the coach rumbled to a stop in front of Lady Clarissa Terrebonne's Curzon Street town home, Steven crossed his arms over his chest and glared at Delaroux. "I'll wait here."

"Have it your way, old man. I'm just going to hand this note to Mr. Greville."

But as the carriage door swung open, Steven saw a man hurrying down the walkway toward the street. With his head ducked and his shoulders slumped, the man looked as if he were making a getaway of some sort. Instantly suspicious, Steven pushed to the edge of the bench seat and peered at the man. When he saw the shock of blond hair that spilled from beneath the brim of the man's beaver hat, Steven's heart stopped.

He leapt from his equipage. His boots hit the cobbles and he ran into the street just as the blond-haired man jumped into a carriage waiting halfway down the block. As soon as the carriage door slammed shut, the rig jolted forward, its team of grays breaking into a gallop before they'd gone a block.

Staring at the departing equipage, Steven swore colorfully. Anger fueled his urge to give chase, but the fleeing carriage grew small in the distance as it picked up speed. There was precious little chance Steven's driver could overtake it. Returning to the walkway where Delaroux stood, Steven expressed his frustration with a salty string of curses.

"Couldn't agree more!" Delaroux stood in the walkway, where the blond man had barreled past him. Brushing invisible lint from his jacket, he frowned indignantly. *"Who was that?* Monstrous rude of the fellow. I nearly fell down trying to avoid a collision. Now my cravat is ruined!"

Steven pinched the bridge of his nose. "Well, you'll just have to go home and have your valet tie a fresh one on, won't you?"

Oblivious to Steven's sarcasm, Delaroux nodded. "Bloody well right. But what am I to do about delivering this message? What if one of the girls sees me? I can't have Lady Jane seeing me like this. I look a fright!"

"Since when is Lady Jane Bowlingbroke the arbiter of all things fashionable? Besides, you said she was too high in the instep for your tastes. Have you changed your mind?"

With his bottom lip poked out, Delaroux shot his cuffs. "What do *you* think about her?"

What Delaroux thought about Jane was immaterial. What he thought about her father was crucially important. "I haven't given her much thought at all, to tell the truth. But she's fairly pleasant to look at and she is exceedingly wealthy. I suppose a man could do much worse than marry a girl the likes of her."

"Do you like her?"

"Do I like—"

"Yes, do you like her? I've seen the way she looks at you, Steven, and believe me, it pains me to say this, but she stares at you with cow eyes, as if you were the most handsome man in the world! If you feel anything toward her, I've no right to stand in the way. I wouldn't. But if you are merely toying with her, if you have no serious intentions of courting her, then I think you should turn your attentions elsewhere. It isn't right to lead a lady on, Steven. It isn't fair."

Startled, Steven stared at Delaroux through narrowed eyes. "I hadn't really thought about it, Robert. I hardly know her. I don't know whether I like her or not. Not in the sense you are talking about, anyway."

"Well, think about it, that's all. Just think about it." Afternoon shadows lengthened on the walkway, and Delaroux's face suddenly darkened.

If Steven had been the sort of man to embrace another, he might then have thrown his arm around Delaroux, so sympathetic was he to the man's plight. But Steven wasn't long on displays of affections, especially toward members of his own gender. Nodding curtly, he swallowed hard and averted his gaze. Embarrassment for Delaroux engulfed him. He wished he didn't have to interfere in Delaroux's courtship, but he had no choice, not if he meant to get closer to the Earl of Bowlingbroke.

"Deliver the message, Robert. I will wait in the carriage." But as Steven turned to go, a movement above him caught his eye. Pausing, he looked back at the house. Lady Eugenia Terrebonne, standing at the third-floor window, stared down at him. In the dimming of the day, her gaze was wistful. It pained Steven that the pluck she'd possessed when he first met her was now replaced by agitated sadness. She loved her mother, but she dreaded the woman's arrival. Conflicted feelings of love and loyalty were something Steven understood.

Eugenia pressed her fingertips against the glass pane. She threw a quick look over her shoulder; she was speaking to someone in the room with her. Steven's breath caught in his throat. He wished he could restore a smile to her lips. But he was determined to resist her charms and befriend Lady Jane. Reminded of his own duplicity, he was filled with self-loathing.

The curtains moved and she was gone.

Trevor Sparrow tried to tell him as he burst through the front door, but Sir Steven ignored the little man's nervous babblings. "Leave me alone, Sparrow, I'm in a foul mood!"

He stalked into his library, slamming the door shut behind him. For a moment, he stood in the late-afternoon semidarkness, his back pressed to the door. "Damme," he muttered. And then, without knowing precisely why, he whispered, *"Eugenia."* The sound of her name on his own lips nearly caused him to explode with frustration.

At the sideboard, he poured himself a healthy dose of whiskey, quaffed it, then poured another. Warmth slowly spread through his veins.

He lit a lamp and stood behind his huge mahogany partner's desk. As light flooded the room, Sir Nigel Pennyworthy faded into view.

"How the hell did you get in here?" Steven growled.

Pennyworthy sat in the armchair opposite Steven's desk. "Mr. Sparrow saw me in, of course. I was told you were not in. I didn't mind waiting."

"What the devil are you doing here?"

"I've come to obtain an intelligence report on your investigation. Are you making any progress, Steve?"

Sir Steven slowly lowered himself into his leather wingback chair. Something in Pennyworthy's smug expression rubbed against the grain. "Very little, as a matter of fact. As you know, my plan was to insinuate myself into the earl's inner circle by befriending his only daughter, Lady Jane."

"Yes, a pretty little minx, wouldn't you say?"

"Fair. A bit toplofty for my tastes."

An elongated span of silence ticked by. "You prefer her friend, Lady Eugenia Terrebonne."

Beneath the desk, Steven's hands curled into fists. "I do not prefer Eugenia. I do not prefer any woman. In fact, I am not interested in women at all."

Pennyworthy arched his brows. "Oh? Are you telling me that you prefer—"

"Take care, Nigel. I wouldn't want to have to shoot you. I am simply saying that home and hearth hold no appeal for me. I take my pleasure with women who are willing, but I make no promises to any of them. Lady Eugenia is not that sort of woman. Therefore, I have no interest in her."

"Ah. You are determined not to fall in love. Ever again."

"Once in a lifetime is enough for any man."

Pennyworthy steepled his fingers beneath his chin. "You have never forgiven her, have you, Steve?"

"If you are referring to Lady Catherine, I prefer not to discuss her."

"Do you know where she is now?"

"I do not care to know," Steven bit out.

"She is back in London, dear boy."

The hair on Steven's nape bristled. *Lady Catherine in London?* A surge of dreadful excitement swept through him. He hated her, yet the thought of seeing Catherine was perversely thrilling. He had a million things he wanted to say to her, yet no words could express the depth and complexity of his emotion. He hoped she missed him. Guiltily, he hoped she was miserable.

Casually, he said, "Last I heard, she was in Scotland. With Fitzhaven."

"It appears her liaison with Fitzhaven has ended. Rather badly, I hear."

"She has left him?"

"Let us say she has *escaped* him."

Steven's breathing grew more shallow; his chest ached. When he spoke, he could not control the rasping anguish in his voice. "Escaped him? Are you suggesting that he was abusive to her, that he misused her?"

"Beat the hell out of her on a regular basis, from what I understand."

"How do you know these things?"

"I make it my business to know such things. Fitzhaven has long been on our list of suspected French sympathists, you know."

"But the Home Office exonerated him!" Steven leaned forward, his clenched fists now on the top of his desk. Hot blood pulsed through his veins and sharp pain stabbed his temples. He couldn't comprehend Pennyworthy's remark. It made no sense.

When Steven had turned in his report to the Home Office five years earlier, Pennyworthy had ripped it to shreds. Instead of recommending a charge of treason against Fitzhaven, Pennyworthy had denounced St. Charles as *reckless* and accused him of harboring a vendetta against the man who had cuckolded him. Steven's career ended in disgrace. Obsessed with his failure to bring down Fitzhaven, he fell into a dissolute life of drinking and debauchery—and would have continued had Pennyworthy not offered him a second chance to bring down Fitzhaven.

Was Pennyworthy admitting he'd been wrong?

"Is it possible, Nigel?" Steven asked. "Are you telling me that you believe Fitzhaven is a traitor?"

"I am telling you that since Lady Catherine has returned to London, her tongue has not ceased wagging. She will tell everyone who will listen what a scoundrel Fitzhaven has been to her."

"A scoundrel is not necessarily a traitor."

"Rumor has it that she is willing to give testimony against her former lover. Don't ask me how I know this. My contacts among the *ton* are legion. There is only one condition, my friend."

"You are not my friend. What is the condition?"

"She will only talk to you."

The pressure in Steven's head was excruciating. He felt as if he were ten thousand leagues beneath the sea. Swallowing hard, he flexed his fingers and tried to regulate his breathing. How he managed to control the tone of his voice, he would never know. "Why does she want to talk to me? For God's sake, she as much as told me she despised me. She chose Fitzhaven over me. Why would she want to talk to me now?"

"Perhaps she recognizes her mistake. Perhaps she is remorseful. Perhaps she still loves you."

Steven stood abruptly. Every nerve in his body stretched to the point of snapping, every muscle tensed. "Someone else can talk to Catherine. I do not want to see her."

"She has important information, Steve. She has lived with Fitzhaven for years. She knows him, his friends, his contacts, and his connections in France. Her testimony could lead to Fitzhaven's arrest and, eventually, his execution. Depending on the depth of her knowledge, she might lead us to an entire network of spies."

"No! Someone else—"

"There *is* no one else, St. Charles!" Pennyworthy uncrossed his long legs, and stood. Eyes burning brightly, he pointed a boney finger at Steven and spoke with the unyielding passion of a zealot. "This is a job only *you* can perform, and you *will* perform it. That is an order from the Prince Regent himself!"

Hot tears blurred Steven's vision, but anger immediately vanquished them. As quickly as his emotion had flared, it subsided. Having no choice in the matter, he would accept his duty with dignity and grace. Never again would he give Sir Nigel Pennyworthy the pleasure of seeing him beaten.

Regaining his composure, Steven quietly replied, "All right, then. Where is she?"

"She is living in rented quarters in Glasshouse Street, not far from here." Pennyworthy passed Steven a small folded slip of paper. "That is her address. I suggest you visit her as soon as possible. Find out everything she knows about Fitzhaven. Assure her that in exchange for her testimony, she will have complete immunity from prosecution and protection from her former lover. Tell her that if she doesn't testify—"

"If she doesn't testify, what?" Steven leveled a malevolent stare at Pennyworthy. He'd never liked the man; now the sight of his gaunt face was sickening, the urge to punch his craggy nose nearly irrepressible.

"You know what will happen to her if she refuses to cooperate, Steven. I am leaving it up to you how best to handle Lady Catherine. You know her far better than I."

"Do you want me to threaten her, Nigel? Is that it? I'm to wheedle as much information out of her, pat her on the hand, and tell her the Prince Regent will reward her for her duplicity. But if she is recalcitrant or too frightened to give testimony that will most likely bring down an entire network of spies, I am to politely remind her that if she refuses, she will be prosecuted herself, or at the least, transported to Australia. Is that it?"

"Do you what you must," Pennyworthy replied tersely. "Just see to it that you win Lady Catherine's trust. Woo her if necessary. God's teeth, seduce her if that is what it takes! Just find out what she knows about Fitzhaven and persuade her to testify against him in a court of law."

With Catherine's address in his balled fist, Steven leaned across his desk. His whispered voice, even to his own ears, was harsh and grating. "Get out of my house, Nigel. And do not ever come here unannounced or uninvited again. I am not your lackey."

"No, Sir Steven. You are Prinny's *gigolo.*" With that parting shot, Pennyworthy pivoted and strode toward the door. Pausing in the threshold, he turned. "Consider yourself fortunate, Steve. You possess the attributes of a great lover. And you are being given another chance to use those talents."

As the door closed behind Sir Nigel Pennyworthy, Steven trembled with pent-up rage and emotion. His throat was parched and his head ached. He crossed the room and stood at his sideboard. He needed a drink. He needed more than a drink. He needed something to numb his fear and assuage his anger. Throwing back a stiff shot of whiskey, sighing as the liquor burned down his throat, his thoughts turned to the comforts which could be found at Mrs. Simca's.

But first he had some business to conduct at Curzon Street.

"Dashie, stand still, dear!" With a grunt, Lady Clarissa bent over to pat her tiny dog on the head. "Oh dear, I am getting old," she said, slowly straightening. "My poor back is killing me."

"Could it be the brass doorstop in your pocket, Aunt?" Standing in the middle of her bedchamber, a dressmaker kneeling at her stockinged feet, Lady Eugenia wore nothing but a thin cotton chemise and a hoop skirt. Pins in the skirt and in the seams of her bodice necessitated her holding her arms out from her sides. Impatience marred her pretty features.

Blushing, Aunt Clarissa removed the object from the folds of her skirt. Only after turning it over in her hands as if it were treasure did the older woman slip it back in her pocket. "I couldn't resist, dear. How often does one get a doorstop from a place like the Fives Court?"

Shaking her head, Eugenia replied, "At any rate, I don't think Dashie likes her costume. Perhaps we should not subject the poor animal to this."

"Nonsense, dear, she loves to get dressed up. Don't you, Dashie?"

But the dog didn't appear thrilled to be wearing the tiny sheepskin coat fashioned for her by Madame Renaud, the mantua maker. Falling prostrate, Dashie whimpered and clawed the air with her tiny paws. When she was unable to rid herself of the sheepskin coat, she scrambled back to her feet, looked up at Clarissa, and sneezed.

Clarissa, apparently interpreting the dog's sneeze as an entreaty, answered by clucking her tongue and saying in a soothing voice, "It will only be for a little while, Dashie, and you will be the most unique little dog in all of Mayfair. La, I know of no other dog who will be in attendance at the Bowlingbroke masquerade. So, come now, be a good girl for Mumsy and stand still for Madame Renaud."

From the bed, where she sprawled on her side, head propped on her hand, Lady Jane spoke around a mouthful of apple. "I think it's the grandest costume I've ever seen!"

Eugenia turned, staring at her friend. "Of course you do. You're not the one dressed in itchy crinoline and a girdle that feels like a tourniquet!"

"You look adorable as Little Bo Peep," answered Jane.

"Now if we could only teach Dashie to bleat." Lady Clarissa chuckled.

Eugenia laughed, too, rather convincingly, as a matter of fact. But in her heart she felt nothing but sadness. Her emotions were topsy-turvy. Her head and her heart were at war.

"Do you really think Mother will have sufficient time to throw together a suitable costume?" she asked Aunt Clarissa. "Perhaps she will not want to attend the masquerade. She'll be weary, after all. Perhaps she will prefer to stay at home and rest."

Lady Clarissa frowned. "I don't know what makes you think that, dear. Your mother has more energy than a charging light brigade. I've no doubt but that she'll rally in time to attend the masquerade. 'Tis the social event of the Season, after all."

Nibbling on the apple core, Lady Jane inserted, "Mother and Father would be disappointed if Lady Terrebonne chose not to attend. You must see that she does, Genie."

With a little huff, Eugenia said, "I pray you aren't suggesting that I have any control over my mother. Or my father, for that matter."

"Don't sound so petulant," said Lady Clarissa. "Your parents adore you and they would do anything for you."

"Then, why don't they live together?" Bitterness spilled into Eugenia's voice. Struggling not to cry, she said, "Then, why don't they act like normal, ordinary people and live together and act kindly toward one another? Why must they always be quarreling and fighting, retreating and regrouping?"

Jane tossed her apple core on the bedside table, and sat up. "Why, Eugenia, I had never thought your parents' situation pained you so!"

"Madame Renaud, will you excuse us please?" said Aunt Clarissa. "And take Dashie to Mr. Greville, if you please. It is about time for her afternoon walk."

When the perplexed seamstress had left the room, Lady Clarissa gave a nod to Jane. The two women quickly helped Eugenia shed her pincushion chemise and slip into a warm woolen robe. Then, as Eugenia and Jane hopped back onto the bed and propped themselves against a bank of pillows, Lady Clarissa pulled the bell cord and summoned a pot of hot tea.

"Is there room for me up there?" she asked, hefting herself and her ballast-filled apron onto the feather mattress.

Snug between her best friend and her beloved aunt, Eugenia released a jagged sigh. "I do apologize. I find it deplorable when others feel sorry for themselves. And here I am, acting like a spoiled child just because my mother is coming to pay a visit."

"I admit, I do not understand your upset," Jane said gently.

"You love your mother, yet you are angry with her because she cannot seem to make peace with your father," Aunt Clarissa said. "Is that it?"

After a pause, Eugenia said, "I can't seem to sort it all out. Of course, I love Mother and I want to see her. I do! But everything is so much . . . so much *easier* when she is not here. Don't you understand, Aunt? She walks into a room and everyone holds their breath, waiting to see what provocative *on-dit* will drop from her lips. And, dear Lord, the stories she tells! It is difficult to listen sometimes, knowing that Father would throttle her if he knew of some of her escapades. She is a light-ning rod for controversy!"

"That is Lady Alexandra to a tee," Lady Clarissa said. "But since when did you begin resenting your mother for being what she is?"

"I do not resent her—" Jane was interrupted by a knock on the door. A maid entered, bearing a tray of tea and crackers. When the servant was gone, Jane contin-ued. "It is just that I was so looking forward to the masquerade. With Mother in attendance . . ."

"Are you saying she will spoil your fun?" Jane asked.

"Yes! No!" Eugenia covered her face with her hands.

"Well, dear me, this is a surprising turn of events," Lady Clarissa said. "I find myself echoing Jane's senti-ments. I had no idea you felt so strongly about your parents' estrangement. I wish that there were something could be done to make everything right for you, Genie, really I do. But I'm afraid the state of your parents' marriage is quite beyond my control, or yours."

Eugenia responded soberly to her aunt's observation. "Yes, I know, Aunt. I learned long ago I could not force my parents to love one another. Indeed, I cannot force *anyone* to feel *anything.*"

"You are wise to understand that," Aunt Clarissa said. "One person cannot control another."

"Perhaps you will simply have to learn to accept your parents' feelings toward one another," Jane said. " 'Tis painful, I am certain. But they are both good people. And your mother is a true original. She'll be the life of the party, you'll see."

Eugenia closed her eyes and hugged herself. Picturing her mother at the Bowlingbroke masquerade, costumed in some outrageous getup and laughing louder than any-one else, she shivered. Yes, Lady Alexandra would be the life of the party. Perhaps she would perform one of her famous parlor tricks and make a coin appear from

behind Lady Bowlingbroke's ear. That was always good
for a laugh. Or maybe she would overindulge at the
punch table and dance the tango with a man half her
age. She'd been known to take snuff, or smoke from a
hookah, if her host would allow it. She had exposed her
naked ankles to Mayfair society more often than Prinny's
Hanoverian she-devil. Lady Terrebonne, or Alex, as she
was known to her friends, invited controversy and gossip. Lady Alex Terrebonne *craved* excitement.

Oh, the Bowlingbroke masquerade was sure to be exciting now. Sir Steven would be there. He would be there
at midnight when everyone's masks came off. And he
would no doubt think that Eugenia's mother was the
most indecorous exhibitionist he'd ever seen.

Gritting her teeth, Eugenia reminded herself that she
could do nothing to control her mother's behavior. Moreover, there was no reason to care what Sir Steven
thought of Alex. He was not, after all, Eugenia's potential suitor. He was Jane's, if she could get permission
from her father to entertain his courtship. That should
have been a consoling thought; Eugenia should have
been relieved to remember that Steven was not her concern but rather Jane's.

But for some odd reason, that thought merely fueled
Eugenia's misery and she wanted nothing but to bury
her head in the pillows and pound her fists and sob.

As her aunt passed her a cup of hot tea, she opened
her eyes. Accepting the saucer, she smiled. Lady
Eugenia Terrebonne was a master of disguises; masquer-
ades were a daily affair for her. She'd hidden her feelings
behind that pretty little smile for years. What difference
could one more night possibly make?

Below stairs, a door was slammed, then hurried footsteps pounded up the stairs. A maidservant entered the
room with a cream-colored envelope in her hand and a
worried look on her face.

"Another letter?" Aunt Clarissa handed her cup and saucer to the servant in exchange for the ivory envelope.

"And there's a gentleman waitin' in the parlor, m'lady."

"A gentleman? Here, Lady Jane, it's come in the post from across town. And it is addressed to you."

"As if I live here!" Jane grabbed the letter, opened it, scanned it, and quickly slipped it in a pocket.

"Who was that from?" Eugenia asked.

"Robert. He wanted me to know that he is going to attend the masquerade dressed as Ro—"

Distracted by the maidservant's fidgeting, Lady Clarissa laid a hand on Jane's arm, shushing her. "What is it, Nellie? You look as nervous as a cat."

"It's Sir Steven St. Charles, m'lady. He's downstairs. Says he's monstrous sorry for calling here at such an impolite hour, it bein' so close to supper and all. But he says he'd like to ask the young ladies a question or two. Asked specifically for Lady Jane, if she was here, which she always seems to be, of course. Oh, I'm sorry, m'lady, I didna' mean nothin' by that remark . . ." The servant twisted her fingers and blushed. "The gentleman said he wouldn't mind seeing Lady Eugenia, too."

"Oh, he would, would he?" Lady Clarissa laughed. "Why, that scamp! Thinks he can court two young ladies at once, does he?"

"What would ye have me tell him, m'lady? Mr. Greville's in the alleyway with Dashie, which is why there was no one to open the front door but me."

"Quite all right, dear. Tell Sir Steven I will receive him in a moment. As for the girls, it is up to them whether they wish to visit with their gentleman caller. His timing is most inappropriate. I wouldn't blame them at all if they chose not to make themselves available."

But there was little chance of the girls being unavailable for Sir Steven's visit. Steeling herself against the unpleasantness of witnessing Jane and Steven's burgeoning romance, Eugenia widened her fake smile.

"I only have to throw on a dress and comb my hair," she said. "Tell Sir Steven I will be down in a trice."

"Me too," said Jane. "I've got a wager on Sir Steven, after all. Perhaps tonight will be the night you make him laugh, Genie. Don't forget our bet. And remember, you only have until the stroke of midnight at the masquerade."

A stream of sourness erupted in Eugenia's belly and scalded the back of her throat. The eagerness in Jane's voice truly made her feel ill.

Nevertheless, her smile persisted.

SEVEN

He stood at the mantelpiece, hands clasped behind his back. Hardly startled by the appearance of Lady Clarissa Terrebonne, he bowed crisply as she entered the drawing room, then thanked her for seeing him at such an inconvenient hour.

"I must admit, there has been more traffic than usual at my front door today." She eyed him speculatively. "Why don't you stay for supper, Sir Steven?"

It was the invitation that took him by surprise. Judging from Lady Clarissa's quick blush, the invitation took her by surprise, too. Concluding immediately that she'd spoken impulsively, and would quickly regret her hospitality, he shook his head.

" 'Tis so kind of you, my lady. But I have an appointment this evening in St. James's. Perhaps another time."

She chuckled. "I shocked you, didn't I? Well, the truth of it is, I shocked myself. But the more I think on it, the more I believe you *should* sup with us. Jane and Eugenia will be delighted. They think the world of you, sir. *Both of them.*"

Steven hesitated. The idea of sitting down to dinner with Jane *and* Eugenia caused a tightening in his gut. Yet he was duty-bound to accept the invitation. "If it is not too much trouble, then."

Clucking her tongue, Aunt Clarissa gave the bell cord a tug, and when Mr. Greville appeared with Dashie in his arms, she informed him that another place should be set at the dinner table.

"Yes, my lady." The dour-faced butler gently placed the little dachshund on the floor, and as it scurried across the carpet toward Aunt Clarissa, he said, "She did her business, ma'am, just like a good girl."

"Good girl, Dashie!" Aunt Clarissa sat on the sofa with the dog nestled in her rather generous lap.

Standing at the mantelpiece, Steven wondered at the phenomenon which compelled pet owners and new parents to marvel over the details of their charges' bodily functions. He saw the disturbing trait a symptom of domesticity, a condition which he vigorously eschewed, and which, in his private musings, he determined was ample justification for never getting married.

Lady Clarissa's question interrupted his thoughts. "Do you have a dog, sir?"

"A dog?" He couldn't imagine. "No."

"A cat, then?"

Steven's only response was a baffled silence.

Lady Clarissa gazed at him as if he were the most pitiful creature. Shaking her head, she murmured, "I am sorry for you then."

"Sorry for me? Whatever for?"

"Everyone needs someone to love, even if it is a furry little four-legged animal."

"Perhaps that is the nature of women," Steven said. "But I need no one."

"Oh? Is that a distinctly masculine trait, this self-sufficiency that you speak of?"

Lady Clarissa's tone, both cynical and patronizing, rankled. Crossing his arms over his chest, Steven met the older woman's gaze. The glint of amusement he detected there irritated him even further.

Harsh words threatened to leap off the tip of his tongue. He wished to tell her that he was not soft or sentimental, that he was not weak or needy. Those were womanly qualities. He, by contrast, was a soldier. And he did not need anyone or anything, much less a furry little four-legged animal!

But it wouldn't do to be rude to Lady Clarissa. Not when he was in her home for the covert purpose of insinuating himself into Lady Jane's good graces.

"I seem always to misspeak in your presence, Lady Clarissa. I pray you will forgive me. I fear my experience in the war has robbed me of my gentility."

Eyeing him shrewdly, Lady Clarissa said, "You are not what you seem, sir. However, my instincts tell me you are an honorable man. I ask only that you take care in dealing with my niece and her friend Lady Jane. They are very young, you know, and despite their seeming sophistication, quite green."

Lady Clarissa's warning was underscored by girlish voices and the light patter of satin slippers on the stairs. Sir Steven, sobered and tense, watched Lady Jane and Lady Eugenia enter the drawing room arm in arm. A quick appraisal of Eugenia's understated gown, and the manner in which it flowed over her hips and legs as she walked, deepened his anxiety. Despite his resolution, he simply couldn't acquit himself of his fascination with Eugenia. He barely noticed Lady Jane.

After a moment of idle chatter, Mr. Greville announced dinner and the party moved smoothly into the dining room. Once seated, Steven found himself staring across the table into Lady Eugenia's huge brown eyes. Disconcerted, he tried not to look at her. Silently, he ate his turtle soup and sipped at his wine. But Eugenia's wide blinking gaze was irresistible, her presence disturbing. By the time he laid down his spoon, Steven was miserable.

Not the least of his irritations was the banal conversation surrounding him. On his right, Lady Jane chattered incessantly about the day's shopping excursion, and particularly the excellent quality of face powders and almond paste she discovered at a small emporium on Bond Street. On his left, at the head of the table, Lady Clarissa fussed over Dashie, who, much to Steven's amazement had been placed in a baby's high chair and was now eating sliced roast beef off a small plate set on the table.

"Have you never seen a dog eat at the table, sir?" Lady Eugenia's lips quirked; she seemed to be stifling a smile.

"I confess, I have not."

"Dashie is one of the family," Lady Clarissa said. "I wouldn't dream of not having her at the dinner table."

Lady Jane giggled. "Mother and Father would have a fit if they saw a dog dining at the table. My parents are far too proper to appreciate such a thing."

"There's much to be said for proper parents," Eugenia replied.

"And there's much to be said for improper ones," Jane rejoined.

"Oh, Janie, I forgot!" Eugenia said, around a mouthful of buttered hot-cross bun. "Did you see the note your mother sent this afternoon?"

Jane nodded. "Um-um. This soup is delicious, Lady Clarissa. My compliments to Cook!"

"Thank you, dear. Do you think it will be warm enough to go out for a ride tomorrow afternoon?"

As the ladies' conversation ricocheted around the table, Steven felt more and more out of place. It seemed to him the ladies never stayed on one subject for more than a minute before they flung themselves to another. And the topics they discussed! Who cared whether Dashie needed her toenails clipped, or whether the aging dowager across the street was really having an illicit love affair with the pie vendor?

"What do you think, Sir Steven?"

Servants had removed the soup dishes and replaced them with plates of roast duck and boiled turnips. As he picked up his knife and fork, Steven realized he'd been spoken to. "Ah, I believe it will be warm tomorrow."

An awkward silence descended. Chewing, Steven became aware that the ladies were staring at him.

"We dispensed with that subject five minutes ago," Lady Eugenia said. "Aunt asked you whether you like the roasted duck."

"Oh." Swallowing, he looked at Eugenia, and again saw that mischievous sparkle in her eyes that told him she was well aware of his discomfort and that she found it amusing. They locked gazes, sharing the joke. The entire tableau was absurd. A dog at the dining table. A conversation so circuitous it would have taken an expert cartographer to map out all the topics.

"Oh," he repeated. "The duck. Yes, the duck is wonderful. Very tender. Not too gamey."

Lady Clarissa smiled gently. "What are you going to do tomorrow, Sir Steven?"

At first, he didn't understand the question. "What am I going to *do?*"

"How do you intend to spend your day?"

Puzzled, Steven looked to Eugenia for help. Her smile, warm and perhaps a bit sympathetic, sent a runner of unwanted desire through him.

"Aunt is merely making small talk." Eugenia chuckled over the rim of her wineglass. "We do not mean to interrogate you, sir. I'm afraid the conversation of three women seems like idle chatter to you, does it not?"

He didn't know what to say. He wondered if the wine had muddled his thinking. Grateful to Lady Jane for launching a sudden tirade against Prinny's debauchery, Steven receded into his own thoughts. He couldn't re-

member when someone had asked him what his plans
were. He couldn't remember when anyone had given a
farthing what he intended to do with his time.

For that matter, he couldn't remember when he'd been
privy to a more trivial, inane conversation. Lady
Clarissa's voice mingled with Jane's, and the ladies
jointly told a ribald anecdote about Princess Caroline's
behavior on the Continent. Eugenia opened her mouth
wide, much too wide to be called ladylike, and guffawed,
her laughter filling Steven with an almost erotic pleasure.

Meeting her gaze, he found his inhibitions loosening.
Perhaps it *was* the wine easing his tension, relaxing his
muscles. Perhaps not. But something peculiar was happening at the corner of his lips. His heart felt light and
his shoulders were relieved of their burdens.

Staring into Eugenia's eyes, Sir Steven smiled.

For a moment, she wasn't certain whether he had
smiled or merely twisted his lips in a grimace of disgust.
Stunned, she stared at him, searching his expression for
a signal of his emotions. But the smile, if it had indeed
been a smile, vanished from his lips as quickly as it had
appeared.

And now, he stared at her, his pale blue gaze penetrating as always, so intense that it filled her with longing and apprehension. As Jane and Clarissa giggled into
their linen serviettes, he stiffened, his face darkening.
Mechanically, he reached for his wineglass and drank
long. When he put the glass down, he touched his linen
to his lips and cleared his throat.

Nodding curtly to Lady Clarissa, he said, "I must be
going now, my lady."

Lady Clarissa dabbed at the tears in her eyes. Still
chuckling, she said, "Are we too much for you, sir? Dear
me, I do apologize if we have run you off. You're more
accustomed to discussions of serious matters, I suppose."

We'd Like to Invite You to Subscribe to Zebra's Regency Romance Book Club and Give You a Gift of 4 Free Books as Your Introduction! (Worth $19.96!)

If you're a Regency lover, imagine the joy of getting **4 FREE Zebra Regency Romances** and then the chance to have these lovely stories delivered to your home each month at the lowest price available! Well, that's our offer to you and here how you benefit by becoming a Regency Romance subscriber:

* **4 FREE** Introductory Regency Romances are delivered to your doorstep

* **4 BRAND NEW** Regencies are then delivered each month (usually before they're available in bookstores)

* Subscribers save almost $4.00 every month

* Home delivery is always **FREE**

* You also receive a **FREE** monthly newsletter, which features author profiles, discounts, subscriber benefits, book previews and more

* No risks or obligations...in other words, you can cancel whenever you wish with no questions asked

Join the thousands of readers who enjoy the savings and convenience offered to Regency Romance subscribers. After your initial introductory shipment, you receive 4 brand-new Zebra Regency Romances each month to examine for 10 days. Then, if you decide to keep the books, you'll pay the preferred subscriber's price of just $4.00 per title. That's only $16.00 for all 4 books and there's never an extra charge for shipping and handling.

It's a no-lose proposition, so return the FREE BOOK CERTIFICATE today!

Say Yes to 4 Free Books!

*Complete and return the order card to receive this
$19.96 value, ABSOLUTELY FREE!*

If the certificate is missing below, write to:
Regency Romance Book Club
P.O. Box 5214, Clifton, New Jersey 07015-5214
or call TOLL-FREE 1-888-345-BOOK

Visit our website at www.kensingtonbooks.com.

FREE BOOK CERTIFICATE

YES! Please rush me 4 Zebra Regency Romances without cost or obligation. I understand that each month thereafter I will be able to preview 4 brand-new Regency Romances FREE for 10 days. Then, if I should decide to keep them, I will pay the money-saving preferred subscriber's price of just $16.00 for all 4...that's a savings of almost $4 off the publisher's price with no additional charge for shipping and handling. I may return any shipment within 10 days and owe nothing, and I may cancel this subscription at any time. My 4 FREE books will be mine to keep in any case.

Name _____

Address_____ Apt. _____

City_____ State_____ Zip_____

Telephone ( ) _____

Signature _____ RN071A
(If under 18, parent or guardian must sign.)

"I suppose."

"Our silly trivialities may bore you," Clarissa continued, "but I, for one, take comfort in the mundane."

"As does the widow across the street." Jane dipped her head, and stifled a snort of laughter.

Eugenia held her breath.

Roughly pushing back his chair, Steven stood ramrod straight. He was not amused. "Good night, ladies. I thank you for a very . . . *interesting* . . . evening. Don't bother ringing for Greville, my lady, I can see myself out."

"Have you forgotten something, Sir Steven?" Lady Clarissa said, without the slightest trace of rancor or surprise at his abrupt farewell.

He looked confused.

"You said you had a question to ask the girls."

"Thank you." His cheeks darkened as he looked from Eugenia to Jane. "There was a gentleman who called here this afternoon. I saw him when Lord Delaroux and I were here earlier. He passed Robert on the walkway, nearly knocked him down, as a matter of fact. Do you know who I am talking about?"

Eugenia and Jane exchanged puzzled glances, then shook their heads.

"Perhaps it was the gentleman who returned Dashie." Noting Sir Steven's frown, Lady Clarissa explained about the dog's mysterious absence and subsequent return. "My little prodigal was brought home by a very kind gentleman who said he found Dashie in the street, of all places. I swear, it made my heart palpitate just to think of the little dear exposed to such danger and filth!"

"And did the gentleman leave his card, or tell anyone his name?" Steven asked.

"His name was Fitzhaven," Eugenia said.

The stormy look that instantly appeared in Steven's

pale blue eyes capped the room like a leaden sky. For a moment, he stood at the table, his fists clenched, tension roiling off his body. At length, he said, "Fitzhaven, then," in so hoarse and low a voice it sent tremors of fear rippling through Eugenia's body. Turning, he strode the length of the room without another word.

"Good night, sir," said Lady Clarissa, seemingly unruffled.

"Good night," Jane and Eugenia murmured in unison to the gentleman's departing back.

At the threshold, he paused, pivoted, and without so much as a glance at Eugenia, said, "Good night, Lady Jane. I look forward to seeing you at the opera."

In a flash, he was gone, leaving behind him a wake of silence.

After a moment, Jane exclaimed, "Well! What happened to him?"

"He ran for the hills, poor boy," Aunt Clarissa replied. "Probably the first time he's ever deserted. The sad thing is, he has deserted himself."

"I don't understand." Eugenia nibbled at her bottom lip, thoroughly confused.

Aunt Clarissa reached over and squeezed Eugenia's hand. "I'm sure you don't. One thing your parents have taught you, whether they intended it or not, is to confront your emotions head-on. I don't believe Sir Steven is capable of doing that. His heart and his head are at war, and he doesn't know what to do about it."

Jane said, "How very romantic, Lady Clarissa! What makes you think so?"

Eugenia watched her friend's eyes sparkle, and wondered whether she would ever be able to feel happiness for Jane's good fortune. Releasing her aunt's hand, she slowly stood, her knees wobbly from the effort of suppressing her emotion. If Sir Steven's head and heart were

at war, it was because he was in love with a young
woman whose father had forbidden him to court her.
His dilemma was obvious. He hadn't even said good
night to Eugenia; he only had eyes for Jane!

She forced a sickly little smile to her lips and pushed
in her chair. "I'm not feeling very well, Aunt. Perhaps
the turtle soup did not agree with my stomach."

Clarissa eyed her shrewdly. The older woman was not
blind to the looks that had passed between Steven and
Eugenia, nor was she fooled by Eugenia's sudden stomach pains. A bubble of friction had surrounded the pair
from the moment they looked across the dinner table at
one another.

Steven's obvious determination not to show any affection for Eugenia was confusing, however. Perhaps the
man truly did have a crush on Jane, but Aunt Clarissa
found that highly doubtful. The two were not suited, she
thought to herself as Eugenia kissed her cheek. Jane was
too concerned about her social position to be attracted
to a man like Steven. Jane needed to be put on a pedestal
and adored.

Eugenia, on the other hand, simply needed love.

The only question in Lady Clarissa's mind was
whether Sir Steven was ready, willing, and able to give
it to her.

There was something about the little brown-eyed
woman at Mrs. Simca's that piqued Steven's interest, and
for a moment, at least, she took his mind off his troubles. He paid a small fortune for the privilege of spend-
ing the evening with her in her tiny bedchamber. Now,
with a glass of brandy in his hand, he lay on her four-
poster bed, fully clothed and booted, watching her as she
moved about the room and slowly discarded her cloth-

ing, item by item, in a dance that he imagined was meant to be erotic.

She peeled off her elbow length gloves and dropped them on her vanity table.

Steven sipped his drink and yawned.

She stepped out of her satin slippers and sat on the edge of the bed, her body nudging Steven's legs. Languorously, she slid the hem of her gown up her thighs in order to display the garter and hooks that held up her stockings.

Mildly intrigued, Steven made eye contact with her and nodded.

She pushed the silken hose down her bare legs and tossed them onto the floor. Then she stood and began to push the bodice of her red velvet gown off her shoulders.

An expanse of creamy *décolletage* glowed in the candlelight.

But Steven's body failed to respond. Somehow, in spite of his iron will to banish thoughts of Eugenia from his mind, he simply could not forget about her.

With a sigh of frustration, he threw one arm over his face.

"Is there anything the matter, sir?" the woman asked.

Unable to witness her nakedness, Steven said, "It has nothing to do with you. Please get dressed."

A rustle of velvet and silk ensued. "The blue devils got you, have they, sir? Has it anything to do with a woman?"

Steven put his arm behind his head and slanted her a curious look. "How did you guess?"

"Hardly a difficult guess, sir. More often than not, men who seek their pleasure at Mrs. Simca's are unhappy at home. Do you want to talk about it? We've got all night, you know. You paid for it, after all. If you leave, I'll only have to go below stairs and find another patron."

Since that notion seemed unappealing to her, Steven decided he was in no rush. Besides, he *was* unhappy at home and didn't wish to be there. Patting the bed beside him, he invited the young woman to lie down, and she did, stretching on her side with her head propped on her hand.

She stared expectantly at him. "What is it then? Wife left you? Girlfriend cheating on you? Spill it all, sir. Whatever you say will never leave this room. I'll go to me grave with your secrets, I swear it."

Steven closed his eyes. It was a heady thought, the idea that he could say anything he wished without fear of repercussion or censure. He supposed that was the essence of why men frequented prostitutes, not so much for the freedom of sexual expression, but for the license to do, be, and say whatever one pleased. This woman was inviting him to let down his inhibitions and say whatever he felt without the worry of being rejected. He'd never felt free to voice his emotions; the very thought of it filled him with anxiety. But the weight of her touch on his arm was reassuring, and he had the need to confide in someone.

"I fear that I have fallen in love," he whispered.

"Does she love you?" the woman asked gently.

"She cannot possibly."

"Why not? You are very handsome, sir. And rich. A bit stern, perhaps, but I'll wager that when you let your guard down, you're a fine sort of fellow."

"That's just it. I will not let my guard down. I can't even reveal my affections toward her, much less tell her that I love her." Steven rubbed his face. "It's all very complicated, you wouldn't understand."

"I might surprise you. Try me."

"She's very young."

"How young?" the woman asked warily.

"Oh, she's of age, I don't mean that! But she's so . . . innocent."

"Is that good or bad?"

Steven stared at the tufted canopy above his bed. "That's bad. Well, it's good, in a way. Damme, I don't know! She seems so vulnerable, and yet when she looks at me, it seems that she can see straight through me."

"That must be very frightening for a man like you."

"What do you mean, *a man like me?*"

"A man who tries to keep his true feelings to himself. You're a sort of, um . . . what's the word? You're a repressed-like sort of man."

"What makes you say that?"

"You never smile, for one thing."

Steven tilted his glass to his lips, draining the liquor and grimacing as it burned a streak down his throat. He *had* nearly smiled that evening, for the first time since he could remember, in fact. Perhaps he *had* even smiled a bit. He knew his lips had turned up and he'd felt as if his face were about to crack. Horrified, he'd quickly schooled his lips into a scowl. But it may have been too late; he wasn't certain, but he feared his body had indeed betrayed him and allowed a smile to flicker on his lips.

What had caused such a bizarre phenomenon?

He struggled to recall. There had been a silly joke told at the dinner table, and Eugenia had laughed. It wasn't the joke that Steven smiled at. He remembered now. It was the way Eugenia's lips had slowly curved and her nose wrinkled and her gaze lighted up with amusement. She had the most miraculous smile, he thought, picturing again the movement of her expression, the amazing way her features always seemed to be melting upward instead of down.

Yes, it was amazing. It stole his breath away, and as

he lay beside the prostitute at Mrs. Simca's, his body grew tense with desire and his heart ached for release. But the desire was not for the woman lying beside him. And the release he needed had nothing to do with sex. What Sir Steven St. Charles needed was a moment alone with Lady Eugenia Terrebonne, just a moment to tell her how he felt, to whisper trivialities in her ear and make her smile. He needed to see her eyes sparkle and her teeth flash in the candlelight. He needed to make her laugh. A delicious chill rippled over his skin at the memory of her laughter.

The prostitute beside him whispered, "What is it that you want from this woman, sir?"

Steven gave the question some thought. When he finally spoke, his voice was hoarse and liquid heat behind his closed eyelids felt dangerously close to spilling. He wanted from Eugenia what he'd never had from any other woman, and even as he said it, he knew it was foolish to believe that it was possible.

"Acceptance." His glass tumbled from his fingers and shattered on the hardwood floor. He threw both arms over his face and through the shudder of self-loathing that wracked his body, said, "I want her to trust me. And yet I am so very afraid that I am not the sort of man she should."

"Ouch!" Eugenia stared at the droplet of blood on her fingertip. In less than half an hour, she'd managed to prick herself three times. Her fingers were bruised and stiff from the violence of her stitching, and to show for her efforts, the underside of her embroidery looked like a chicken had worked on it.

She looked over at Jane, who, bent over the keyboard of the pianoforte, was managing to make Hayden sound like chopsticks. Sucking on her fingertip, Eugenia stared at the winsome blond beauty and for a fleeting instant, thought, *Why is she still here?*

Then, a backlash of guilt assailed her as she realized Jane was still in Curzon Street because the Earl and Countess of Bowlingbroke were attending yet another raucous dinner party and hothouse route. Jane preferred to spend her otherwise lonely evenings with Eugenia at Aunt Clarissa's. The girls were, after all, best friends. Why Eugenia should suddenly begrudge her dearest confidante the sanctuary of her own home was inexplicable.

Well, not inexplicable, Eugenia thought, studying the pad of her finger. Satisfied by the absence of blood, she stabbed her needle through the linen canvas stretched taut in her embroidery hoop. In her own mind, she easily explained the resentment she felt toward Jane.

A pause in Jane's recital, followed by a frantic flipping of sheet music, then a resounding chord of mismatched sharps and flats, drew Eugenia's irritation to a head. Gritting her teeth, she reminded herself that Jane had always been an atrocious piano player. Yet Eugenia's nerves had never been so frazzled by the pounding of the keys as they were tonight. And she'd never felt as suffocated by Jane's fussy presence as she did tonight.

Yanking needle and thread through the underside of her embroidery, Eugenia muttered a mild curse under her breath. Jane had not become a nuisance overnight; it was simply that Sir Steven liked Jane better than he like Eugenia. And that was something Eugenia found unbearably painful.

Her mind flashed on his face, to the way he looked at dinner when the ladies bored him to tears with their silly chatter of pampered dogs, bored widows, ribbons, and the weather. She saw the look on his face when Aunt Clarissa asked him how he'd spent his day. His eyes had widened slightly, then narrowed in a hooded, almost suspicious look—as if he didn't trust the question, or as if he thought Clarissa was trying to trick him, or make a fool of him. Was it possible that he took offense at the question? Or, Eugenia wondered, her fingers frozen over her sewing, was it simply as Clarissa had later suggested, that no one had ever made that particular inquiry of him?

In her mind, she turned over Clarissa's theory that Sir Steven had bolted from the dining room, or "run for the hills," because the cozy intimacy of the evening and the comfortable banality of the conversation unnerved him. Clarissa thought the intimacy unnerved him because he wasn't accustomed to letting other people see so much of himself. She surmised—and shared her musings sotto voce with Eugenia while Jane was above stairs in the water closet—that the man was so accustomed to suppressing his emotion that he couldn't bear the gay candor or the trivial chatter of the ladies' dinner table. It disturbed him. It provoked him. It made him smile.

A half-triumphant, half-sympathetic little grin wavered at the corner of Eugenia's mouth. When she glanced at Jane, however, her lips pressed firmly together. It wouldn't do for Jane to ask why she was smiling. Jane hadn't even noticed Sir Steven's smile. The smile itself, the way Steven's mouth had curved, the way the lines in his face had smoothed and the tiny creases at his eyes had crinkled, sent a frisson of excitement through Eugenia's body. But the thought that Steven smiled in response to Jane's silly joke made Eugenia's stomach roil.

Sighing, she pulled a strand of yellow wool through the coarse canvas. The colorful pastoral scene she embroidered would be a small pillow cover, but the creative process left her totally unfulfilled tonight. She simply could not forget Sir Steven's abrupt departure, or the fact that he bid good night to Jane and not her. His actions were proof of his feelings, weren't they? She had no alternative but to believe that Jane was the object of his deeply disguised affections.

And if that were true, wasn't it her obligation as Jane's best friend to facilitate the romance? Despite the earl's opposition, Jane and Stephen were clearly infatuated with one another. Or, so it seemed. Eugenia looked up, caught Jane's gaze, and smiled.

"Your needlepoint is beautiful, Genie. Much better than my piano playing!" Jane's laughter swelled throughout the room.

The pretty blonde really was quite guileless. Another wave of guilt washed over Eugenia. Her resentment toward Jane was petty, childish, and misplaced. A true friend would act in Jane's best interest, assisting her without complaint in her efforts to snare Sir Steven. It would be a measure of Eugenia's character to see if she could put aside her own selfish interests and focus on the wants and desires of her friend.

Setting aside her needlepoint, she stood and walked to the pianoforte. "Jane, your playing is"—a giggle erupted at her lips—"truly awful!"

Jane's mouth formed a little O and her eyes rounded. For an instant, she looked wounded. Then her smile returned and her fists fell like hams on the keyboard. The discordant noise startled Eugenia and, with a yelp, she jumped so violently that her teeth chattered.

"It serves you right!" Jane cried.

The girls laughed together until tears ran down their cheeks. By the time they ascended the steps, they were arm in arm and as close in spirit as sisters.

At the landing, they paused. Eugenia kissed her friend's cheek and said good night without the slightest outward hint of disappointment. If the good Lord meant for Jane and Steven to be together, it was not Eugenia's place to second-guess Him. Nor was it the Earl of Bowlingbroke's prerogative to abrogate the romance—even if Jane was his daughter. If the couple was thwarted in their efforts to be together, it was Eugenia's duty as Jane's friend to do everything in her power to help them.

"You are the very dearest friend a girl could wish for," Jane said, unwittingly deepening Eugenia's confusion and guilt. Then she turned and headed for the guest bedchamber that had become her own headquarters away from the Bowlingbroke town house.

Tossing herself in bed, Eugenia flashed on the image of Jane in a gorgeous white wedding gown, walking down the aisle of some grand cathedral toward her handsome lover. She pictured Sir Steven's face, his serious, somber, unsmiling expression. A sob racked her body. Her imagination tortured her. In her mind's eye, Steven's lips twitched, quirked, thinned . . . then curved upward in a slow, sensual smile.

But the smile was for Jane, not Eugenia.

And the cruel, self-punishing fantasy Eugenia conjured for herself produced nothing but a flood of scalding tears.

For no matter how noble and selfless Eugenia tried to be, she could not lie to herself. The thought of Steven loving anyone but her filled her with hot dread and disappointment. The thought of Steven's dark brooding gaze staring at her across the dinner table filled her with longing.

And the thought—the vivid image that was burned on her mind—of his smile, so fleeting and so quickly suppressed, filled Eugenia with a desire so compelling and so relentless that she feared her aching body would melt from the heat of her desire.

EIGHT

Twelve hours and several bottles of whiskey later, Steven remained at Mrs. Simca's, sequestered in the tiny bedroom of the buxom brunette whom he now knew as Harriet. Flat on his back, he lay bare-chested, with his naked feet cradled in the capable hands of Harriet, who clad in a thin chemise, kneeled at the foot of the bed.

He took a long drink, then reached to set his empty glass on the bedside table. Unfortunately, just at that moment, Harriet, who had been kneading the sole of his foot with her fist, applied a new force of pressure which sent a shard of pleasure up his spine. His fingers relaxed too quickly and the glass fell to the floor with a crack.

"That's the third glass you've broken, sir." Harriet's tone was mildly admonishing, her smile slow and sweet, as she languorously pulled his toes.

He grimaced, then sighed his satisfaction. The fact that he hadn't had sex with Harriet did not diminish the physical pleasure she'd given him during the night and throughout the long, lazy day. Nor did their lack of bed sport reduce the comfort he'd found in talking to her.

"Sorry, Harro." He had even coined a pet name for her. "I'll pay. What time is it?"

She didn't answer, but rather offered to pull the bell cord and summon a plate of food. Famished, Steven managed to push himself to his elbows and crow his delight when a maidservant appeared with a tray laden with sausages, tiny cakes, and hothouse fruits. While he and Harriet ate, supine on the bed with the food between them, like decadent Roman emperors, they continued a conversation that had lasted throughout the night.

"Why on earth would someone want to know what I *did* during the day?" Steven asked, popping a grape into his mouth.

Harriet giggled. "Was it Lady Eugenia who asked you?"

"No, it was her Aunt Clarissa. Wanted to know how I spent my day, for God's sake. Don't think anyone has ever asked me such a silly question. Didn't rightly know how to answer it."

"This woman, Catherine—didn't *she* ever say to you, 'Darling, how was your day?' "

"Of course not. 'Twas none of her concern. She had her own interests, I had mine. We went in different directions, and it suited us well. We got along that way, you see, never imposing on one another, never intruding."

"Yes, I see." Harriet crumbled the top of a muffin with her fingers and in a rather unlady-like fashion, crammed the sweet bread into her mouth. Brushing crumbs from her lips, she said, "You've never been in love before, have you?"

"I loved Catherine."

"Did you? What did you love about her?"

Steven hesitated, his mind reeling back to the days when he and Catherine were together. "She was very beautiful, with her long raven hair and flashing eyes. Her sense of fashion was exquisite. Everywhere I went with her, heads turned and people stared. She always appeared perfect, like a China doll. I warrant, sometimes it was nearly bloody impossible for me to keep my hands off her—even in public!"

A shrewd look gleamed in Harriet's eyes. "Was she sweet and kind?"

Sweet and kind? A long moment passed while Steven nibbled on strawberries and considered the question. A burst of sourness on his tongue drew a frown to his lips. Hothouse fruits were often underripe; removing the pit from his mouth, he sighed.

"I remember once when she discharged a young footman for being absent from work so many times in a week. Later, I discovered that the boy missed work because he was severely ill from the flux. His illness resulted from standing for hours in a rainstorm at the Oxford-Cambridge cricket match, just to hold an umbrella above Catherine's head. When I told Catherine she should reemploy the child, she looked at me as if I had lost my senses. I later hired the boy as my tiger, but Catherine ridiculed me each time she saw the ragtag little creature in his striped vest and baggy pants."

"All right, then, charity wasn't her greatest moral attribute. Was she at least intelligent? Witty? Or, perhaps clever?"

"Oh, she was clever," replied Steven. "Clever enough to conduct an affair with a man I had accused of . . . well, you needn't be privy to all my secrets, Harro. Suffice to say, Catherine knew what she was about and never passed up an opportunity to advance her own interests."

"Forgive me for saying so, sir, but your Lady Catherine sounds positively dreadful."

The truth of Harriet's statement pained Steven, yet it also provoked a perverse urge to defend Catherine. "Oh, she wasn't that bad. A bit vain, perhaps, but what woman of fashion isn't?" Perhaps he simply didn't want to admit he could be such a poor judge of character.

"She hadn't a selfless bone in her body, if what you are telling me is true. And you, sir, are equally at fault for tolerating such superficiality."

"Are you questioning my ethics, woman?" Steven ate another strawberry, savagely chewing the hard, bitter little fruit, ignoring the tart acidity that puckered his lips and brow.

"I'm questioning your motivation and your honesty. You didn't love Catherine, you couldn't have!"

The sudden urge to leap out of the bed and end this disturbing conversation was quickly suppressed by Steven's self-punishing nature. It struck him as absurd that he allowed Harriet the prostitute to talk to him in such a familiar manner. A man who challenged his integrity would have been called out. But Harriet's interrogation brought the dawn of a certain clarity, and though accompanied by the discomfort of brutal self-realization, the past illumined was far more instructive than a history clouded in denial and bitterness. For once, instead of evading and escaping his own feelings, Steven chose to confront them and fight.

"I thought I loved her. And if I thought I did . . . well, then, I did, didn't I?"

She shrugged one shoulder. "Ask your heart, sir."

He fell quiet, confused and frustrated. His thoughts darted from past to present, from one puzzling woman to another.

At length, Harriet said, "What are you thinking about now?"

Taken off guard, he answered frankly. "Eugenia."

She reached over and, with the back of her hand, caressed his cheek. "Speak your mind, sir. Tell me. Your secrets are safe with me."

Closing his eyes, Steven pictured the pretty doe-eyed girl he'd met at Nigel Pennyworthy's just a few nights earlier. Her swanlike neck, the tumble of chestnut hair atop her head, the fragile yet intrepid quality of her being . . . her sweetness . . . all these, her considerable charms, conspired to breach Steven's hitherto impenetrable defenses.

Grasping Harriet's fingers, he beat back the wave of emotion that threatened to consume him. In a hoarse whisper, he confided, "I wonder where she is. I wonder how she has spent her day. *God in heaven have mercy on me.* I wonder what Eugenia is doing this very moment."

"Have you decided what you are going to wear to the opera tonight?" Lady Jane Bowlingbroke paused in her stroll down the aisles of the traveling library. Running her finger down the gilt spine of a book, she glanced sideways at Eugenia.

"Um? I hadn't given it any thought, to tell the truth." The lines in Sir Walter Scott's latest novel blurred before her eyes as Eugenia felt the glare of Jane's scrutiny. She looked up from the leather-bound volume she held. "Why are you staring at me like that?"

"I've been thinking."

"About what I should wear?"

"No, silly. About what *I* should wear!"

Eugenia stifled a giggle. "I should have known. And what have you decided?"

"I think I should wear something very daring and eye-catching."

"Do not forget, Jane, that you are going to be sitting for several hours. I plan on dressing comfortably."

"A woman must suffer for beauty."

"If that is the case, I am relieved to be thought of as plain. I'm afraid I haven't the energy to be beautiful."

Jane snatched the book from Eugenia's hands and snapped it shut. Shoving it back into place on the shelf, she stood beside her friend and said, "Do you think he fancies me, Genie?"

"How could he not?" Eugenia met the pretty blue gaze that stared back at her. "The question is, are you certain you love him? Is it possible that your parents' opposition has made him more attractive to you than he would be otherwise?"

A dreamy look drenched Jane's eyes. "Not possible, Genie. I love him, plain and simple."

"Well, then, that is that."

"But Father thinks he is too far below my station to be seriously thought of as a potential husband."

"There are only so many dukes, marquises, and earls to go around," Eugenia pointed out.

"Yes, yes, but Father knows at least fifty men who are earls or better. According to Father, a viscount is barely above the salt. A baronetcy is no good at all."

"How enlightening," Eugenia murmured.

"Oh, he doesn't mind associating himself with men of inferior rank. 'Tis necessary in the ordinary course of business, commerce, and politics. He has befriended men from all walks of life—your father, for example, and Sir Nigel Pennyworthy. It is just that Father does not want *me* to marry *down,* do you understand, Genie?"

"I think I am beginning to." A trickle of sympathy for poor Sir Steven began to seep into Eugenia's heart. She wondered if the man knew what he was letting himself in for. A life of being snubbed by his father-in-law? Was it worth it?

"I have a plan." Jane's face was lit with mischief. "It will require your cooperation, though. Will you help me, Genie? Oh, dear, dear, dearest friend, will you please help me?"

Swallowing hard, Eugenia nodded. "Anything for a friend. What must I do?"

"I want you to deliver a message to my father. Oh, don't worry, I will have it written down on a piece of paper, and you will merely slip it into his hand when

you greet him. Tell him not to open the message until
midnight. You will be in costume, with your face disguised. Father will think you are a flirt, playing some
naughty game, and he will go along, I have no doubt."

"And what will the message say?"

"I cannot tell you now, dear," Jane whispered. "The
details are not entirely clear. But when all is said and
done, my father will know the true measure of a man.
Rank will not signify when my hero rescues me."

"When your hero *rescues* you? From what? What sort
of caper are you plotting, Jane?"

"Best you not know everything just yet."

An older woman brushed past, scowling in disap-
proval of the girls' idle chatter. Smiling at her, Jane
added, "And do not forget our bet, Eugenia. You have
tonight at the opera and then until midnight at the masquerade to coax a chuckle from our handsome friend."

"Impossible." Eugenia's throat constricted. Jane
hoped to lose the bet, of course. If Steven did laugh,
then Eugenia would have the prerogative to name whatever man she chose and Jane would have to kiss him.
Jane was counting on Eugenia to choose Sir Steven, but
in the mood she was in, Eugenia might very well force
her friend to kiss Lord Delaroux!

"Anything is possible, Genie. We ought not to let con-
vention stand in our way of happiness."

"You sound suspiciously like Aunt Clarissa," Eugenia
noted glumly. "And for once, I am not sure that is a
good thing."

Jane grasped Eugenia's hands and held them tightly.
"Oh, dear, dear, dearest friend . . ."

"Enough!" Half teasingly, Eugenia shook off her
friend's embrace. "You are too reckless by half, Jane!
When your father catches wind of this wild escapade,
whatever it is, he will turn you over his knee!"

"On the contrary, dear. When the Earl of Bowlingbroke comprehends how brave and heroic my true love is, which result I am confident of now that I have conscripted you into my conspiracy, he will have no choice but to alter his views concerning my marriage. He *is* brave and heroic, Genie."

"Who?"

"Romeo. Oh, it is so romantic. I dare not even whisper his true name. We are like the Montagues and Capulets, Genie. But my Romeo is all that is good and kind and . . . oh, it doesn't matter that Father thinks him a paperscull."

"A paper—" Eugenia laughed out loud at the absurdity of the earl's snobbishness. Then, taking Jane's arm, she walked leisurely toward the subscription counter of the library, where she purchased a copy of Sheridan's *The School For Scandal.* "For you," she said, presenting the tiny folio to Jane as they emerged in the afternoon sun. "I think you will find it amusing, and perhaps, like Georgiana, you will recognize yourself somewhere in that make-believe cosmos."

"The Duchess of Devonshire?" Jane took the proffered gift and held it close to her bosom. "Now there was a great lady of fashion, Genie."

As they gracefully embarked Lady Clarissa's waiting carriage, Eugenia said to her friend, "There was a lady who learned her lessons the hard way. I hope you do not find your future life to be so painfully instructive, dear."

"Dearest, dearest, dearest friend," Jane said, closing her eyes, and imagining, Eugenia was certain, her beloved Romeo sweeping her into his arms and spiriting her away from her own, perfectly wonderful, tightly corseted, mundane little existence.

With a sigh, Eugenia tossed off her bonnet and stared out the window at the Georgian mansions that swept past the moving equipage. The uneasy resentment she felt at playing Cupid for her friend was not alleviated; in her heart remained a deep sense of disappointment at Steven's lack of interest in her. But the idea of teaching the Earl of Bowlingbroke a lesson in democracy held a wicked appeal.

If she couldn't have love, Eugenia reckoned, at least she would have some fun.

Perhaps there was a bit of the old Georgiana in her as well.

Lady Catherine Malloy-Fitzhaven was not surprised to find Sir Steven St. Charles in her drawing room. The butler had merely announced the arrival of a "gentleman who wouldn't give his name, m'lady," but Catherine had been expecting him. He was, above all else, a man of duty and honor. It was inconceivable that he wouldn't come to her now. And it was inconceivable that he wouldn't come angrily.

What did surprise her as she ushered her servant out, then gently drew shut the doors behind her, was the affect his broad shoulders and rigid bearing had on her. With his back to her, he stood at the mantelpiece, his hands clasped behind him, his head slightly bowed. She knew that posture well, knew that he was deep in thought, mulling over some serious problem, contemplating some unpleasant task that lay ahead. It was Steven's classic pose. It was one of the many ways he had locked her out of his private world.

"Steven."

Slowly, he turned. Facing her, his gaze swept her entire length, and though he probably wished he could suppress it, his eyes held a grudging look of masculine approval. "You haven't changed, Cat."

But he had. His face was deeply lined, his features more angular, his pale blue stare even icier than she remembered. The thick blond hair she'd curled her fingers in so many times before was now cut unfashionably short in a style that could only be called Spartan. His mouth turned down. Even his eye sockets seemed bonier, more skeletal.

A dryness clutched at her throat. Tentatively, Catherine took a step toward him, noting his still lean legs, his narrow hips . . . the provocative fit of his buff breeches and the nearly obscene prominence of his masculine anatomy.

"You haven't changed either."

"A lady wouldn't stare at a gentleman that way."

Lifting the trajectory of her gaze, Catherine met his stare. Cold though it was, it filled her with heat as it had always done. "Then, I don't care to be a lady."

A long moment of silence stretched between them. At length, Steven said, "I think you should know that Sir Nigel Pennyworthy asked me to come here. No, *ordered* me to come. Otherwise, I wouldn't have."

"I need you, Steve."

"I wouldn't have come absent Nigel's orders," he repeated, emphasizing each syllable. "He has instructed me to offer you help—"

"I need a place to live. These are temporary quarters. I cannot stay here much longer."

"—in exchange for information."

"I've already told Nigel what I know. Which isn't much. Nothing in fact."

"He wants to know where Fitzhaven is hiding and who his contacts are. According to Nigel, Fitz may be concealing an entire network of French sympathizers, men who, if they are not out-and-out spies, would be willing to pass on sensitive information to the French concerning the British War Department's state of readiness, or Prinny's secret strategies."

Catherine pressed her lips together. "I know of no such network."

"—men who are well placed in government and society," Steven continued. "Wealthy men who might provide financial aid for the French cause, or contribute funds to one of those ultrafanatic cults that would resurrect Robespierre if possible."

"Rubbish! There is no such cult! The newspapers spew that sort of trash to frighten the populace and entertain the *ton!* Besides, why would I divulge the names of such men, even if I knew them. I would be signing my own death warrant, Steven. You know that."

"You would have my protection, Catherine."

"Would I?"

Before she knew it, Steven had closed the distance between them and grasped her upper arms. Gasping, she looked into his angry eyes. His nearness filled her with desire, yet his anger frightened her. Pressing her palms against his chest, she arched her back a little so that their bodies touched and their lips met.

She felt his body stiffen.

"Damn you, Catherine," he whispered.

"Without you, Steven, I am already damned."

His expression tightened; he drew back and gave her one last searching, scalding look before he lowered his head and kissed her.

Her lips yielded beneath his mouth while her pliant body melted into his arms. Steven pulled her into his embrace, his kisses rough and hungry. A flood of erotic desire rushed through him. And a hundred emotions he couldn't identify peppered his thoughts.

His hands traced the familiar curves of her hips and bosom. Memories of their lovemaking stirred him. A raw, physical need compelled Steven toward unreasoned passion. Despite her betrayal, or perhaps because of it, he still wanted to possess Catherine. Her feline aloofness captivated and challenged him. But as always, she was perfectly in control.

Pushing him to arm's length, she murmured, "Come above stairs with me, Steven."

Blood roared in his temples. Without speaking, he took Catherine's extended hand and followed her to the drawing room doors. On the landing, he drew to a halt, staring at her, wondering what the devil he was about to do, wondering if he dared give in to Catherine's seduction.

He wanted her. God, how he wanted her!

As if sensing his hesitation, she tilted her head and slanted him an alluring half smile. "For old time's sake, Steve. Please."

"I didn't come here to rekindle our affair, Cat."

"I know that. But lie down with me awhile and I will tell you what you wish to know. That's why you came here, isn't it, Steven? To fulfill your duty to your country?"

"I cannot lie to you. I do not love you."

"Here I am offering to share all my secrets with you, and you are worried about your *ethics.*" She clucked her tongue. "You always were too serious, sweetling."

She moved toward him, lifting her face. Surrounded by her perfume, a lush aroma of moss and musk, he felt trapped, weakened by his own frustrating urges. "No, Catherine," he managed.

Her mouth found his again, her arms wound round his neck, and her fingers coiled in the hair at his nape. Hoarsely, she whispered, "I will tell you everything. Just come upstairs with me."

Then her hands moved down the length of his body, stroking and caressing him as only Catherine knew how to do. Expertly, she brought him to the brink of his desire. His breath caught in his throat, and in a blinding flash, physical hunger consumed him. Brusquely, he swept Catherine off her feet and gathered her in his arms. As her hands linked behind his neck and her head fell against his shoulder, he marched up the steps and toward the bedroom she indicated. Inside, he kicked the door shut and tossed Catherine on the bed.

On her back, raven hair splayed across the pillow, hands thrown up in a gesture of feminine capitulation, she purred her arousal.

Steven hovered over her, mindless of anything but his sexual need. Slowly, deliberately, he lowered his mouth to hers.

But just as their lips met, and their gazes locked, and their breathing mingled, a crack of gunfire sounded below stairs.

"He shot me! He bloody well shot me!" Lord Robert Delaroux, standing in the center of Catherine's entry hall, clutched his chest.

Steven bounded down the steps and, taking in the shocking tableau with one glance, rushed past Delaroux toward the gaping front door. Not surprisingly, he saw a fair-haired young man sprinting away from the house, down the walkway, and toward the street, where a carriage awaited. But now was not the time to give chase. Treating Delaroux's injuries was the prime concern.

"What the hell are you doing here, and where were you shot? Move your hands, for God's sake, and let me see." When Catherine appeared on the scene, Steven made an elliptical set of introductions while continuing his examination of Delaroux's shirtfront. It was difficult, given Delaroux's general state of agitation.

"I'll get some hartshorn," Catherine suggested, disappearing.

"Christ on a raft," Steven muttered. "Your wound is

on your upper arm, Robert. It's nothing but a scratch, thank God."

"But there's blood all over my chest! I've been shot in the heart, Steven." Delaroux's face was pale as a bleached larch. "You will tell Lady Jane that I loved her, won't you?"

"Tell her yourself," Steven growled. "You'll live another fifty years, at least, if someone else doesn't see his way clear to shoot you. The blood on your shirtfront is from your fingers. Your wound is not life-threatening, I assure you. Once it's cleansed and bandaged, you'll forget all about it."

"What precisely happened?" Catherine had materialized with a small brown vial of smelling salts. "Who shot this man? And why on earth would someone shoot him in my house?"

"First things first." Steven took the lead in directing the small party to the first-floor drawing room. With Robert settled comfortably on a small settee, and Catherine perched on gilt chair, he found a bottle of whiskey at the sideboard and helped himself. Then he handed a drink to Robert and, standing before the mantelpiece, watched the wounded man gulp it down. "Feel better? Good. Tell me, then, Robert, why you came here tonight."

"Been looking all over for you." Delaroux wiped his mouth with the back of his sleeve. Gingerly touching the gash in the upper arm of his bottle green jacket, he frowned. "Don't you think we should summon a surgeon, or a barber?"

"You're more in need of a tailor," Steven replied impatiently. "Why are you here, Robert?"

"I went to your house to fetch you for the opera. Had you forgotten, Steven? Trevor said he hadn't seen you since yesterday. Don't mean to embarrass you in front

of your lady friend, but your valet said he feared you
were on another bender."

"A bender?"

"According to Trevor, you haven't gone on a binge
in weeks; he figured you were due one."

Sighing, Steven pinched the bridge of his nose. No,
he hadn't gone on a binge since Pennyworthy enlisted
him to spy on Lord Bowlingbroke. The prospect of nab-
bing Fitzhaven and bringing the diabolical villain to his
knees had given Steven a new purpose in life. But now
everything seemed to be leading toward a disaster, and
the whiskey burning down his throat merely magnified
his sense of failure.

He'd fallen in love with Lady Eugenia, yet duty demanded he ignore her. He'd nearly succumbed to Catherine's seduction, and might yet, in some bizarre and
perverted attempt to get even with her. He had even put
Lord Robert Delaroux in harm's way. And still, he hadn't
a damn bit of evidence to show to Pennyworthy that
Bowlingbroke was a French collaborator.

"Anyway," Delaroux continued blithely, "Trevor said
he didn't know where you were. So, I went to Mrs. Pommard's. Thought you might be playing cards. But you
weren't. I went to Brooks's, but the doormen said they
hadn't seen you in ages. Then I remembered Mrs.
Simca's."

"Mrs. Simca's?" Catherine shot an accusatory glance
at Steven.

"As luck would have it," said Robert, "you were just
getting into your carriage to leave when I drew up. My
driver pulled to a stop and I hopped down. I tried to
catch your attention, but you didn't hear me yelling.
That's when I told my driver to follow you. I'm surprised you didn't see my rig drawing up when you
knocked on the front door here."

"I'm afraid I was bit preoccupied." Avoiding Catherine's scorching looks, Steven made another trip to the sideboard. This time, he poured himself a more generous drink, downed it, and poured another. Back at the mantelpiece, his anger barely suppressed, he said, "All right then, what happened next?"

"I waited in the carriage." Delaroux's face darkened. "None of my business what you do in your private life, you know."

"Indeed."

"But after an hour, I began to get worried. The opera begins at ten o'clock."

"It is only eight o'clock now, Robert. Why the rush?"

"Rush? How long does it take you to dress, Steven? If I had managed to get home by seven-thirty, I should have had a difficult time being ready to leave my house by eight-thirty. And we told the ladies we would pick them up—"

"What ladies?" Catherine interjected.

Sheepishly, Lord Delaroux said, "Lady Jane Bowlingbroke and Lady Eugenia Terrebonne."

"Would that be the earl's chit? How interesting," Catherine said, folding her arms across her chest and staring at Steven.

"They'll be furious with us, Steven. We're going to be late."

"I don't care!" The harsh tone of Steven's voice drew startled, slightly frightened stares from Robert and Catherine. With tremendous effort, Steven ground out, "What happened next, Robert?"

"I knocked on the door and it opened. Well, it must have been ajar, and when I knocked, it swung inward. I called out for you, Steven, but no one answered. I know it was rude, but I stepped into the entry hall. I just meant to wait for you, truly I did! Suddenly a man came rushing toward me. I don't know where he came from, down the steps perhaps, or from the drawing room."

"You didn't see which direction he came from?" Steven questioned.

"I was looking in the mirror, straightening my cravat."

"Of course." Steven swallowed more whiskey.

"He shot me, Steve. At arm's length, I tell you. I saw him from behind, in the mirror, of course. I whirled just in the nick of time. Otherwise, I suppose he would have put a bullet in my back."

"Then he ran," Steven said flatly.

"And I started howling bloody murder. That's when you came tearing down the stairs." Delaroux shot his listeners a foolish grin. "I think I frightened him off, to tell the truth."

"Yes, I'm sure you put quite a scare into him. Would you recognize the man if you saw him again?"

Delaroux shrugged. "I think so. Perhaps."

Catherine, eyes snapping, stood abruptly. "I think I've heard enough. The two of you will find your own way out, I trust." She turned and stalked toward the door.

Pushing off from the mantelpiece, Steven followed and caught her arm. Roughly, he drew her outside the drawing room and out of earshot of Robert, and said quietly, "We have a bargain, Cat. Your information in exchange for my . . . protection."

She jerked her arm from his grasp, and fairly hissed. "Protection, Steven? A strange man just walked into my house and was shot by another—"

"Fitzhaven."

Her eyes narrowed. "How do you propose to protect me, then, Steven, when you can't even keep the enemy away from my doorstep? What will happen the next time Fitzhaven returns?"

"I won't let him hurt you, I promise. I'll go straight to Pennyworthy and see that you have round-the-clock bodyguards. I'll have Trevor bring round my pistol, Cat.

If Fitzhaven corners you, you must swear to me that you will use it. I can't bear to think of your being hurt . . . I can't bear it."

She moved away from him, backing toward the staircase. Watching her, Steven was mesmerized, not only by her stealthy movements and wary expression, but by her disturbing sexual appeal. His body tensed as she floated beyond his reach; his chest tightened with the fear of losing her again. Yet even as her lips curved upward in a curiously inviting smile, even as her eyelashes flickered and her cheeks flushed, he knew he had lost her.

She paused at the landing and arched her eyebrows. "Lie down with me awhile," she whispered huskily.

And he was tempted. Sorely tempted. He wanted her and needed her. But something deep within him warned him off. How queer that the woman who knew him better than any other was the one he could not trust. The thought chilled him, and he shook his head. "No, Cat."

"I need you, Steven."

"You must give me all the information you possess," he replied. "You will have my protection, and that of the Prince Regent, in the bargain."

She studied him, apparently considering his offer. At length, she said simply, "I will be at the Bowlingbroke masquerade, Steven. Oh, don't look surprised. Getting an invitation wasn't difficult at all. I still have some old friends in Town, dear. Meet me there, and I will pass the information to you in a letter."

"Why?" He took a step toward her. "Why not tell me what you know now, Cat? Why risk being discovered—"

But she placed a finger on his lips and stilled his protests. "All will be explained. Just look for me at the masquerade."

His heart squeezed as she drew her touch from him and turned away.

"How will I know you?" he asked her as she silently padded up the steps.

But she didn't answer and she didn't look back. He thought he heard a deep-throated chuckle as she faded from view. Above stairs, the door to her bedchamber opened and clicked shut. His hands tightened into fists and sharp pain jabbed the back of his skull. When Lord Robert Delaroux burst out of the drawing room, babbling about how furious the ladies were going to be because of the late hour, Steven came perilously close to slapping him.

Somehow he restrained his violent impulse. He had a duty to fulfill. And though duty required him to live a lie, hiding his feelings for Eugenia while pretending to care for Jane, he would perform his obligations. Sir Steven St. Charles was a man well trained in the art of ignoring his own emotions.

NINE

The letter came in the post from Southampton, its author clearly identifiable from the precise little letters that spelled Eugenia's name on the envelope. "It's from Father," she cried, ripping open the thick vellum.

But as she read the message, her eyes filled with tears.

Grateful that she was alone, having just climbed out of a hot bath, Eugenia sat at her vanity, alternately staring at her reflection and the letter Sir Albert Terrebonne had mailed three days earlier. It seemed impossible, but the words remained indelibly imprinted on the writing paper no matter how many times Eugenia read them. After a half-hour there was nothing she could do but face reality: Sir Albert Terrebonne was on his way home and would reach London within a fortnight.

She dressed mechanically, somehow managing to get her sturdy half boots on her feet, and her hair piled loosely atop her head. Luckily, Eugenia's mode of dress was so simple and conservative, she rarely needed an abigail's assistance. Tonight, she wouldn't have been able to tolerate the attentions of a servant, so fidgety and nervous had she become as a result of her father's letter. It took every ounce of strength she had just to leave her room, descend the stairs, and enter the drawing room, where the rest of the opera party was waiting for her.

Crossing the threshold, she put a counterfeit smile on

her lips. "Good evening, gentlemen." She dropped a
small curtsy to Sir Steven and Lord Robert, who stood
before the mantelpiece. Then she lowered herself into a
chair opposite the sofa, where Aunt Clarissa and Lady
Jane sat, smiling back at her as if all were right with
the world.

"Lord Robert was just telling us about last year's
Derby race," Aunt Clarissa said, prompting Delaroux to
perform his imitation of Lady Jersey batting her eyelashes at the triumphant jockey.

Jane's giggles were subdued, but her reddened cheeks
betrayed the true extent of her amusement. "How you
could not laugh at that, Sir Steven, I will never understand," she said.

Eugenia shot a look at Steven, wondering what his
reaction to Jane's jibe would be. Noting that his lips
hardened in an ever firmer, straighter line, she felt a tiny
surge of satisfaction. At least Jane hadn't lured a chuckle
out of him so easily tonight. There was, Eugenia told
herself, *that* to be grateful for.

And with her pettiness came that familiar backlash of
guilt. Struggling to hide her unease, Eugenia stood and
crossed the room to the sideboard. Behind her, Lord Delaroux continued an animated description of the Duke
of York attempting to feed apples to the horse that won
the St. Leger at Doncaster only to have his fingers nearly
chomped off. Apparently, this dissertation was deemed
hilarious by Aunt Clarissa and Lady Jane, for they
laughed so heartily that Dashie became agitated and began barking in chorus.

From her reticule, Eugenia extracted her silver flask.
Uncertain when she'd filled it last, she gave it a good
shake.

"Have you emptied it already?" The deep, throaty
voice behind her belonged to Sir Steven.

Startled, Eugenia froze. She hadn't realized he left the

mantelpiece; his nearness to her was a shock. Slowly, she lowered the flask to the sideboard, her fingers clutching the silver so tightly she might have dented it. For a moment, Eugenia's throat constricted so violently she couldn't speak. Her heart, battered by a multitude of emotions, squeezed painfully. The urge to escape the drawing room and simply run away was strong.

When she did manage to speak, her voice was a strangled whisper. "I fear you have got the wrong impression of me, sir. I am not a tippler, not by any means."

He moved around her, facing her. "I did not mean to imply—"

"Don't apologize." Her back was to the others. Staring into Sir Steven's gaze, she could almost pretend that they were alone. "Can I pour you a drink?"

His frown deepened. "I've had quite enough for one day, I believe. 'Tis an evil vice, immoderation. I admit, I have struggled with it in the past."

"Truly?" Eugenia recapped her flask without pouring more liquor into it. "Few men admit to their faults, sir. I am amazed that you are willing to do so. Particularly in light of your obvious dislike of our dinner conversation last evening."

"I am full of apologies tonight. I hope that you will forgive my behavior at your aunt's dinner table. It is just that I so rarely dine with friends . . . much less ladies. I am afraid the intimacy of the conversation left me feeling . . ." He stared intently at her, his pale blue eyes rimmed in red, his face careworn.

"Feeling what?"

"Naked."

The word, the mental image it conveyed, shot an arrow of physical awareness through Eugenia's body. Then after that initial jolt, a convulsive little laugh bubbled in her throat. "You have an odd way of expressing yourself, sir," she finally said between chuckles. "Why on earth would you say you felt naked at Aunt Clarissa's dinner table last night?"

"I am not accustomed to letting my guard down, Eugenia."

Her fingers itched for a glass of whiskey, but she suppressed the urge. If Sir Steven was attempting to avoid an old temptation, the least she could do was leave the whiskey bottle alone. "I think I understand," she heard herself saying. "I feel that I am constantly pretending I am happy when I am not. If I were to show my true feelings, people would be shocked or repulsed. They would think me rude or ungrateful."

"I believe that if I were to express my true feelings, I would be tossed into jail." A slight, almost indiscernible quirking of Steven's lips accompanied this remark.

"Are your private thoughts so terrible?"

"My dear, they are murderous."

Eugenia drew a quick breath. "Really? And who do you fantasize about murdering, sir?"

The side of his mouth twisted. "Oh, I do not really want to murder anyone. But I have spent the last few years nurturing grudges and harboring black emotions. 'Tis an unhealthy habit, never thinking about what is good and correct in one's life, always dwelling on the past."

"I didn't take you for such a philosophical man, sir."

"I confess, I am rarely so." He took a half step toward her, banishing the rest of the world with his closeness. "But I have spent the last twenty-four hours contemplating my life, past and future. I have made many mistakes, Eugenia. The problem is, I don't know whether I can rectify any of them."

"One can always be redeemed. If one wants redemption badly enough."

"Do you think so?"

Swallowing hard, she took a tiny step backward.

Steven's nearness made it difficult to think, impossible to reason intelligently. His leathery aroma captivated her, provoking her imagination to some of the most wicked thoughts she'd ever conjured. Yet her conscience pricked at her, reminding her that this man was out of bounds. Jane had already fallen in love with him. Eugenia had no business talking so intimately with Sir Steven. She had far less right to imagine the man's lips pressed against hers.

"I shouldn't be speaking to you this way." Glancing over her shoulder, he stiffened. "I have no right—"

She presumed he was referring to his courtship of Lady Jane. "Nor do I."

"But there is something about you, Eugenia. Something that makes me want to tell you how I feel. Something that I seem to recognize in you."

"I would be honored to be your friend, sir."

His gaze was penetrating. "You're unhappy."

She gasped. "How would you know such a thing? I smile all the time. You're the one who never smiles."

"We have both learned to hide our feelings, haven't we, Eugenia? Yes, that's what it is. We're alike, the two of us. You, pretending to be happy even when you're sad. Me, refusing to love anyone out of fear they will not love me back."

His candid words elicited the most sympathetic response from Eugenia. Hugely moved, she could only stare at Sir Steven, her thoughts reeling at the vulnerability his speech revealed. After a moment, the tears she had beaten back all afternoon threatened to spill over. Inhaling deeply, she closed her eyes, willing the floodgates to close. Crying was sloppy, she told herself. Self-pity was unforgivable. Grown women didn't burst into tears in the middle of a drawing room with a small party raging in the background.

The party was, albeit small, in full swing. Lord Delaroux whinnied and snuffled in imitation of the horse who won at Newmarket the previous Season. Aunt Clara proudly displayed the doorstop she'd acquired at the boxing match, and Lady Jane eventually gave way to outright laughter. But at the sideboard the ambience was anything but frivolous. A sort of airborne friction held Eugenia in a trance; she couldn't cease staring into Sir Steven's eyes, despite the apprehension his pale blue gaze caused her.

"I suppose we'd best return to the party," she whispered, her voice betraying more emotion than she wished to divulge.

"Eugenia." Her name on his lips was erotic, evoking an intimacy that she could only imagine. "I am sorry—"

She pressed a finger to his mouth, only briefly, but long enough to feel the moist heat of his lips against her skin, long enough to sense the anguish inside him. "Do you care for her?"

His gaze darted to Jane. Suddenly, his eyes were hooded, his expression stony. "She is . . . very pretty."

"I know her father is a thorn in your side. But she is determined to insinuate you into the earl's good graces. She is a sweet girl, not at all as toplofty as she is given to be. You are a good judge of character to have chosen her as your intended bride."

"You cannot possibly understand." He reached for the whiskey bottle.

She grasped his wrist. "I know what it is like to be thwarted in love. And that is why I have committed myself to helping you."

Withdrawing his hand, he closed his eyes for an instant, and Eugenia fancied that he was deeply touched by her offer and so embarrassed by her generosity as to render him unable to express his gratitude.

At length, he looked at her and said simply, "Thank you."

Eugenia fought the urge to touch his lips again, to caress the corners of his mouth, to feel his warm skin against hers. Instead, she merely smiled. And though Sir Steven did not return the smile with his lips, his gaze drank in her warmth. She felt him respond to her; an invisible connection formed between them. In her heart, she longed to cast off her mask and tell Sir Steven that she loved him.

But the duties of friendship demanded loyalty to Jane. Eugenia slipped her flask back in her reticule, turned on her heel, and returned to the gathering before the mantelpiece with a perfectly schooled look of gay contentment on her face.

The opera house in Orange Street was packed full. In a box situated directly across from Prinny's, the four young people and Lady Clarissa sat fanning themselves and peering at the patrons below. With the peanut and fruit vendors hawking their concessions, the fancy ladies of the night advertising their wares, and the *haut ton* ostentatiously quizzing one another, the overall effect was that of a circus.

When the Prince Regent appeared in his box with three ladies not his wife, the crowd buzzed with amused interest. Seated between Sir Steven and Lady Jane, Eugenia allowed herself a chuckle. Her dread of attending the Bowlingbroke masquerade with both her warring parents in tow slowly receded. The novelty of the opera and the pleasure of Sir Steven's company captured her attention.

She touched Jane's elbow, and leaning close, spoke behind her fan. "Would you care to trade places with me, dear?"

Jane shot her a puzzled look. "I'm quite satisfied with the seating arrangement, Genie." Lord Delaroux sat on

Jane's other side and Aunt Clarissa on the farthest end of the row. "Is there something the matter?"

Slightly confused, Eugenia murmured, "Why, no." But her question seemed to be answered a few moments later when the Earl and the Countess of Bowlingbroke appeared in the neighboring box. Jane smiled sweetly at her parents and her mother blew her a kiss. To any casual observer, it would have looked as if Jane and the older couple who waved back at her were simply friendly acquaintances.

Concluding that Jane meant to divert attention from her courtship with Lord Delaroux, Eugenia resigned herself to sitting beside Sir Steven for the duration of the opera. She wished for darkness, but the bright glare of the overhead candles was unrelenting, and the continual drip of wax, a glob of which occasionally landed on a gentleman's shoulder or in a lady's coiffure, was annoying. Still, as the performance began, Eugenia dared a sidelong glance at Steven.

He looked past her at Jane, then at the Bowlingbrokes, who with their entourage of friends, made quite a ruckus as they settled into their box. His brow was deeply furrowed, his jaw set in granite. Forcing herself to look at the stage, Eugenia wondered what thoughts produced such an expression of discontent on Steven's face. She guessed he was disturbed by the appearance of Jane's parents; now he was forced to be circumspect in his attentions to his beloved. Now he *had* to spend the rest of the evening in Eugenia's company.

Mrs. Partridge, the famous soprano, sang beautifully. With her breasts bound close to her chest, she played the role of Julius Caesar, a part originally written for a male castrato. Her voice lilted through the theater, soothing Eugenia's jangled nerves. Drawn into a fantastic world of make-believe, she forgot her troubles and the fact that her parents would soon descend on London with an entire arsenal of emotional weaponry to use against one another. What she could not forget was Sir Steven's closeness.

Midway through the second act, she was jerked from her reverie by a rasping breath at her shoulder. Looking sharply to her left, she was startled to see that Sir Steven had fallen asleep. With his long, muscular legs crossed one over the other and his arms folded, his head nodded precariously. As Mrs. Partridge's voice warbled and danced, his chin touched his chest.

His breathing deepened. Surreptitiously, Eugenia glanced to her right. Satisfied that Jane, Delaroux, and Aunt Clarissa were unaware of Steven's having fallen asleep, she turned back to him. His body began to lean, until his shoulder was flush against hers.

A feeling that Eugenia couldn't identify, something like *music,* flowed through her. Steven's gentle snoring both calmed and aroused her. His head tilted toward her, slowly, inexorably, finally resting on her shoulder. The weight of his body was comforting, yet disturbing. The smell of his skin, the texture of his thick bristly hair, and the warmth of his breathing excited Eugenia beyond reason.

Swallowing hard, she shut her eyes tightly. One sideways glance from Jane would ruin Steven's attempted courtship. Afraid to move, Eugenia sat as still as a statue. She was terrified that Jane would see, but she could not resist pressing her cheek to Steven's head. She was frightened to death that Steven would awaken and recoil from her touch, but she could not force herself to disengage from him. When she felt his hand atop hers, she nearly yelped. Her eyes flew open and her heart galloped. The sensations that poured through her as his forearm nudged her side and his fingers tightened around hers were indescribably intense.

Minutes ticked by, with Mrs. Partridge treading the

stage in pursuit of another soprano playing the role of
Cleopatra. But the opera was a fuzzy blur to Eugenia's
eyes, the floating melodies a vague buzzing in her ears.

All she heard was Steven's breathing. All she felt was
the weight and warmth of his body against hers.

He shifted in his chair, pressing harder against her
side. His head grew heavier on her shoulder. In his sleep,
he jerked and gave another snort. His fingers clutched
hers so tightly she gasped.

His dream was not a pleasant one. With her chest
aching, Eugenia took his hands in hers and held them
snugly. She massaged his palm and stroked his fingers.
Then she dipped her head and whispered in his ear, "Everything
will be all right, love."

His lips moved. Eugenia wasn't certain, but she
thought she heard him whisper in return, "Please do not
leave me."

A sudden thunderous applause erupted as Mrs. Partridge
hit her high C with vigorous clarity. Abruptly returned
to her senses, Eugenia withdrew her hands from
Steven's. His head bobbed violently. Then he inhaled
deeply, sat ramrod straight, and with a somewhat confused
look, said to Eugenia, "I hope I did not snore."

With the end of the act, an intermission convened and
patrons began to stand and stretch, talking loudly and
laughing.

Lady Jane was on her feet. "Robert and I are going
to get a strawberry ice, Genie. Would you like to join
us?"

"Thank you, but I'm quite comfortable here."

"I'll go!" Aunt Clarissa said, giving Eugenia an inexplicably
puckish wink.

Sir Steven stood, demurring at the offer of a flavored
ice. When Jane, Delaroux, and Aunt Clarissa had disappeared
through the curtains, he resumed his seat next to
Eugenia.

Tugging at his cravat, he said sheepishly, "It's not often I fall asleep at the opera. Julius Caesar is one of my favorites."

She touched his arm. "You must be tired."

He looked away from her, his expression tightening. "Yes. But I'm happy to be here next to you, Eugenia."

Studying his profile, Eugenia held her breath. His words seemed to indicate that he held an interest in her that went beyond friendship, beyond the mere fact that she was Jane's best friend.

Yet it was impossible. "I like you, too, Steven," she finally stammered. "I must confess, I think Jane the luckiest girl in London to have won your affections."

He gave her an odd look. "Are my affections for Jane so . . . obvious?"

"Why else would you be accompanying Lord Delaroux all over town? He does not strike me as the sort of man you would ordinarily form a friendship with. But I suppose he is a harmless creature, and since he has long been a friend of Jane's, he is the perfect companion for her favorite suitor."

"Quite right."

"Besides, she told me how she feels about you."

To Eugenia's surprise, Steven appeared shocked by this revelation. "What on earth did she say?"

"That her father forbade her to entertain your overtures. That she intends to defy the earl. That the two of you are determined to be together no matter what. Like Romeo and Juliet."

"Dear God, I hope our ending isn't that tragic."

Eugenia squeezed his forearm, then withdrew her hand. "I have pledged my assistance, sir. Now there is something I must ask of you in return."

The soft, plaintive note in her voice pained Steven. Facing her, he could not resist reaching for her hands, no matter how inappropriate the gesture. Glancing over her shoulder, he saw that the Bowlingbroke box was empty, a good thing since he would not like the earl and countess to see him holding Eugenia's hands.

But her small slender fingers curled neatly in the larger cup of his hands, her skin felt warm and tender, and her lips parted as he gazed at her. Really, she was quite the loveliest creature he had ever seen, all blinking eyes and fluttering lashes.

He thought he'd like to kiss her, ravish her, possess her, but his circumstances made it impossible. Duty had determined his fate, and he was either too weak or too strong to shirk the obligation imposed on him by Pennyworthy.

Musicians in the pit below tuned their instruments, plucking at strings and offering up a cacophony of discordant notes. It was an appropriate musical score to accompany Steven's thoughts. His *duty* suddenly seemed absurd, his reliance on it cowardly. He'd spent the last twenty-four hours examining his motives and desires, yet he hadn't resolved his feelings toward Eugenia or Catherine. *Why?* Why couldn't he let go of the past and admit to this precious young woman how much he cared for her?

Perhaps it had nothing to do with his duty, or his spy mission. Perhaps it was something buried very deep inside Steven that prohibited him from loving a woman. Steven squeezed Eugenia's fingers, unable to voice what he felt. But he knew that an unfathomable abyss existed in his heart, a blackness so vast that it would swallow up and destroy anything so innocent and young as Lady Eugenia Terrebonne.

He simply couldn't do it to her. He owed it to her *not to fall in love with her.* He wasn't like other men. He wasn't given to fits of happiness or contentment or complete self-love. No, he was melancholy and temperamental, a brooding loner who suffered from sleeplessness, recurring nightmares of heinous battle scenes, and repeated episodes of self-loathing. He wasn't capable of articulating, much less sharing, his most secret fears and emotions. He didn't want to.

Which was why any woman unfortunate enough to become the object of his attentions was bound to wind up brokenhearted, or worse, filled with hate and vitriol. Just look at poor Lady Catherine. He'd neglected her and mistreated her to the point she was forced to find solace and succor in the arms of another man. Now, she needed him and he could only bring himself to use her as bait. The emptiness in Steven's heart would devour anyone he attempted to love.

With a sigh, he withdrew his hands from Eugenia's lap. "You asked me to do something for you in return for your kindness. Of course, I will help you, Eugenia. I would do anything for you."

"This afternoon, I received a letter from my father. He is on his way to London."

Steven searched her expression. "Doesn't that make you happy?"

"Of course! I cannot wait to see Father. But Mother is on her way, too. They are going to descend on Curzon Street at the same time, Steven. Don't you see what a disaster is in the brewing?"

"I'm not sure—"

"They will both be attending Lord Bowlingbroke's masquerade." Eugenia's ubiquitous smile had disappeared.

"And you are afraid they will create a scene at the masquerade?"

"Afraid?" She rolled her gaze to the ceiling. "Dear sir, I have no doubt that they will. If you thought the massacre of the Mamelukes at Cairo a bloody mess, wait till you see what my parents can do to one another."

"And what would you have me do to prevent your

parents from engaging in battle at the Bowlingbroke masquerade?" Steven asked her.

"Only that you would contrive somehow to help me keep them apart. If there is sufficient distance between them, perhaps they will not be able to attack one another."

"Do you have a plan?"

"No." Eugenia nibbled her lower lip, an affectation that made Steven's loins ache. "But I am working on it. I should think that if Mother does not recognize Father, then she should have a difficult time waging war on him."

Steven had the inkling of an idea. "Who is arriving in London first?"

"Mother, I think."

"Then I suggest that when she arrives, you determine immediately what her costume will be. You must inform me as soon as you know."

A tentative smile flickered on Eugenia's lips. "What have you in mind, Steven?"

"Oh, I can't tell you yet. But I think between the two of us, Eugenia, we can make it so difficult for your parents to fight that they will soon give it up. At least for a time."

"A million thanks to you, sir. Truly, you are . . . wonderful."

A warmth seeped into Steven's blood and he felt his lips curve upward. His jaw relaxed, the stiffness in his neck eased, and the muscles in his face surrendered to the pleasure of being beside Eugenia. Then a rustle of curtains behind him announced the return of Jane, Clarissa, and Robert. He found it odd that he had to force a frown to his lips. But when he turned back to the stage, feigning interest in the second half of the opera, he realized something quite amazing had happened to him.

Sir Steven St. Charles had smiled.

* * *

Mrs. Partridge curtsied beneath a deluge of wilted roses thrown by her admirers. The curtains drew to a close amid enthusiastic applause. But for Eugenia the opera's ending signaled her reentry to reality. She stood slowly, allowing Sir Steven to drape her plain black cloak over her shoulders while Lord Delaroux assisted Jane in donning her fashionable blue coat with military style epaulets on the shoulders.

Lord Delaroux's hands lingered on Jane's shoulders. For a moment, Eugenia thought her eyes were playing tricks on her. But after she blinked and looked again, the scene remained the same. Jane, with her back to Delaroux, smiled over her shoulder at him and laid her hand atop his fingers. He whispered something in her ear, and she smiled.

Shocked, Eugenia tore her gaze off them and led the party out of the box and down the stairs. A heavy rain had started and a congregation of patrons jammed the lobby, waiting for their carriages to be brought round. Sir Steven, having volunteered to fetch the driver, instructed Delaroux and the ladies to wait inside. Then he pressed through the crowd and disappeared outside.

"You're awfully quiet, Genie," Jane said.

Eugenia stared first at Jane, then at Delaroux. In her state of confusion, she hadn't noticed that Lady Clarissa lagged behind. When her aunt appeared, face flushed and hair disheveled, Eugenia released the breath she hadn't realized she'd been holding.

"Aunt, where have you been?"

"Oh, never mind me, Genie. I got what I wanted."

Another doorstop. Suppressing a smile, Eugenia said, "Would you like for Lord Delaroux to carry it for you? Surely, it must be too big and heavy for you to carry in your reticule."

Delaroux, looking a bit confused, nevertheless offered a wobbly smile. "Can I help?"

"No, no." Lady Clarissa shook her head. "Come, there is Sir Steven at the door. Our carriage is here."

The small party moved through the tightly woven throng. Outside, they gripped their coats tightly and bent their heads against a gust of cold wind. Eugenia wrapped a protective arm around Aunt Clarissa, but Steven's firm grasp on her own elbow as they walked the ten steps or so to the carriage was reassuring. Clambering in, she slid down the squabs and nestled in the corner. Clarissa, Jane, and Delaroux followed, leaving Sir Steven to embark last.

Giving his instructions to the driver, Steven hovered in the open doorway of the carriage compartment, one booted foot on the step, one suspended in midair. Against the darkness, backlit by the new gas lamps outside the theater entrance, his figure was solid and commanding, his shoulders broad, his legs long and sinewy.

As always, when she looked at him, a bud of desire opened within Eugenia's body. She wished she didn't crave Sir Steven's attentions. She wished she didn't long for the man's touch or yearn to hear his voice. But she was a green plant and he the sun. With each passing day, she grew more keenly in his direction.

Without warning, a pistol shot split the air. The window next to Eugenia exploded, spraying tiny bits of glass all over. Spooked, the horses bolted and jumped. The carriage rattled and jerked forward. Sir Steven threw himself inside, landing on his back as the tiger slammed shut the door. Then the rig took off at a gallop, the ladies bouncing helplessly on the squabs, the driver shouting obscenities from his perch.

The outside carriage lamps dimly lit the interior compartment. Scrambling to his knees, Steven paused, touched his throat, and muttered his favorite imprecation, "Christ on a raft." Slowly, as if his muscles ached, he pushed back onto the leather seat beside Eugenia. His head lolled against the cushions and his eyelids fell shut. Only then did she see the stain of crimson on his cravat.

"He's been shot!" Eugenia put her arms about him as the carriage barreled through the streets of West London. His head fell against her shoulder, and his weight pressed against her. She didn't care whether Lady Jane hated her for holding Steven. A thousand strongmen couldn't have pried the man from her embrace.

TEN

The veil of black evaporated while the voices surrounding him sharpened into focus. As he drifted lazily back to consciousness, Steven's eyes blinked open. He was in Lady Clarissa's drawing room, sprawled on a sofa, his head supported by a velvet bolster. Staring down at him were Eugenia, Jane, and Clarissa. Curled up beside him was a worried-looking Dashie. And leaning against the mantelpiece was Lord Delaroux, looking a bit irritated.

"His eyes are open," Delaroux said. "See there, I told you, he is fine."

"The surgeon cleaned the wound and bandaged it as best he could," Eugenia said. "You lost consciousness because of the blow to your head when you landed inside the carriage compartment. Would you like a drink?"

"Are you in terrible pain?" Jane asked.

Clarissa said, "No, don't touch your ear, dear! The bullet took off the bottom half of your earlobe. Could have been worse, sir. Had the shot strayed an inch to the right, you might have lost your life."

"My head aches," Steven croaked. It was a struggle, but he managed to sit up, forcing Dashie to rearrange herself, in order to accept the glass that Eugenia offered him. The whiskey scalded his throat, but it dulled the sharp pain in his head and burned the fog from his senses.

Delaroux impatiently tapped his fingers on the mantelpiece. "Who shot at you, Steve? You must have an idea."

"I do not."

Jane and Eugenia sat on either side of Steven, while Aunt Clarissa gathered Dashie in her arms and sat in the chair opposite the sofa. The glass-domed clock that graced the mantel ticked loudly, punctuating the lull that settled in the room. Steven cleared his throat, aware that everyone waited for him to explain why he had been shot at, and by whom, but there was nothing he could say that would satisfy his listeners.

Thankfully, a loud crash on the front door snapped shut the gaping silence. Dashie erupted in a fit of yelps and Aunt Clarissa sprang to her feet. Below stairs, Mr. Greville's boots clapped hurriedly across the foyer. Then the door opened and a woman's voice could be heard shouting, "I am here! Eugenia! Where are you?"

"Mother!" Eugenia didn't make it halfway across the drawing room before her mother burst across the threshold, arms thrown open. The two women met in a bone-rattling embrace that lasted several minutes, then they held one another at arm's length and studied the changes wrought by several months.

At last, Lady Alexandra moved further into the room, distributing quick hugs and kisses to Clarissa and Jane before turning her frankly curious look on Lord Delaroux and Sir Steven.

She was a handsome woman, not beautiful in the classic sense, but arresting nonetheless. Despite his aching body, Steven stood and made an abbreviated bow. Taking Lady Alexandra's hand in his, he met her dark-eyed gaze, and in a flash, understood Eugenia's ambivalence concerning her mother.

Her face was that of a woman who had spent a great deal of time in the sun. Crevices bracketed her mouth and nose, yet the youthfulness of her expression offset any premature aging the elements had caused. A shocking lime green and pink scarf was draped negligently around her neck and shoulders; a widow's peak of silver ran straight down the middle of her head.

Overall, Steven thought, Lady Alexandra presented as a confident, eccentric, and friendly woman. He also thought that being married to her was probably extremely difficult, and he understood in a flash why Eugenia was so apprehensive about her parents' imminent confrontation.

She looked him up and down, then arched her brow. "Caught a bullet in your ear, eh? Well, that should make an interesting story. I cannot wait to hear tell of it."

To Lord Delaroux she said, "Hello, you handsome devil. Met you last year. Nice jacket."

Mr. Greville and a serving lady shortly reappeared, and pots of hot tea and coffee, along with trays of sandwiches and cookies, were offered as a late night repast. Lady Alexandra tossed off her hat and gloves, gave a flurry of instructions to the staff, concerning her trunks and packages, then ensconced herself on the sofa, patting the cushions and inviting the girls to sit beside her. Clarissa returned to her chair while the men bracketed the hearth.

"Well, somebody bring me up to date! What has been going on in London these last few months? Has Prinny rid himself of that awful German woman? Are you enjoying the Season, Genie? And, Jane, have you fallen in love? Come, come, tell me everything! I am sorely in need of some good gossip." Lady Alexandra popped another sandwich in her mouth, signaling she was ready to be regaled.

It fell to Eugenia to give her mother the news. "You've arrived in Town just in time for the Bowlingbroke masquerade, Mother. We'll have to discuss your costume, of course. I'm certain we can throw together something."

Lady Alexandra swallowed half a sandwich whole. "How exciting! That always is the best party of the year! What is everyone else wearing, dear?"

Eugenia hesitated. "It is customary to keep one's disguise a secret, Mother."

"Pish-posh," Jane exclaimed. "We won't tell anyone outside this circle. I am going as Juliet."

Sir Steven, aware of Lady Alexandra's scrutiny, passed the baton to Delaroux. "What are you wearing, Robert?"

"I—I do not know yet. Haven't decided."

"Come on, man! I don't believe it. It takes you three days to get your cravat tied properly and that's when you're dressing for no special occasion! You must know what you are wearing to the masquerade." Steven suddenly remembered his earlier conversation with Delaroux. Snapping his fingers, he said, "Didn't you tell me you are going as Ro—"

"I've changed my mind!" Delaroux's face turned red. "Can't a man change his mind, sir? And I do resent your insinuation that I am a fop! I'm no such thing."

Delaroux's outburst silenced Steven. He hadn't meant to hurt the man's feelings. Belatedly, he realized that Lord Robert Delaroux had very little sense of humor about himself, especially concerning his vanity. "Sorry, then," Steven muttered.

"And you, sir?" Eugenia's mother looked pointedly at Steven. "What are you wearing?"

"I confess, I have not yet decided what my costume shall be." Unnerved by the tension that hung over the gathering, Steven turned to their hostess. "Have you decided what you are wearing, Lady Clarissa?"

"I'm Mother Goose, dearie, author of such rhymes as the one about Old Mother Hubbard. She went to the cupboard, you know, to fetch her poor dog a bone. But when she got there—"

"The cupboard was bare," said Steven.

"And now the poor dog has none," finished Eugenia.

Steven held Eugenia's gaze, saddened by his inability to hold her hand, or touch her, or even act as if he cared for her. "And you, Lady Eugenia. What are you wearing to the masquerade?"

"I'm Little Bo Peep, who has lost her sheep. Dashie, bless her heart, is going as a lamb."

Lady Alexandra look taken aback. "How tame you ladies are. One tragic Shakespearean heroine and two nursery book characters. Well, I suppose I shall bloody well shock you all with my choice of costume."

Her language shocked them well enough. Eugenia blushed beet red while Aunt Clarissa choked on a tea biscuit.

Lady Alexandra seemed not to notice. "I don't have much time, do I? Well, then, I will make do with what is in my traveling trunks. And since I have just come from Egypt, where the French are overrunning the place, and there is not a good cup of tea to be found anywhere, I assure you, I believe I will go to the masquerade as . . . Cleopatra."

A tiny smile curled on Eugenia's lips. Steven would have smiled, too, but for his habit of not doing so. A warm feeling of intimacy, the pleasure of a private joke shared, passed between them. So, she'd been correct in her prediction. Eugenia Terrebonne evidently knew her mother very well.

"Excellent!" cried Aunt Clarissa, and the sentiment was echoed by Jane and Delaroux, the latter of whom appeared happy again.

"There is one other bit of news, Mother." Setting down the cup of tea she'd been sipping, Eugenia turned a serious look on her mother.

"Out with it, dear. You look as if you're about to inform me of someone's passing."

"It's about Father."

Lady Alexandra, her china cup rattling in her trembling hands, paled noticeably. "He hasn't—Oh, God! What was it? A bullfighting accident? Did he fall off his skis in Switzerland, or get hit in the head with a golf ball in Scotland? Spit it out, Genie, I can't endure the suspense. How did my beloved husband die?"

"He isn't dead. He's on his way to London. He'll be here day after tomorrow, just in time for the masquerade. You'll both be attending—"

"Then, I shall kill him!"

"Mother!"

Backbone stiff, and color up, Lady Alexandra bristled with anger. "How dare he? 'Struth, I haven't been in London one hour and already he is vexing me."

"I don't see how you can say that," Lady Clarissa said in defense of her brother. "After all, Alex, this is his home."

"He must have known I was coming. Have you corresponded with him, Genie? Did you tell him?"

"No, Mother, why would I?" Eugenia responded. "Do you think I relish these confrontations?"

Lady Alexandra took no notice of that remark, however. It occurred to Steven that, despite her obvious intelligence, Eugenia's mother was often oblivious to the effect her behavior had on others. Clearly, she was blind to the discomfort written on her daughter's face. To Steven, though, Eugenia's pain was palpable. Staring at her, he knew he would do anything he could to ease it.

"Ladies, it is late," he said, throwing a friendly arm around Delaroux's shoulder, careful not to touch his injured upper arm. "I believe it is time for Robert and me to take our leave."

Startled by the show of companionship, Delaroux grinned. "I look forward to seeing you all again."

"When?" Lady Alexandra asked.

Lady Clarissa chuckled. "There is nothing subtle about you, Alex."

"Never has been," her sister-in-law returned. "That is why your brother married me. Oddly, that is why he despises me now. But enough of that. I believe I would like to see you gentlemen again, both of you. Someone name a time and place, quickly!" She pointed her finger at Steven. "That one appears to be getting away!"

Indeed, Steven was making his exit, bidding good night and backing toward the door. Delaroux made an elaborate leg, then threw kisses to the ladies as he followed.

"Why don't you accompany us for a ride in the park tomorrow?" Jane flashed a bright smile.

The men exchanged looks.

"We will pick you up at three o'clock," Steven replied. "All right with you, old man?"

Unable to contain his pleasure, Delaroux slapped Steven on the back. Hard. The jolt set off an explosion of pain in Steven's head, reminding him that he'd been shot just a few hours earlier. He needed rest badly. He needed to sort out his feelings. And he needed to plot his next move in connection with the Bowlingbroke investigation.

With a sigh he met Eugenia's gaze just before departing the room. She made a face, communicating her misery. Silently, he returned the signal. For an instant, they were connected by an invisible touch. Then he was down the stairs and out the door.

In the carriage, seated across from Delaroux, Steven point-blank asked the obvious question. "Are you in love, Robert?"

"With Jane? Yes, of course. Who wouldn't be? What do you think my chances are? Do you think she loves me, too? I know her father dislikes me, but I believe I can change all that. I have a plan."

But Steven's head ached too violently to listen anymore. Holding up his hand, he quelled Robert's further confessions. "I'm sorry, but my ear hurts."

"Understandable. My arm hurts."

Into the chilly darkness, the carriage rattled on, its wheels splashing though puddles left by the night's downpour. A sense of dread overtook Steven. His sideboard conversation with Eugenia rang in his ears. According to her, Jane was very much in love, but not with Robert.

Jane's misplaced affections saddened Steven beyond all logic. It occurred to him that he did not want to see Robert's heart broken. He knew what a broken heart felt like, and he didn't wish it on his worst enemy, much less Delaroux, a harmless puppy if there ever was one.

With a growing sense of wonder, Steven realized he had developed a sort of affection for the man. He couldn't understand how that had happened, but his heart seemed to have opened up. Some new and unexpected feelings had crept inside him. He wasn't certain he liked that; it meant pain could steal its way in, too.

He said good night to Delaroux with mingled feelings of relief and regret. Trevor Sparrow met him at the door with a hot toddy, but Steven turned down the offer of more alcohol. He needed a clear head to analyze his feelings. For once, he had no desire to blunt his own emotions.

* * *

Jane was unusually animated. "I saw him, Genie, don't deny it! He was smiling! At the opera. I saw it!"

Lady Alexandra said, "Good heavens, what is this about? I am bone weary, but I can't go to bed until I hear it all."

"What else did you see, Jane?" Eugenia asked warily.

Lady Clarissa spoke up. "Not as much as I did. Lady Jane was too busy whispering with Lord Delaroux to see much of anything."

Eugenia smiled gratefully at her aunt. So Jane hadn't seen Steven fall asleep on her shoulder. But Aunt Clarissa had. The old woman seemed to have eyes in the back of her head.

"I'm totally in the dark," cried Lady Alexandra.

"We're talking about the opera," said Clarissa evasively. "We'd just returned from seeing Julius Caesar when you arrived."

"How lovely," Lady Alex said. "And what is this about Sir Steven smiling? Is there something uncustomary about that?"

"Oh, yes," replied Jane. "He never smiles. He is the most serious man I have ever seen. So Eugenia and I placed a bet. I wagered she couldn't make Sir Steven crack a grin."

"And I did not," Eugenia inserted.

"Well, he smiled tonight."

"Even if he did, it doesn't signify. We upped the ante if you recall. The wager was on a laugh, not a smile."

Jane nodded. "Quite right. Well, he didn't laugh, that much I'll allow."

"And what happens if you coax a chuckle out of the poor man?" asked Lady Alex.

"The loser of the bet has to kiss a man," Jane said.

"Now *that* is scandalous," Lady Clarissa murmured in a tone that merely bordered on reproaching.

Lady Alex appeared favorably impressed. "You don't

say! And which man would the loser be obliged to kiss? Or is it to be any man?"

A muscle in Eugenia's stomach tightened. Her instincts had warned her against making Lady Alex privy to this wager. The chances for mischief were far too high. But Jane had already let the secret out, so there was nothing for it but to give Lady Alex a full explanation.

"If I lose the bet, Mother, then Jane may choose any man she pleases, and I must kiss him. However, if I succeed in making Sir Steven laugh, then I will name the man whom Jane must kiss."

"How very wicked," Lady Alex said approvingly. "But did I understand correctly that Sir Steven smiled this evening?"

"Perhaps," Eugenia said carefully. "And perhaps not. At any rate, he did not laugh, so the bet is still on."

"You have only until midnight, the night of the masquerade," reminded Jane.

"Yes, I know." Eugenia noted her mother's compressed lips. The woman was hatching a plot, she was quite certain. "And there will be no interference from you, Mother. I must be the one who makes Sir Steven laugh."

"Oh, I understand, dear. I wouldn't dream of interfering!" Lady Alex touched her throat and gave a look of wounded shock. "You know how I am about bets, Genie. The sureness with which one meets her gambling debts is a measure of one's character. But it is a sign of cowardice to shirk a wager. Oh, no, dear, I quite agree, you must see this through to the end." She smiled warmly at Jane. "And may the best young lady win!"

And with that, she leaned over, gave Eugenia a warm kiss, and rose. "Good night, all. We have much to do tomorrow. I understand we have been invited to ride in the park with our gentleman friends. And I wouldn't miss that for the world!"

Lady Alexandra floated out of the drawing room, leaving behind her the scent of sun, sand, and exotic spices. Eugenia released a pent-up breath and shivered. With her mother home and her father en route to London, she felt as if a tempest were brewing. And she knew from experience that the force of her parents' respective natures was too powerful and too inexorable to resist. All she could do now was ride out the storm.

Lady Clarissa's practical phaeton accommodated one coachman and four passengers. The seating arrangements left much to be desired. While Eugenia, Jane, and Lady Alex scrunched together on one bench, Lord Delaroux and Clarissa, with Dashie in between, sat opposite them, riding backward behind the driver. Sir Steven, mounted on a glistening black gelding, rode alongside the open-air equipage, his profile handsome and unsmiling beneath the short brim of his beaver hat.

Decked out in a hunter's red jacket, elaborately tied neck scarf, and high-topped riding boots, Lord Delaroux was full of exuberant optimism. "What a beautiful day to be out-of-doors! Sorry there wasn't room for you in the carriage, Steve. Are you certain you're all right?"

Sir Steven nodded curtly.

"That's a fine horse you've got there, Sir Steven." Lady Alex was resplendent in a pearl gray morning gown set off by an Indian madras shawl. As the breeze rustled her hair, the fresh flowers she had tucked in her upswept coiffure fell loose and fluttered behind her, so that it seemed she was strewing rose petals in her wake. Appraising Sir Steven, she tilted her head and cocked a brow. "I rode an Egyptian stallion in Cairo. It was the wildest beast I have ever known."

"Your impressions of Egypt, my lady?" Steven returned Lady Alex's gaze.

"Romantic, profound, dangerous. I galloped along the banks of the Nile at dusk with the Pyramids looming in the distance . . . it was thrilling. It seemed the secrets of the universe lay just beneath the surface of the earth, and the eyes of God shimmered in the purple sky. Yet there was not a good English pudding to be found in the whole country."

Sir Steven, his mouth twisting, touched his hat. Nudging the sides of his horse, he moved ahead for a bit, then gradually adjusted his animal's gait, so that after a few minutes, he was abreast of the carriage's occupants again.

Looking at him, Eugenia was, as always, moved by his rugged masculinity, his good looks, and aloofness. Stiff-spined, head erect, chin jutting, he looked as humorless as a sphinx.

But beneath that tough outer skin, she knew, was a gentler soul than anyone could imagine. Eugenia thought of the way Steven had gazed at her in Madame Truffaut's when it was announced Lady Alex was going to be attending the Bowlingbroke masquerade. His kindness had comforted her when she learned Sir Albert would be there, too. He'd understood the difficult position her parents placed her in. He offered to assist in any way he could.

Well, that's what friends were for, weren't they? Reflection on her parents' unhappy marriage, a too-frequent obsession of Eugenia's, brought her to the conclusion that friends were more important than lovers. Romantic love was a fleeting, volatile, ephemeral thing, as difficult to hang on to as the tail of a comet. Her parents were living proof. Yet friendships lasted through the years, despite hardships and differences of opinion. Friends could be relied upon. The spousal relationship was, by its nature, mercurial and uncertain.

She should be happy that Sir Steven was her friend. The fact that he might one day be her friend's lover should cause her no *unhappiness*.

But it did.

Deep in thought, Eugenia barely noticed that Dashie had left her post beside Aunt Clarissa and had crawled into Lord Delaroux's lap. She paid little mind when Lord Delaroux sneezed loudly, whipped out a linen kerchief, and dabbed his nose. What did grab her attention was Jane's elbow jabbed into her side.

Startled from her reverie, Eugenia watched in amusement as Delaroux attempted to tactfully shoo Dashie away. Each time he gently pushed Dashie off his legs, she clambered back onto him. Jane dipped her head and stifled a giggle.

Delaroux's face darkened and his eyes watered. It seemed that Dashie's determination to sit in his lap grew in direct proportion to Delaroux's opposition to the idea. With her front paws resting on the carriage side, she could see every passing landau and buggy, every rider on horseback, every dog and squirrel that raced through the park. Her little tag wailed furiously, batting Delaroux's pristine jacket and occasionally swishing his face, as well.

Meanwhile, Aunt Clarissa and Lady Alex prattled on about the necessary preparations for Sir Albert's arrival.

"Perhaps he should go to a hotel or boardinghouse, Clarissa."

"He is my brother, Alex. I'll not be sending him to a hotel."

"Then I shall move to Limmer's for the duration. It won't be long. When Albert learns I am in London, I suspect he'll continue on his version of the Grand Tour."

"You will do no such thing. You will remain at Curzon Street, Alex, with the rest of your family. Don't be silly."

"But there isn't room, Clarissa! Bless you, dear, but you can't be expected to board my entire brood, plus—"

Clarissa gave her sister-in-law a quelling look. "There is plenty of room for all of those currently residing at Curzon Street, and there is plenty of room for Albert. If you don't want to share a bedchamber with him, you may sleep in your daughter's room."

"Perhaps I should return to my own home," Jane said quietly.

"You'll do no such thing, Jane." With a sigh, Eugenia found Jane's hand and closed it in her own. The lines of battle were being drawn. Whose blood would be spilled remained to be seen. "Not unless you want to, that is. I can't expect you to stay with me forever, but you're more than welcome."

"Don't your parents miss you, dear?" Lady Alex asked.

"I don't suppose they have noticed how long I've been gone," Jane replied. "They are very much engaged with one another at the moment, arranging the masquerade, planning their costumes, that sort of thing."

"And what are their costumes to be?" Alex asked.

"They haven't told anyone." Jane spoke matter-of-factly. "Certainly not me."

Alex slanted a curious look at Jane. Eugenia half smiled, knowing that her mother was sizing up the situation, attempting to deduce the nature of Jane's relationship with her parents. But no matter how peripheral Jane's proximity to her parents seemed, the fact remained that the Earl and Countess of Bowlingbroke did not place their daughter in the middle of their own private war. Perhaps they excluded Jane from their intimacy, but that was because they were so deeply and vividly in love. Eugenia considered that a far more tolerable situation than her own.

An ear-splitting yelp gave everyone, including the coachman, a start. Dashie, standing in Delaroux's lap, had spotted a dalmatian running alongside a gentleman's equipage. The little dachshund growled and yapped while Delaroux clutched at her harness. The spotted dog abandoned its post and raced over to the ladies' carriage.

Eugenia's neck lashed forward as the carriage skid to a halt. Suddenly, there was a huge black-and-white beast throwing itself against the side of the carriage. Dashie, her lips pulled back in a vicious snarl, strained against Delaroux's hold while Aunt Clarissa wrung her hands and wailed.

Eyes round with horror, Delaroux hugged Dashie tightly in an effort to protect her. Infuriated, the dalmatian sprang up on his hindquarters and nipped Delaroux's arm, ripping his jacket. Delaroux and Dashie now howled in unison. Relaxing his hold on Dashie, Delaroux screamed, "I've been bitten!"

Sir Steven yanked his horse's reins, rounding the carriage just as Dashie leapt from Delaroux's lap. The tiny dog flew over the side of the open carriage like a diver leaping from a great height. Eugenia held her breath, certain that the beloved pet was throwing herself in the jaws of death.

Aunt Clarissa cried, "Save her! Save my baby!"

On the ground, and thankfully out of sight, the two dogs barked, growled, and snarled at one another. Dismounting, Steven thrust his gloved hand into the fray and grabbed the dalmatian's collar. The big dog fought against restraint, but Steven managed to jerk its head up so that its snapping jaws were no longer a danger to Dashie.

On the opposite side of the dirt track, the owner of the spotted dog stopped his cabriolet and disembarked.

A young Corinthian, judging by his stylishly cut coat, buttery riding gloves, and polished Hessians, he approached with a look of concern and apology on his face.

"Sorry for the trouble, old man! I've never known Danton to run off like that before."

Steven thrust the dog toward its owner, then scooped a wriggling Dashie in his arms. "No harm done. Though I don't think it is a good idea to let that animal run loose in the park."

"Danton's not a bloodthirsty dog, I assure you." The man's face reddened as his dog fought against him. When Danton took another leap toward Dashie, his arm nearly jerked out of its socket. "Had he wanted to, he could have torn that little morsel to shreds."

Silently, Dashie showed her teeth. From the safety of Steven's embrace, however, the little dog did not appear eager to engage the dalmatian again.

Steven gave the man a steely-eyed look. "Sir, if your dog had harmed a hair on Dashie's head, I would have called you out."

"You are joking."

"Do I appear to be joking?" Steven handed Dashie into the carriage, and Delaroux passed the dog into Clarissa's waiting arms. Dusting his gloved palms, Steven continued. "Now keep your dog on a tether, or leave the beast at home. Do you understand me?"

The younger man swallowed hard and, dragging his struggling dog, backed away. Quickly, as if he were anxious to get away from Steven, he shoved Danton into his rig and drove off.

Steven was still standing in the middle of the track when the sound of galloping hooves reached his ears. His head snapped up and his muscles tensed. From behind a copse of trees materialized a black-clad horseman, his face obscured by a swath of black silk tied around the lower part of his face. The rider's many-caped coat swirled around him as he bore down on Steven.

ELEVEN

Steven reacted without hesitation. "Get this rig out of here!" he ordered Lady Clarissa's coachman. Then, as the carriage lurched and accelerated, he swung himself onto his horse's back.

The villainous horseman flew in a cloud of dust. A flash of silver appeared within the folds of a black cape. A sword glinted in the sunlight. Thunderous hoofbeats reverberated from the ground up, pouring through Steven's body.

Goading his horse with his heels, Steven rode hard at his assailant. His reactions now were purely animal, purely instinct. He hadn't fled the field of battle; he rode toward danger without fear.

Surprised at Steven's onslaught, the horseman reared back in his saddle. As the two horses passed one another, the black-clad rider swung his sword wildly. Steven ducked, and the blade clipped the top of his bristled hair. Then Steven drew back on his reins and turned his horse around for another pass at his opponent.

But the villain rode on, his horse pounding the earth. Steven watched with mingled relief and disappointment as the mysterious horseman disappeared into the woods that bordered the track. As his heart slowed, so did his gait. He easily caught up with Lady Clarissa's carriage and trotted alongside, sheepishly running his hand through his ruffled hair. His hat was left for tatters in the trodden road behind him.

"Are you all right?" Lady Eugenia asked, clutching at the sides of the carriage, half leaning out of it, her expression fraught with anguish.

Unexpected pleasure shone through his bones. Steven met her gaze, so warm and anxious. "Of course, my lady. Nothing to be overset about."

"You could have been killed! That man tried to run you down!"

"He missed."

She sat down hard, taking up more space than she had before, causing Lady Jane and Lady Alex to fidget. Her brown eyes snapped with an emotion Steven couldn't identify. She looked angry, but that made no sense to him.

"He missed?" Eugenia's voice rose an octave. "Is that all you have to say for yourself?"

"Eugenia, calm yourself," her mother admonished.

Lord Delaroux, red-faced and breathing heavily, said, "Did you see the man's face, Steve? Do you know who he was?"

He hadn't seen the man's face, but he knew it was Fitzhaven. "I have no idea who it was," Steven lied.

"Got any enemies?" Delaroux asked, his tone half joking.

"Too many to count," Steven replied lightly.

"Owe any gambling debts?" Lady Alex asked.

"No, my lady."

"Well, I don't suppose it was an accident," Lady Clarissa remarked benignly. "Although it pains me to think that someone would deliberately attempt to run you down."

"I wouldn't worry about it," Steven said. But of course the significance of the attack worried him greatly. It meant that Fitzhaven had determined to kill him. It meant that Fitzhaven was maintaining a close surveillance on Steven. Worst of all, it meant that Fitzhaven knew who Steven's friends were. Delaroux was now a known acquaintance of Steven's. He'd already suffered for being in the wrong place at the wrong time. The next time Fitzhaven took a swipe at him, the cut could be fatal.

Acid burned in Steven's throat. Lady Eugenia was in danger now, too, simply because she'd been seen in Steven's company by the ruthless and evil Earl of Fitzhaven.

He looked away from her, unable to face the compassion in her eyes. He ought never to have befriended her. He ought never to have developed feelings for her, or allowed her to treat him with such kindness and tolerance.

She would only get hurt in the end.

Steven drew his horse to a skidding halt. "I'm afraid I must take leave of you all. Business to attend to, I'm sure you understand. I'm delighted that Dashie wasn't injured, Clarissa. Looking forward to seeing you all at the masquerade."

"Steven"—Eugenia reached for him—"you cannot just—"

But met by the coldness he projected, she quickly recoiled. Shoulders hunched, arms hugging her chest, she pressed herself into the corner of the carriage. Her eyes squeezed shut, and her lips became a firm little line cut sharply in her face.

The others looked quizzically from Eugenia to Steven.

He turned his back and galloped toward Mayfair.

Thankfully, the wind dashed away his tears. If he had any integrity at all, he would abandon this silly mission Sir Nigel Pennyworthy had thrust on him. He'd leave England on the next packet and never show his face in this country again. He'd leave Lady Eugenia Terrebonne alone and not trouble her with his needs.

If he possessed an ounce of integrity . . . but he doubted that he did.

And he hated himself for it.

"What the bloody hell are *you* doing here, Nigel?"

Sir Nigel was visibly startled by Steven's entrance, but quickly regained his composure. He got to his feet self-assuredly, and crossed half the room to shake Steven's hand. Grasping Steven's upper arm, he leaned forward and whispered, "Trying to help you, Steve."

Steven looked past Nigel to where Catherine sat on the sofa, a mane of black hair flowing about her shoulders. She lifted her chin in greeting, but made no attempt to interrupt the muted conversation between her guests.

"Trying to help me? Why?" growled Steven.

"You haven't been particularly successful, Steve. Surely, you'd admit to that." Sir Nigel's brows puckered. "Perhaps you've lost your touch."

"I need more time."

"We have no more time. Prinny wants the information now."

"She will only talk to me. You said so yourself."

"I thought you could wheedle it out of her. But we can't wait forever."

"I know that," Steven said. "Fitzhaven is here in London. He has located Catherine's hiding place, and he knows she has talked to me. He's made several attempts on my life."

Sir Nigel's expression was inscrutable. "You've seen him, then?"

"Yes."

"Well, then. Perhaps we no longer need one another,

Steven. Our bargain called for you to get the information we needed from Lady Catherine. In exchange, I agreed to tell you Fitzhaven's whereabouts. If you already know—"

"He knows where I am!" Steven's blood boiled. Jabbing a finger in Nigel's chest, he backed the man across the carpet. They stood beside the sofa where Lady Catherine sat quietly, her posture amazingly serene. "He knows where Catherine is, too!" Steven continued. "But that does not mean *I* know where *he* is!"

"No doubt *he* will find *you.*" Nigel's voice was shaky, as if he feared Steven's violence. But his eyes were as narrow as slits in an armored helmet. "In the meantime, there is this business of Lady Catherine's debriefing. And her safety."

"Don't worry about her safety. I've taken care of that."

"You can't be her bodyguard round the clock, Steven. You have other pressing matters to attend to."

Like finding out whether the Earl of Bowlingbroke is a French sympathizer. Nigel's insinuation ground into Steven like broken glass. He hadn't got the information that Prinny wanted from Lady Catherine. Nor had he discovered one useful thing about the Earl of Bowlingbroke's political leanings. He was a failure, a washed-up dilettante who couldn't get it right. Anger burst inside him like fireworks. His fists coiled as he fought against the urge to punch Nigel's face—or head for the sideboard and the inevitable bottle of whiskey he knew was there.

"You came here . . . without telling me." Steven's voice was menacingly quiet. "Why did you do that?"

"I told you."

"She won't talk to you."

"You have your methods," Nigel said sotto voce. "I

have mine. Mine are a bit more . . . shall we say . . . crude."

Lady Catherine spoke at last. "I'm not a deaf mute, you know."

The men turned and stared at her. She really was beautiful, Steven thought, yet today her cold loveliness gave him a chill. "If you want to talk to Sir Nigel alone, Cat . . ."

"No." She looked from one man to the other. "I want him to leave. He was just leaving when you arrived. Weren't you, Sir Nigel?"

The man's expression looked as if it had been sheared off by a dull ax. Stiffening, he gave Lady Catherine a look of icy warning. Then he brushed past Steven and stalked out of the room. His boots pounded the steps, and the front door slammed behind him a moment later.

"Did he threaten you, Cat?" Steven ignored the empty spot beside her on the sofa, the spot she patted with her hand. Standing at the mantel, he looked blandly at her, trying hard to disguise his admiration for her glossy hair, full lips, and expertly advertised *décolletage*.

"No." She ran the back of her hand along her throat, then let her fingertips rest on the delicate pulse point at the base of it. "But he would have. You saved me, Steven. Thank you."

He swallowed hard. "I did not save you, Cat. The government still wants that list. You've got to name Fitzhaven's coconspirators. Otherwise, I cannot protect you."

"If I divulge that information, Fitzhaven will kill me."

"He will if he can get to you. I won't let him hurt you, Cat. I promise."

"You'll have to kill him, then."

Steven stared at her in abject silence. The weight of Catherine's words pressed against his chest like a wall

of stones. *You'll have to kill him, then.* So that was what
it had come down to.

The Earl of Fitzhaven, spy *extraordinaire,* not only
cuckolded Steven, but ruined his career as well. No one
had believed Steven when he said Fitzhaven was a Bonapartist. They'd ridiculed him, told him his jealousy had
warped his perspective. But now that the government
realized Fitzhaven was a traitor, they wanted Steven to
use his seductive influence over Catherine to persuade
her to betray her lover. The only problem was, that put
Catherine's life at risk. So in order to protect the woman
who'd betrayed him, Steven would be forced to kill the
man who had ruined his life.

The irony of the situation nearly made him smile.
Something cold crept into Steven's bones. Shivering, he
thought of the comfort a bottle of whiskey could bring
him, and he wanted a drink. No, he *needed* a drink.

"Care for a shot of whiskey?" Catherine asked, read-
ing his mind.

He pinched the bridge of his nose. There was much
to do in the next few days. Matters vital to the security
of the country rested in his hands. Lady Eugenia was
overset about the simultaneous arrival of her parents in
London, and he'd promised to assist her in averting a
nasty, embarrassing scene. Yes, he did need a shot of
whiskey.

But he thought he could survive without it, and he
wanted to.

"I need the list, Catherine." His voice was rough-
edged, his determination smooth and sharp.

"At the masquerade, Steven. I will give it to you then.
No sooner."

"Why? Why not give it to me now?"

"Because I want to go the masquerade. It is the best
and most exclusive party of the Season." Catherine's
voice was kittenish, but there was not a hint of kindness

in her tone. She had as much compassion for him as a cat toying with a dead roach. "It's as simple as that."

Flinching, Steven turned away. An ugliness he would never have thought Catherine capable of made it impossible for him to look at her. But it was that ugliness which brought clarity to his mind. Suddenly, he saw her for what she was, a cold, calculating minx whose only interests were her own.

A new perspective illuminated Steven's thinking. He realized that his bitterness had only weakened him, but it had empowered his enemies. By allowing his wounded pride to consume him, Steven had permitted Lady Catherine to hobble his emotions. By letting his anger control him, he had allowed Pennyworthy to use him.

He slammed one fist into his open palm. A streak of pain, along with a blinding clarity, shot through him. "Damme!"

"What is it?" Catherine asked. "Look at me!"

Turning, he faced her. It struck him as odd that her features were the same, yet her looks were entirely changed. Catherine's lovely features no longer stirred him.

An inexplicable peace of mind descended upon Steven. Self-awareness expanded his thinking. He knew what he wanted.

He knew he loved Lady Eugenia Terrebonne. He craved her company, the warmth of her dark brown gaze, the lilt of her voice. He saw her famous smile, that sweet unhesitating curve of her lips that never failed to move him. To think that he could inspire that smile, or even be the recipient of it, was a dizzying and foolishly romantic hope. Yet in that instant he knew that he would spend the rest of his life studying Eugenia's smile . . . if she would let him.

"Whatever is the matter with you?" Catherine purred.

"Ah . . . it is just that I am worried for your safety. And very frustrated by my inability to protect you."

"Stay awhile, then." She palmed the cushion beside her.

"No." Steven withdrew a small pistol from the back of his waistband. Handing it to her, he asked, "Do you know how to use this?"

Her fingers closed silkily around the ivory handle. "Yes. You taught me. Do you remember?"

He did. But Steven couldn't remain a moment longer in Lady Catherine's presence. Nodding curtly, he said, "If Fitzhaven threatens you, you must shoot to kill. Do you understand?"

"Shoot to kill. Um-um." She smiled provocatively.

If he remained a moment longer, the temptation to tell her what he thought of her might prove overwhelming. Steven said, "Good-bye," and showed himself out, stepping into the afternoon sun with as much relief as if he'd just been released from prison.

Eugenia walked down Curzon Street, Dashie trotting alongside on a leash. It was unseasonably warm, surprisingly so after the recent rains that had swept through London. With a light shawl wrapped around her shoulders, Eugenia lifted her face to the sun and inhaled deeply. Passing a couple of climbing boys, she made it a point to meet their gaze and smile. Smiling was the first step toward making oneself happy; that was her belief. And Lady Eugenia Terrebonne had no desire or intention of being a sullen puss the rest of her life.

Even if Sir Steven St. Charles was not in love with her.

Recounting the incident in the park, she drew her shawl more closely around her shoulders. Even the afternoon sun could not quell the shiver that ran through her body as she recalled her fear. The evil-looking horse-man who nearly galloped over Steven had meant to kill him.

Someone had tried to kill him outside the opera house, too. Eugenia knew that Steven, a veteran of the wars, was a taciturn man who never smiled and rarely appeared to be anything less than desperately unhappy. Sadly, it wasn't hard to imagine that someone wanted to kill him. What was shocking to Eugenia was her own reaction to that threat. If anything happened to Sir Steven St. Charles, she would likely never smile again.

She loved him. It was hardly a revelation; she had loved him for some time. Since the first time she met him, she supposed, at Sir Nigel Pennyworthy's party.

But he'd had eyes for Jane that night. And since that time, Jane had evidently developed a *tendre* for him as well.

Eugenia's smile slipped a bit.

Coming toward her was a man selling scissors and knives, pushing a rickety cart ahead of him. As they passed, Eugenia said, "Hello." The man seemed surprised, and tapping his battered hat, smiled in return. His wistful greeting gave Eugenia pause; she had much to be grateful for. It was foolish to indulge her self-pity and make herself unhappy by pining for a man who didn't love her.

Besides, Jane needed her help and Eugenia intended to give it.

With a sigh, she turned up the walkway that led to Aunt Clarissa's town house. Dashie pulled at her lead, stretching toward the door, but Eugenia wasn't terribly eager to go back. Still, she forced a pleasant expression on her face as she stepped inside and unhooked Dashie's leash. She gave the tiny dog a pat on the head and chuckled as it took off in search of Clarissa.

Yanking off her gloves, she stood in the foyer, her

thoughts still spinning around images of Steven, her heart still aching at the thought of his loving Jane. Head bent, she started up the stairs in search of her mother. But at the first landing she paused, eerily aware of some-one above her, watching. She felt his presence before she saw him. She knew he was there, his loving gaze awaiting her.

"Father!" Lifting her skirts, she pounded up the stair-case and threw herself into his arms.

For a long time Sir Albert hugged her tightly to his chest. Then he held her at arm's length and studied her face. "Eugenia, my love. You look beautiful. Come, now, don't cry! Why the sad face? I should have thought you'd be happy to see me!"

"I am!" Eugenia allowed her father to brush the tears from her cheeks. She looked closely at him, too, noting the stubborn set of his jaw, the new streaks of silver in his thick ginger hair, the tiredness in his gaze. The crin-kles around his eyes bespoke his age, but to Eugenia he was more handsome than ever. "Oh, Father, I'm so happy to see you! It's just that . . . well, have you seen Mother yet? You do know she's here, don't you?"

Sir Albert Terrebonne led her toward the drawing room where they settled side by side on the sofa. "Your mother went out shopping the moment my carriage ar-rived. Says she doesn't want to speak to me, or lay eyes on me." Taking her hand in his, he peered intently into Eugenia's eyes. "But I'm sure she will return soon, and eventually she will relent." He sighed. "She always does."

Laying her head on her father's shoulder, Eugenia sniffled. "Please don't fight with her, Father. I don't think I can stand it."

But her head popped up at the sound of footsteps outside the room. Mr. Greville, taking stock of the situation, entered cautiously, a small calling card clutched in his extended hand.

"What is it?" Sir Albert said gruffly, clearly unhappy at the intrusion.

"Forgive me, sir. But there is a Sir Steven St. Charles below stairs."

Eugenia straightened. "He's here to see Jane, then. I believe she's in her room, Mr. Greville."

"No, my lady, the gentleman says he is here to see *you.* Would you like me to send him away?"

Startled, Eugenia cast a nervous glance at her father. Why would Steven be visiting her? Mr. Greville must be mistaken. But her pulse skittered at the thought of sending him away. "Father, do you mind—"

"A gentleman caller? Of course not! Send him up, Mr. Greville. I should be happy to meet any man who has the good sense to court my daughter."

"No, Father, you are wrong." Eugenia spoke quickly, anxious to inform her father of all pertinent facts before Mr. Greville returned with Steven. "He likes Jane and she likes him. Only he never smiles. And Jane has wagered that I cannot make him laugh before midnight at Lord Bowlingbroke's masquerade. Oh! And Lord Bowlingbroke is against a match between Jane and Steven. So, I have agreed—"

When Steven stepped into the room, her speech faltered and her throat constricted. Steven, devilishly handsome in his buff breeches and dark blue coat, strode into the room. Watching him walk, Eugenia felt the first wave of arousal shimmy through her bones. Her cheeks warmed and her skin prickled. Something about the man's mere presence made her slightly insane.

Her father's quick appraisal was not subtle; he looked at Steven, then met his daughter's guilty gaze. Embarrassment suffused her cheeks. Sir Albert Terrebonne was not a man easily fooled. To him, Eugenia was transparent.

Sir Albert stood and shook Steven's hand. Then the men sat, Sir Albert beside Eugenia, Steven in a chair opposite the sofa. There was a moment of awkward silence while Eugenia and Steven stared at one another, silent questions filling the air.

"I understand you have just returned from abroad, sir," Steven finally said, uncharacteristically deferential.

"Athens, to be exact. Sketching the ruins. Marvelous scenery. Hot as hell. And not a decent cup of English tea to be found in the entire country."

Eugenia and her father chuckled. Steven's lips curled in what could have been a grimace or a grin.

So, he *could* smile! A pervasive warmth flowed through Eugenia's veins. Irrationally, *his* smile seemed to reflect *her* happiness. Locking gazes with Steven, she smiled sunnily in return. Amazingly, he held her gaze and stared at her with all the intensity she was accustomed to from the serious Sir Steven.

But there was something else shining behind his eyes. There was a new and lingering softness in them, a *yearning*, yes, but not one borne of sadness and self-defeat. For the first time since she had known him, Eugenia saw unalloyed pleasure and contentment in Steven's eyes.

"Well." Sir Albert rubbed his knee. "Well, well."

Sir Steven cleared his throat. "Has Eugenia told you about the masquerade?"

"The Bowlingbroke masquerade? Don't tell me I've arrived in London just in time to make an appearance at the grandest celebration of the Season? Dear me, how lucky can I be?"

Eugenia's senses were on full alert. Sir Steven's unexpected visit suddenly had a purpose. So, *this* was why he had appeared in Curzon Street unannounced—he came to learn what Sir Albert intended to wear to the costume party. He had promised Eugenia he would help her avert a disaster at the masquerade; he was fulfilling his pledge.

God, but Jane was a lucky woman!

"You *are* lucky, Father," Eugenia said. "That is, if you intend to grace the *ton* with your presence. You don't have to go, you know."

"Is Alex going?"

"Yes."

"Then I must also attend."

"What shall you wear?" Eugenia asked, attempting to sound nonchalant.

"Oh, I don't know. I suppose I have plenty of time to decide."

"No, you don't!" Eugenia stammered to explain herself. "I mean, you must make a decision quickly. There isn't much time, you know, and if a seamstress is required—"

Steven spoke up. "There is hardly a seamstress or mantua maker in Mayfair who is not overloaded with orders. I daresay, you will be hard-pressed to find anyone who can stitch up a costume on such short notice."

"Then I shall improvise."

"How so, Father?"

Sir Albert rubbed his lower lip and frowned. "Let me think on it overnight, Eugenia. I am certain that I can come up with something suitable."

Snapping her fingers, Eugenia said, "Something that will reflect your personality, Father . . ."

"Something no one else would ever think of," added Steven.

"A costume that will show off your best features, Father!"

"But something simple," said Steven.

"What is Lady Alex going as?" Sir Albert asked.

Eugenia swallowed hard, hesitating. She knew her father so well. At length, she said weakly, "Mother is going as Cleopatra, Father."

"Cleopatra, eh?" Sir Albert's expression turned impish. "Well, then. I believe there is only one disguise that will suit me. I shall go as Julius Caesar! I want you to be sure and tell your mother, Genie! She won't agree to ride with me to the masquerade, but surely she will be touched by my choice of costume."

"Why won't she accompany you to the party?" Eugenia asked.

"Seems she is a mite overset at something I said months ago during one of our many battles. But I intend to set things to rights, Genie. It is time your mother and I reached an accord."

Eugenia's stomach floated queasily as she recalled the fight that had precipitated her parents' most recent separation. It had been unusually bitter, and though Eugenia was not privy to everything that was said, she knew that when it was over her mother's feelings were deeply, and perhaps irreparably, wounded. "Oh, Father, please don't start another controversy—"

Holding up his hand, Sir Albert said, "Now wait a moment, Eugenia. Hear me out. I didn't travel halfway around the world to pick another fight with your mother. I came here to woo her."

"Woo her?" Eugenia looked from her father to Steven.

"You might as well hear this, too, young man," Albert said. "Perhaps you will learn something from my mistakes. At any rate, I have had time during this last trip to think long and hard about my wife, Alexandra. A fine woman, full of spirit. I love her desperately."

"You love her? Then, why—"

But Eugenia's father squeezed her hand tightly and shook his head to quiet her. "I don't know what happened, and I don't know when. But somehow, sometime, I forgot *why* I loved your mother. I know it sounds strange, but you see, when I met Alexandra, I thought she was the most exciting, ravishing woman I'd ever met. She was brash and outspoken, a true original. Wherever we went, people were attracted to her. Everyone laughed at her jokes, our friends depended upon her to make their parties a success."

"And then?" Eugenia murmured.

"And then, somehow, sometime, the very things I loved in her began to gnaw at my self-confidence. I realized it was Alex who drew in our friends, and held them close to us. I saw the world falling in love with her, and I was jealous. I wanted her all to myself. I tried to hold her more closely to me, but I only succeeded in wounding her."

Stricken, Eugenia could only gulp and stare at her father in stunned silence. Emotion threatened to spill out her lips and eyes, but she didn't want to cry in front of Steven. Gripping Sir Albert's hand, she clung desperately to her equilibrium.

Steven slowly stood, his own gaze full of stifled emotion. With an awkward movement, he touched Sir Albert's shoulder, then straightened. "Sometimes God is good to us," he said softly, "and we get a second chance, sir."

"It is all I can hope for, isn't it?" Albert replied.

"I suppose it is all any of us can hope for." Steven hesitated, then leaned down and gave Eugenia a kiss on her cheek. "I shall see you at the Bowlingbroke masquerade, my lady. And I will be looking forward to seeing you . . . and . . . well, to putting everything to rights."

"Everything?" She looked up at him, her heart pounding.

"Everything."

At that moment, the front door crashed open. Packages were dropped on the floor, a flurry of activity sounded, and servants began to scurry about the foyer.

Lady Alexandra's voice stormed up the staircase. "Where is he?" Her hurried footsteps followed.

In the threshold, she stood, gripping both sides of the door frame, her face angry and pink, trembling with barely contained violence. She glared furiously at her husband, but said nothing.

Sir Albert leapt to his feet and started toward his wife.

But she recoiled as he neared her, and releasing her hold on the door, pivoted. Her boots were heard stomping the steps, then the door to her bedchamber slammed shut above stairs.

The deafening roar of Lady Alex's silent anger rocked the house in Curzon Street.

TWELVE

The night sparkled. Carriage lamps formed a cordon of candle bursts that snaked from the Bowlingbrokes' town house all the way down Park Lane and into Hill Street. Overhead, stars winked with merry mischief while laughter wafted on the breeze. Eugenia thought the evening sky itself had spruced up for the Bowlingbroke masquerade. It was even rumored that the Prince of Wales would turn out for this exclusive celebration.

A shiver piqued her nerves as she stepped from Aunt Clarissa's carriage. Dressed in a pale blue pinafore and white underdress, a miniature shepherd's staff crooked over her arm, she led the sheepskin-clad Dashie down the walkway. Beside her strode Lady Jane, an apparent guest at her own father's party, dressed in Renaissance garb. With her pale green flowing gown, daring bustline, and tall pointed cap with veils, Jane made a very arresting Juliet.

Aunt Clarissa as Old Mother Goose and Lady Alexandra as Cleopatra brought up the rear of the group. Entering the glittering town house, the foursome adjusted their masks so that their identities were totally obscured. Had they not arrived together, they would never have recognized one another.

Shifting Dashie's weight to her opposite hip, Eugenia drew to a halt. For a moment, she stood in the foyer, gaping at the crowd of people that flowed through the house.

"Come, Genie, we should find the punch table immediately," Jane urged her.

The two girls threw smiles over their shoulders at Clarissa and Alex, then pushed through the throng. Shortly thereafter, they stood in the ballroom, sipping lukewarm drinks laced with fruit and rum. At the edge of the dance floor, they watched a multitude of masked revelers, many of them already deep in their cups, laughing, dancing, mingling, and in general behaving as if they hadn't one inhibition in the world.

"It's incredible, is it not?" Eugenia gazed at the spectacle, searching the room for a Julius Caesar—or two.

"I see him, Genie!" Jane indicated a tall, well-built gentleman wearing an Elizabethan ruff, a bright green quilted doublet and matching hose. Distinguishable as much by the patch of hair on his chin as by the peacock manner in which he strutted, Lord Delaroux spotted Jane at the same instant. "Here he comes. Now please do not forget your promise, Eugenia. You won't, will you?"

Eugenia laid a hand on her friend's arm. "Of course not."

Lord Robert Delaroux approached the ladies with a jaunty smile on his face. "Juliet, you are a vision," he said, bowing low to Jane.

"Romeo." Jane's expression was invisible, but her nervous curtsy and the trembling of her hands betrayed her emotions. Behind her disguise, she spoke the beautiful words Shakespeare had written for her hundreds of years earlier. " 'Thou know'st the mask of night is on my face, Else would a maiden blush bepaint my cheek.' "

"Are you certain you wish to go through with this elopement, Jane?" Delaroux—*or rather Romeo*—asked.

"Elopement?" Eugenia's jaw fell slack and incredulity

strained her voice. "Jane, pray tell me what this is about! I thought you were in love—"

"I am, dear. Very much so. With Robert." A calmness had befallen Jane. She stood beside Lord Delaroux, staring worshipfully at him.

Only the color of their eyes were visible behind their masks, but the couple held one another's gaze, their hands entwined.

Lord Delaroux turned toward Eugenia. " 'Tis so good of you to assist us in our plan. Here is the note which you must give to the earl." Releasing Jane's hands, he withdrew a small envelope from the pocket sewn onto his doublet.

"But I do not recognize Lord Bowlingbroke!" And Eugenia wasn't certain at all whether she wanted a part in this preposterous scheme. Lord Robert Delaroux and Lady Jane Terrebonne? In love? The match would be the talk of the Season, that was certain, but hardly for reasons the Bowlingbrokes would like.

And the implications of this love-match were just beginning to seep into Eugenia's befuddled brain.

"You won't have any trouble spotting *them*. Mother and Father are dressed as Marie Antoinette and King Louis the sixteenth," Jane said. "Mother sent me a note a few days ago informing me of her identity. She wanted to be certain I would recognize her."

"Will she recognize you?" Eugenia asked.

Jane nodded. "She helped me choose the trim for my costume, remember? Of course she knows who *we* are, Genie. But she doesn't know that Lord Delaroux is dressed as Romeo."

"What precisely does this note say?" Eugenia asked, dropping the missive in her apron pocket. Dashie was growing restless, so she placed the small dog on the floor and held the long ribbon that served as a leash.

Lord Delaroux slanted a nervous look at Jane.

"It's . . . well, suffice it to say that the note I have written to the Earl of Bowlingbroke will convince him, once and for all, that I am a man of courage. After tonight, he will know beyond a shadow of a doubt that I love Lady Jane above all else."

"How noble," Eugenia said, thoroughly confused. "Why not simply tell the earl how you feel? Or if you are unable to express yourself to the man face-to-face, why not hand him this letter yourself? Forgive me, but I do not understand the reason for a go-between in this instance."

Jane spoke in urgent tones. "You must slip the letter to my father so that he does not know where it came from."

"How am I to do that? And why?"

"He mustn't know the identity of the letter's author, Genie. 'Tis crucial that you pass the note to him without revealing your identity."

"When the masks come off at midnight, he will know who Little Bo-Peep is," Eugenia argued.

"Then he must *not* know that Little Bo-Peep gave him the letter," Lord Delaroux said.

"But that will be impossible—"

Squeezing her arm, Jane said, "Genie, will you do it?"

Just then, a tall, broad-shouldered man wearing a long Roman toga and a golden laurel around his head appeared at Eugenia's elbow. Despite the man's mask, she knew immediately it was Sir Steven. The air surrounding him was charged with friction.

"Good evening, ladies. Hello, Delaroux . . . I mean, Romeo." The deep, masculine voice was undeniably Steven. Only *his* voice had the power to make Eugenia's insides quiver.

"Steven!" Lord Delaroux clapped his friend's back. "What a clever costume. Only look . . . there on the

other side of the room! There is another man dressed
just as you are."

"Yes, an unfortunate coincidence," Steven said dryly
as Lord Delaroux escorted Lady Jane to the dance floor.

Following Steven's gaze, Eugenia easily picked her
father out of the knot of people surrounding the punch
table. As expected, he wore a costume that was identical
to Steven's.

But to her eye the man across the room was a mere
mortal, her *father,* an ordinary-looking man dressed in
a formless sheath. Sir Steven, by contrast, exuded sen-
suality. The sight of his well-muscled shoulders and
slender hips stirred a tempest of desire deep within
Eugenia's loins.

And Jane was not in love with him!

The realization struck her like a flaming arrow. As
heat suffused her cheeks, she stared at Steven. Though
she could not see his expression, she met his pale blue
gaze and shivered. His penetrating stare, which never
failed to rivet her, now held an element of promise and
yearning.

Perhaps she misread him. Maybe she was imagining
what she wanted to see, but it occurred to Eugenia that
Sir Steven might want her, too.

Her conversation with him at the sideboard in Aunt
Clarissa's house echoed in her head. She told Steve that
Jane was in love with him! His initial reaction, now that
Eugenia thought about it, was one of surprise. But he
didn't deny that the two were secretly in love. He didn't
dissuade Eugenia from her promise to help them.

Did that mean that Sir Steven nurtured an unrequited
love for Lady Jane?

Pain arced through Eugenia as she sipped her treacle
and tried to make sense of all that was happening around
her.

She had every right, now that Jane's affections for

Lord Delaroux were known, to reveal her feelings to Sir Steven. But telling him how she felt was an enormous risk. He might yet harbor a *tendre* for Jane. Worse, he might simply feel nothing for Eugenia.

He leaned toward her, his very nearness filling her with a sexual apprehension that she'd never before experienced. His whispered voice was low and husky. "Have you the love notes?"

She opened her lacy reticule and extracted two folded and sealed vellum papers. Discreetly, she gave Sir Steven the note she had penned to her mother. Signed "Caesar," it was a flowery apology for every slight, real or imagined, Lord Albert had committed against Lady Alexandra since the inception of their marriage.

The other note was addressed to Sir Albert and signed, "Cleopatra." Eyeing her father, Eugenia determined now was as good a time as any to deliver it to him. Recalling the poetic language she had used to express her mother's love for Sir Albert, Eugenia blushed. Lady Alexandra would never speak in such self-effacing terms to Sir Albert.

"Is there any chance this little game will be successful in reuniting my parents?" she asked Sir Steven, her voice shaky.

He shrugged one magnificent shoulder. "If nothing else, sweetling, it will get them to the settlement table. Eventually, they will discover they've been duped."

"Yes. But I hope by that time they won't care." Eugenia paused, uncertain what to say. "Steven . . . I want to thank you. . . ."

He shook his head. Then, after a length, he tucked the letter he was to deliver to Lady Alex into the gold belt that cinched his waist. He took Eugenia's arm, turned it over and scraped the pads of his fingers over the delicate skin between her wrist and elbow.

She gasped with startled joy.

"No need to thank me, Eugenia. You see, I want only what is best for you. I want whatever you want, my lady. I want to make you happy."

Before she could utter another word, the velvet rasp of a lady's voice interrupted.

Sir Steven would have known Lady Catherine anywhere, no matter her disguise. Her voice, catlike and throaty, raised the hairs on the back of his neck.

"I would have known *you* anywhere," she purred. With her bosom displayed to great advantage in a scarlet gown that appeared to be painted on her voluptuous body, Lady Catherine looked from Steven to Lady Eugenia.

"Would you care to be introduced?" said Steven. "Or should I allow the two of you to be surprised at midnight?"

"I think I should like an introduction," Lady Eugenia answered, her tone surprisingly brittle.

Female jealousy was not a trait Steven associated with Lady Eugenia Terrebonne. Taken aback, he stumbled over Lady Catherine's name.

"Never mind," she interjected. "I am Guinevere tonight, Arthur's wife and Lancelot's lover. And you, dear girl? Some storybook character, I presume?"

Dashie let go a low growl. Amused, Steven murmured, "At least the dog has good instincts."

Bending down to scoop the little dog in her arms, Eugenia said, "I am costumed as Little Bo-Peep, madam. And this is one of my sheep."

"How quaint."

Displeased by Catherine's pettiness, Steven said, "Do you have something for me, Cat?" He held out his hand, expecting a note, letter, or list of some sort to be placed in his palm. It was all he wanted from her. Her presence at the masquerade was an irritant. Her insults toward Eugenia were offensive.

Behind her mask, Lady Catherine's feline eyes glittered. "Not here, Steven. Meet me in the library at a quarter after eleven o'clock."

It was not a good time. "Catherine, I insist—"

"Darling, your insistence will gain you nothing. I will see you in the library at the appointed time. There you will receive what is due you. You must trust me." Lady Catherine gave Eugenia a long, appraising stare. Then, in a condescending gesture, she patted the top of Dashie's head, and cooed, "What a sweet little thing. A little ragged, perhaps, but I'm sure she is capable of great devotion and gratitude. Pathetic little creatures like that usually are."

A chill slithered up Steven's spine. He would have liked to shake Lady Catherine till her teeth rattled. But he didn't have to. Dashie lifted her head, curled her lips, and bit the tip off one of the fingers of Lady Catherine's beautiful red silk glove.

"Oh! You beastly mongrel, you!" Lady Catherine yanked back her hand, turned on her heel, and flounced away.

When she had gone, Steven turned to Eugenia. "My lady, there is something I must say to you . . . something I must ask you . . ."

But Eugenia's gaze, even through the narrow slits of her mask, was filled with hurt and anger. Shaking her head, she said, "No. I have something I must do. It cannot wait."

And with that, she, too, turned and crossed the room.

Steven's heart squeezed painfully. He had to tell Lady Eugenia he loved her, even if it meant risking his pride, even if it meant jeopardizing his mission and the military security of his country. He simply couldn't contain his feelings any longer.

Watching her walk away, back straight, carriage proud, her brown curls in delightful disarray, he released a pent-up breath. He *would* tell her loved her . . . tonight. Right after he had a long talk with the Earl of Bowlingbroke.

Fingering the other note he had hidden beneath his belt, he thought of his promise to Sir Nigel Pennyworthy. Sir Steven's duty was to find out whether Lord Bowlingbroke was a French sympathizer. According to Pennyworthy's instructions, Steven had planned to insinuate himself into Lady Jane's good graces, then worm his way into her father's inner circle and find out everything he could about the earl. But because of his infatuation with Eugenia, Steven had been wildly unsuccessful in his scheme.

Now, stalking toward the punch table, Steven's resolve firmly hardened. His mission remained paramount, but his method was altered. He *would* know the true nature of Bowlingbroke's patriotism before the night was over. But he would obtain that information honorably and without subterfuge. The note Steven had penned for the earl simply invited the man to meet him in the library at half past eleven o'clock, before the unmasking began. There, Steven would question Bowlingbroke about his allegiance. And afterward Stephen would be free to tell Lady Eugenia he loved her.

Lady Jane's parents were magnificently costumed, but poorly disguised. As Marie Antoinette and Louis XVI, they seemed to be dressed, at least to Eugenia, perfectly in character.

But passing a note to the earl without his knowing where it came from was hardly a simple task. Eugenia sidled up to Lord and Lady Bowlingbroke, half certain they would recognize her. What if Aunt Clarissa had described Eugenia's costume to the countess? What if Sally Bowlingbroke recognized Dashie, whose sheepskin coat did little to disguise the fact she was a dachshund?

But the exalted couple, apparently intoxicated by the success of their party, and as always, highly distracted by one another, did not see through Little Bo-Peep's disguise.

Beneath a towering powdered wig studded with tiny silver birds and Empire bees, the Countess of Bowlingbroke stood in the center of her admirers. Her gown, an extravaganza of silver silk, satin, and lace, would have embarrassed the Bourbon monarchy. With its whalebone stays and hoop skirts, it was as much a marvel of engineering as it was a parody of the fashions of the fallen French court.

Beside her presided the earl, wearing an equally ornate wig, satin knee pants, and high heel shoes. Clutching an empty champagne flute, he exuberantly related an anecdote about the former French king. Twice, he lifted the glass to his lips and frowned at its emptiness. When he looked anxiously around the room for a servant, an idea occurred to Eugenia.

A man clad in medieval garb and a jeweled crown approached the earl, tapped him on the shoulder, and whispered in his ear. Noting the glinting sword strapped to the newcomer's belt, Eugenia deduced that he was costumed as King Arthur. When she saw the earl half turn and give the man his full attention, she made her move.

A servant passed with a tray laden with glasses of champagne. Eugenia stopped him, slipped her tiny envelope on the silver tray, and said, "You had best supply the Bourbon king with more champagne. His throat is becoming parched and he is more than a little agitated that no one has appeared with drink in the last half hour."

The young servant quickly collected the earl's empty flute and presented his tray. The earl, having closed his conversation with King Arthur and waved him off, lifted a full glass of champagne, paused, stared curiously at the vellum envelope, then picked it up.

Eugenia turned, eager to flee the scene, just as Lord Bowlingbroke ripped open the envelope and let out a ferociously harsh bark of outrage.

Crossing the room in search of Jane, she wasn't surprised by the earl's reaction. The man was most likely reeling from the shocking news that his daughter was in love with Lord Delaroux. Where had the two love birds flown to, anyway?

Eugenia skirted the orchestra, then strolled along the row of potted palms that screened one side of the ballroom. She smiled at unknown maskers dressed as historical figures, animals, and exotic characters. But she never took her eyes off the well-muscled Julius Caesar with the bristly blond hair.

She watched him tap Cleopatra's bare shoulder. She turned as serenely as an Egyptian monarch, her head swathed in the traditional white crown, her figure sheathed in gold-trimmed linen. Clutching a crook and flail in one hand, she accepted Caesar's proffered letter in the other. Her reaction was one of surprise, slight hostility, and suspicion. But Steven, playing his role, bowed gallantly and disarmed her.

He reached for Cleopatra's hand, drew her knuckles to his lips and kissed them. When she reared back, he held her. A long moment passed as the two considered one another. Then Caesar released Cleopatra's hand and disappeared in the crowd.

But Eugenia's soft laughter quickly died. The lady dressed as Guinevere circled the room like a tiger in search of raw meat. Watching her, Eugenia saw that she, too, studied every movement Julius Caesar made.

Guinevere, whoever she was, posed an inexplicable threat to Eugenia's peace of mind. A wave of panic and jealousy consumed her. Then she spotted her father, a shorter, less brawny version of Julius Caesar, and as she drifted toward him, she calmed herself and smiled.

What the devil was the matter with her anyway? And where was Jane when she needed her?

"Here, Father. Cleopatra asked me to give this to you." Eugenia guiltily handed her father the forged love letter. She was playing deep and she knew it, but where her parents' marriage was concerned, she concluded she had everything to gain and nothing to lose.

Her father neatly broke the wax seal and scanned the letter. As his eyes grew large and limpid, Eugenia, embarrassed, averted her gaze. On the dance floor, a lively reel partially obstructed her view, but as a couple dressed in bright harlequin costumes flashed past her, she caught a glimpse of something exceedingly strange.

Near the punch table, on the other side of the room, the man costumed as King Arthur stood beside Guinevere, the lady in red. They were joined by a man wearing a chain metal tunic beneath a scarlet gambeson emblazoned with a golden lion—*a knight of the Round Table?* With heads together, their expressions worried, the threesome looked from one Julius Caesar to another. Their confusion was evident. Then King Arthur gripped the hilt of his sword and removed it from its sheath. He passed the weapon to the younger man, who gave a curt nod, turned on his heel, and marched from the room.

Eugenia knew the lay out of the Bowlingbroke house as well as she knew her own. The man with the sword headed directly for the library, where Sir Steven planned to meet the lady dressed in red. Shortly thereafter, the mysterious lady turned and strode in the same direction. Eugenia had no rational reason to fear that the woman would harm Steven, but a chill ran up her spine.

Her father's voice interrupted her thoughts. "Genie, we must talk—"

"Father, I think it is Mother you should be talking with."

Sir Albert's mask could not conceal his raw emotion. But Eugenia, bewildered and worried for Steven's welfare, blew her father a kiss, then circled the room again. Whatever fate awaited Steven in the library, she intended to be there to share it with him.

Every fiber in Steven's body thrummed with tension. His future hung in the balance. He would tell Lady Eugenia he loved her tonight, or he would never have the courage to do so.

Discreetly, he left the ballroom and walked the length of the corridor to the library, where he was to meet Lady Catherine. Their rendezvous would not take long. He simply wanted to obtain the information she had for him and tell her good-bye forever. The brevity of that meeting would leave the library vacant for his meeting at eleven-thirty with the Earl of Bowlingbroke. Then, with a little luck, Sir Albert and Lady Alexandra would meet alone at midnight for the assignation Eugenia had concocted for them.

Steven had earlier asked a butler where the library was. Now he crossed the threshold and stood in the center of the room, deeply impressed by the richness of the furnishings, the glossy mahogany paneling, the thick velvet draperies that covered one wall, and the faded family portraits that stared so ominously at him. A dense silence settled on him as he made a leisurely perusal of the room's treasures.

The clock on the mantel ticked loudly. It was a quarter past eleven o'clock. Behind him a voice purred, "Really, Steven, you are so predictable."

He turned. "You haven't changed much either, Cat."

She drew the library doors shut, then crossed the room. Her expression was hidden behind her mask, but her hips and breasts, moving seductively beneath her crimson gown, were inviting. Standing before Steven, she removed her mask. Then she crooked her finger beneath the chin of his and tipped it up.

"I want to see your face."

He tossed his mask aside. "Where is the list, Catherine?"

"Not so fast, Steven. We have some old business to clear up, you and I."

"We have nothing to discuss." He took a step back.

She moved forward, pressing her body to his. "Why do you hate me?"

"I do not hate you. I have no feeling for you." His mouth felt dry and his heart hammered in his chest. "It is just . . . I no longer love you, Cat. You have no power over me any longer. Just give me the list, and go."

She ran a finger down his cheek, drew a line of gooseflesh along his neck, then laid her palm flat against his chest. But as she rose on her toes, her face lifted to his, lips parted, the door to the library crashed open.

Little Bo-Peep, mask pushed back on her head, tiny dog clutched in her arms, stared back at him. Her horrified expression betrayed her thoughts as clearly as if she'd shouted them.

The next minute, in which Catherine turned and chuckled, slid by in agonizing slowness.

Frozen in the door frame, Eugenia appraised the damning scenario. Her head told her to leave. She'd been crazy to think that she had a chance for happiness with Sir Steven. Even with Lady Jane out of the picture, there was still the question of his affection for her. Didn't this tawdry tableau answer that?

She thought of her own parents and wondered if there

were such a thing as true love. A thousand doubts assailed her. She felt humiliated and confused. Perhaps loving Steven wasn't worth the emotional pain she felt. She had a fleeting impulse to flee, to run away, and never speak to him again. At least her heart would be protected. At least her suffering would end.

But Eugenia's heart wouldn't let her go. She'd come here to protect Sir Steven, and to tell him she loved him, too. She didn't like what she found, but she was willing to stay and fight.

Blinking back tears, she softly drew the doors shut behind her. "Steven, I thought—"

He roughly put the lady in red aside, and crossed the room. "Eugenia," he whispered hoarsely, grasping her upper arms.

When Dashie yelped, Eugenia bent down and dropped him gently to the floor.

Then, full of questions, she clung to Steven. "I wanted to tell you—"

He pressed a finger to her lips. "No, it is I who must tell you . . . this." His gaze pressed into her, and he dipped his head to kiss her.

But before his lips touched hers, the doors burst open behind them. The Earl of Bowlingbroke as King Louis XVI and the tall, bony man dressed as King Arthur barreled into the room, their expressions shockingly unpleasant.

But if that were not excitement aplenty, behind them trundled an obviously drunken Humpty-Dumpty, his mask pushed to the side, revealing a very puffy, very *royal* countenance.

The Prince of Wales halted in the doorway. Eyes bleary, lips glistening, he slurred his salutation. "Well, hel-loo, everyone! What have we here?"

"Good God, he has ravished this young thing as well!" Bowlingbroke cried, jerking off his mask.

The older man put aside his mask, too, and Eugenia was stunned to see that it was Sir Nigel Pennyworthy disguised as King Arthur.

Prinny's eyes widened, his gaze leaping from Steven to Bowlingbroke.

Steven took a protective stance, putting his body in front of Eugenia's. "What the hell are you doing here, Bowlingbroke?"

Eugenia peeked around him, her pulse racing as much from the excitement of Steven's near kiss as the rude oddity of the interruption. Bowlingbroke looked as if he could murder someone, Pennyworthy looked insanely happy, and Prinny appeared vastly amused.

"You meant to kidnap my daughter, you scoundrel," Bowlingbroke snarled.

"Rapscallion! Villain!" Sir Nigel cried. "It is as plain as the nose on my face what he intended!"

"It was just a kiss," the prince murmured.

"Kidnap your daughter?" Steven exploded. "Have you gone stark raving mad? I don't know what the devil you are talking about!"

Sir Nigel couldn't be outshouted. "And to think he would seduce Lady Jane's friend as well! 'Tis heinous, I tell you! He is not to be trusted. He is not to be believed at all, I tell you! Do you see, Your Highness? Do you see that you can no longer trust anything that Sir Steven St. Charles says?"

"Traitor!" Steven bellowed at Pennyworthy.

Bowlingbroke held up his fist and shook a crumpled piece of vellum in the air. "Here! The kidnap note! You threatened to spirit my daughter away!"

"I did no such thing!"

Terror struck Eugenia's heart as she recognized the writing paper clutched in Bowlingbroke's fingers. Tugging at Sir Steven's elbow, she nearly choked on her remorse and embarrassment. "Steven, I must tell you something," she whispered.

He put his hand over hers, but did not respond to her entreaty. Instead, he spoke as calmly to Bowlingbroke as a man accused of kidnapping could be expected to. "You are mistaken, Your Grace. I passed you a note, asking you to meet me in the library at half past eleven. I wanted to discuss a very delicate matter with you."

At that point, the lady in the red gown stalked across the room. Standing beside Sir Nigel, her arms crossed over her ample chest, she pinned a hostile stare on Steven. "Be careful where you tread, Steven. I don't have to warn you, do I? You are on thin ice here."

Eugenia was amazed by the venom that sounded in Steven's voice.

"No, Lady Catherine, it is you who are on thin ice. Do you think I care for one moment what happens to my career now? I'm finished spying on my fellow citizens—"

"Spying?" The Earl of Bowlingbroke gulped his confusion.

"Oh, dear," said Prinny.

"You are finished as a spy, sir," said Pennyworthy. "Your word can never be trusted again! We've caught you red-handed now—kissing Lady Eugenia Terrebonne after threatening to kidnap her friend Lady Jane and leave the country!"

"I've done no such thing," Steven said in a quietly menacing voice. Turning to the Prince of Wales, he said, "It's a conspiracy, Your Highness. I'm not sure I can explain it all, but surely you can see that I've been trapped. I did not threaten to kidnap Lord Bowlingbroke's daughter. But I did pass him a note requesting that he meet me in the library at eleven-thirty."

"Why?" Prinny asked, his huge bulk swaying from side to side.

Steven sighed. "Because I am weary of this subterfuge and duplicity. I thought it best to simply ask the earl whether he was a French sympathizer and be done with it."

The earl was clearly perplexed. "Now it is my turn to ask you. What the devil are you talking about?"

Steven's body tensed beneath Eugenia's touch. She felt his spin stiffen and his shoulders square. As she stood beside him, a sense of pride roiled through her even though she didn't understand the intrigue that had brought this situation to a head. She only knew that Steven was acting with honor and courage, while Pennyworthy and the lady in red were aligning their forces against him.

"Did you know that you are currently under investigation by the British government, Your Grace?" Steven met the earl's steely gaze without flinching. "You are suspected of being a spy, or at the very least, a Bonapartist in your heart."

"Herbert said so," Prinny mumbled.

"Herbert? Who on earth is Herbert?" the earl asked.

"Herbert Smythfield," replied the prince. "Hasn't anyone a drink, or a least a snort of snuff? Well, anyway, Herbert is stationed in Cairo. He wrote to his wife and told her that the earl is a Bonapartist, and she reported it to . . . well, let us just say that the information came to the attention of the Crown. And I requested that an investigation be conducted."

The earl turned and stared at Pennyworthy in abject amazement. "Nigel! You knew about this?"

"I have always argued in favor of your innocence, Your Grace," Sir Nigel said, his face as red as a beefeater's coat.

Prinny turned and blinked in Nigel's direction. "But Nigel, dear, you were the one—"

"Your Highness, these are matters of national security!" Sir Nigel patted the air with his hands. "With all due respect, I plead with you to protect your sources!"

Just then, Lady Alexandra Terrebonne, dressed as Cleopatra, strolled through the open doors of the library. Relieved, Eugenia realized in an instant of clarity how much respect and reverence she harbored for her own mother, a woman of such self-commanding respect that everyone in the room fell silent.

"Did I hear someone mention Herbert Smythfield's name?" Lady Alex chuckled throatily as she removed her mask. After giving the lady in red a scathing head-to-toe evaluation, she added, "My dears, didn't you know? The poor man was eaten by crocodiles six months ago!"

THIRTEEN

"Eaten by crocodiles?" everyone echoed, astounded.

"Quite by design, I'm afraid." Lady Alex removed her mask to reveal an even more exotic visage, beautiful eyes rimmed in dark kohl and lips painted a deep reddish brown. "He killed himself, you see. By means of crocodiles."

"Killed himself!" Prinny's Humpty-Dumpty face suddenly cracked.

"The poor man was mad at the end," Lady Alex said. "From grief and public humiliation. Remember, the British community in Cairo is quite small," Lady Alex said. "There are very few secrets among us there!"

"Herbert never could keep a secret," Prinny inserted.

"The man was not to be trusted!" Sir Nigel expostulated.

Lady Alex stood beside Eugenia and Steven. "Perhaps not. But before he threw himself into the Nile, he publicly lamented that he'd been cuckolded. He couldn't bear it, he said. He would rather be dead. That's what he told everyone and that's how he ended up. Dead. And he's been that way for six months."

"I doubt his condition will change," Prinny muttered.

"Cuckolded?" The Earl of Bowlingbroke scratched his powdered wig and frowned his displeasure.

"Might we inquire by whom?" Sir Steven asked.

Lady Alex paused dramatically. "By Sir Nigel Pennyworthy," she said, at length.

"That's a lie!" Sir Nigel shrieked.

Prinny's mouth formed an oval of slow comprehension while Bowlingbroke stared in bewilderment.

Sir Steven said, "So, it was *you* who persuaded Herbert Smythfield's wife to inform the Prince that Bowlingbroke was a French sympathizer."

"You devil!" Bowlingbroke accused the ashen-faced Pennyworthy.

"Not true!" Sir Nigel responded, his expression frantic.

Prinny stroked his wobbly chin. "Now that I think on it, it did seem a bit strange to me that Mrs. S. would pass on such a silly piece of gossip. Sir Nigel, you have a heap of explaining to do!"

But before the Prince could say more, Sir Nigel turned and bolted from the room. Picking up her skirts, the lady in red fled behind him.

Prinny stared after the two in amazement while Bowlingbroke shook his head.

Eugenia tugged a little harder on Steven's elbow. This time, he squeezed her fingers and bent his head to her. Pressing her lips to his neck, she whispered, "I'm afraid I'm the one who passed that kidnapping note to the earl. Jane asked me to. I didn't know what was in it!"

He looked sharply at her, questioning.

Quickly, she continued. "You see, Jane and Robert are in love! Yes, I know it sounds ridiculous, but they are, and they asked me to pass that letter to Jane's father. I thought it was a declaration of Delaroux's intentions for Jane. How was I to know—"

"I think I am beginning to understand." Steven's features relaxed, but there was still quite a bit of mystery to clear up. He pinched the bridge of his nose and addressed the earl. "Your Grace, I believe I can explain the origin of the kidnapping note you are holding in your hand."

"No, it is I who must explain." Lord Robert Delaroux, unmasked, strode into the room.

Jane, her eyes red-rimmed, her mask long since disposed of, walked beside him. She took a deep breath, looked her father straight in the eye, and announced, "We are in love, Father, and we plan to be married."

"Jane! You cannot mean it!" But the Earl of Bowlingbroke saw immediately that his daughter had deserted him. His face turned even paler than his powdered wig and his body trembled with emotion. The silver lace of his shirt cuffs trembled as he clutched at his chest. "Dear God, I do not believe my heart can withstand this shock!"

The Countess of Bowlingbroke smiled benevolently as she entered the room. "You will survive, dear."

"Sally, do you see what has happened? She has fallen in love with that, that—"

Calmly removing her mask, the countess replied, "Yes, I see, and I fear there is very little we can do to change the course of Jane's destiny. She is very like you in one respect, Your Grace. That is, she is very stubborn."

"I have already confessed everything to Mother," Jane said sheepishly. "She told me I must explain it all to you now, Father."

"No, I must explain." Robert drew himself up and bravely faced his future father-in-law. " 'Twas my madcap scheme. I must bear the responsibility for it."

"Your scheme?" the earl stammered.

Lord Delaroux explained his plan. He had penned an anonymous note and enlisted Eugenia to pass it to the earl. "I thought if I could demonstrate my good intentions to you . . ." His voice faltered.

"He meant to stage her rescue," Sally Bowlingbroke interjected. "To prove his worthiness to you."

"In the end, all I have done is upset and frighten you,"

Robert said. "The truth of the matter is, I am not worthy. It was a foolish, foolish plan, and one that has cost me dearly. There is no possibility that you will consent to allowing me to marry your daughter, I understand that now."

"Then why are you confessing?" boomed the earl.

"Because I cannot stand idly by while you accuse my friend Sir Steven of committing such an egregious crime. Steven would never do such a thing! He would not!"

Silence muffled the room as Lord Delaroux's words seeped into everyone's understanding. Prinny cleared his throat nervously while Sally Bowlingbroke linked her arm through the earl's and blinked back tears. Jane and Robert steadfastly held one another's hands, but the expression on Robert's face was one of untold miseries and regret.

After an interminable length, the earl muttered, "Oh, hell, if the two of you are that deeply in love—"

"Then you have our blessing," the countess finished.

Gratitude flushed Lord Robert Delaroux's face. A wide grin suddenly flashed on his face. Releasing Lady Jane, he bounded over to the earl and threw his arms around him. "Thank you, Your Grace!"

"Oh, for God's sake, get off me!" the earl cried.

Nervously, Delaroux backed away, nodding and bowing as if he were a medieval serf paying obeisance to his overlord.

Jane rose on her tiptoes and clapped her hands. "Oh, thank you, Father!" Then she, too, threw her arms around the man, adding to his fluster.

Eugenia noted that the countess dashed a tear from her cheek. Watching the poignant family scene, she felt a twinge of envy. Why couldn't her family love one another with so much passion and devotion?

"Are you all right, dear?" Lady Alex asked Eugenia.

"Yes, Mother. And there is something I must tell you,

too." Eugenia couldn't bear the charade any longer. "It is about the message you received tonight. From Father. Well, from a man pretending he was Father."

"Do you mean the message Sir Steven handed to me?"

"You knew it was I?" Steven asked.

"You make an excellent Julius Caesar," Lady Alex said. "But not nearly so fine an emperor as Albert. He has the pompousness to carry it off; you don't. Did you really think to fool me, though?"

"Mother!"

Lady Alex laughed heartily. "Good heavens, I would know your father anywhere, Eugenia. Were you that desperate to force a reconciliation that you would resort to trickery in order to get us in the same room?"

"I thought if you knew how Father felt—"

"But these are not his words," Lady Alex protested, holding up the note Caesar had passed to her.

"No, and these are not yours." Sir Albert Terrebonne's voice turned everyone's head. He waved his letter like a flag, then entered the room and stood beside his wife. "I passed a gentleman in the corridor who seemed in an awfully big hurry to escape this library. Has something tragic happened in here?

"I believe we have unmasked a double-crosser," Sir Steven said. "Though I have yet to comprehend his motive."

Eugenia held her breath, mesmerized by the prickly friction that passed between her parents. She vaguely heard Sir Steven talking to Bowlingbroke and the Prince, but her attention was captured by the soulful glances Sir Albert and Lady Alex exchanged, and by the invisible crackling that ricocheted from one to the other.

Tentatively, Sir Albert cupped his wife's shoulders and drew her to him. Eugenia strained to hear all that was said, but her parents' whispers were low and intimate. She thought she heard her father make an apology, but such a thing seemed outside the realm of possibility. When she heard her mother murmur the very same sentiment, Eugenia was quite certain she was fantasizing. Her parents had never before, as far as she knew, admitted their foibles or apologized for anything. Whatever was happening between them now was entirely unprecedented.

They moved to the other side of the room, away from earshot. Eugenia craned her neck to watch them.

But Sir Steven wrapped a protective arm around her and held her close to him. "I think they would like to be alone."

"But—" Eugenia's protest was stilled by Steven's penetrating gaze. Merely by looking at her, he held her in his thrall.

Behind him, the Prince sighed and said, "Back to the party for me. I believe I saw Mrs. Fitzherbert disguised as Joan of Arc."

The Earl of Bowlingbroke, obviously fatigued, said, "Fifteen minutes to midnight. Come, Sally, we must return to our posts." Awkwardly, he shook hands with Lord Delaroux again, then led his wife from the room.

Turning to Eugenia, Jane offered a watery smile. "I do apologize, Genie. To put you in such a compromising position was unforgivable. But can you? Forgive me, I mean?"

Eugenia left the safety of Steven's embrace just to take her friend's hands and peer into a pair of pretty limpid eyes. "Oh, Jane! Of course, I forgive you. I only want you to be happy."

"I am." The ladies kissed each other's cheeks and hugged.

Delaroux, still grinning like a Cheshire cat, extended his hand to Steven. "Sorry, old man. Didn't mean to cause you so much trouble."

Steven grimaced as his hand was pumped a bit too enthusiastically. "Quite all right, Robert."

"I hope there will be no hard feelings—" Delaroux's gaze shot quickly to Lady Jane.

"Oh, no! None at all. To the victor goes the spoils. The best man has won, and all that. On the contrary, Robert, I wish you and Jane nothing but happiness."

Relief spread across Delaroux's features. "Thank you," he said, his hand on the small of Lady Jane's back.

"Don't forget our wager, Genie." Jane smiled cryptically as she allowed Delaroux to lead her from the library.

"We are going now, too," Lady Alex announced, her arm linked in Sir Albert's. The couple radiated as they crossed the room, gliding across the threshold behind Lord Delaroux and Lady Jane. Over her shoulder, Lady Alex called, "And, Genie, darling, next time you decide to play matchmaker, I suggest you work on a couple who are not already in love!"

Sir Albert drew up short, turned, and from the corridor, faced Eugenia. "You see, dear, we always have been in love and we always will be."

"But I thought—" Eugenia shrugged her shoulders, thoroughly confused.

Lady Alex explained. "You thought we did not love one another because we fought. But dear girl, we fought because we were so deeply in love."

"Deeply in love, but too thick-headed to admit it," added Sir Albert. "It took desperate measures to bring us back together. I suppose your actions gave us both the incentive we needed to talk things out, Genie. For that, we will always be eternally grateful to you." He looked at Steven. "And to you."

Tamping down her emotions, Eugenia blurted, "But why? Why didn't you talk things out before? It doesn't make sense, Mother! I've spent so many years worrying about you!"

"Your father wounded my feelings, Eugenia." A wistful, faraway expression replaced Lady Alex's smile. But then she looked at her husband and, slowly, her smile returned. "But that was many years ago. I am sorry for the pain we caused you."

"Years wasted," Sir Albert said. He blew his daughter a kiss. "If we have taught you anything, I hope it is that you should never let the sun go down on a fight with your beloved. Cherish him, Genie. Yes, *him*. Oh, you can't deny you love him."

"And he loves you." Lady Alex chuckled. "Do you think a pair of lovebirds are blind to that?"

Eugenia's insides melted as her parents faded down the hallway toward the wild laughter and frivolity spilling from the ballroom. The masquerade would soon crescendo at midnight. And then, what would become of her and Steven? Was the emotion she saw in his gaze *real?* Or had her love for him distorted her perception?

Confused beyond anything, Eugenia pressed the back of her hand to her eyes and staved off the tears. She didn't want to cry or appear weak. It wasn't in her character.

She didn't want Sir Steven St. Charles to pity her.

But she was tired of pretending she was happy for others when she was aching for someone to love *her*. And she was weary of smiling when she didn't feel like it.

Gazing into Steven's pale blue gaze, Eugenia finally said what she'd been wanting to say from the day she met him. "I love you, Steven. Desperately. Painfully. And so *wholly* that I no longer know who I am."

At five minutes to midnight, Lady Clarissa experienced a strange preternatural sensation. Standing on the edge of the dance floor, her hooded cape and mask uncomfortably warm, a chill streaked up her spine. With a shudder, she shifted the bulk of her straw basket, an accoutrement of her Mother Goose costume.

Surprisingly, the basket had been a great convenience. Its weight made her back hurt, and she felt a pang of guilty pleasure as she thought of its contents, but the glow she'd obtained from the punch she had drunk warded off any serious misgivings she might have had about increasing her collection of doorstops at the Bowlingbrokes' expense.

Turning, she searched for the source of her inexplicable chill. As her gaze scanned the crowd, her alarm grew. There were Louis XVI and Marie Antoinette, masked and regal in their presumptions of grandeur, entering the ballroom hand in hand. By now everyone recognized the earl and the countess. Lord Bowlingbroke's domineering manner and Sally's queenly demeanor were simply impossible to disguise.

But where were Lady Eugenia and Sir Steven?

Their absence alone could not justify Lady Clarissa's nervousness, but when she spotted Jane and Robert, then Alex and Albert, reentering the party, she worried.

She had *been* worried about Eugenia for days, if the truth be told. The girl's infatuation with Sir Steven was so obvious that it was painful to watch. Yet Steven's intentions had remained unclear. Though he appeared helplessly attracted to Eugenia, something undercut his emotions and restrained him from expressing his feelings. Clarissa had guessed and theorized as to the cause of Steven's repression, but she had no clue whether he would triumph in the struggle with his own demons.

Dashie's appearance in the corridor outside the ballroom nearly set her hair on end. Gasping, Lady Clarissa watched as her faithful little dog, unleashed, unsupervised and unprotected, trotted toward the ballroom. Immediately, Clarissa crossed the floor and headed for the hallway. But when she reached down to pick up Dashie, the dog turned and ran away.

"Oh, you little rascal!" Clarissa trundled after him, her basket slowing her down, her back aching.

The old dachshund was uncharacteristically spry. She ran the length of the hall, then stopped outside the library doors. With her tongue hanging to one side, she wagged her tail, then looked through the open doors and back at Aunt Clarissa.

Clarissa followed, her senses alert. She'd lived with that dog too long to ignore the signals it was sending.

Steven gathered Eugenia into his arms, inhaling her scent, pulling her warmth into his bones. His difficulty with words hampered him. Expressing his emotions did not come naturally for him, but for the first time since he could remember, he wanted this woman to understand what she meant to him. His willingness to admit he needed her frightened him, and he feared it would frighten her, too. She would skitter away if she knew the depth of his love or the neediness of it. But there was no turning back now. Steven loved Eugenia, and now he couldn't rest until he added words—and a promise—to that emotion.

She touched his lips, his face, his eyes. "What is it?" she whispered. "Tell me, love."

"Eugenia." He nuzzled her neck, burying his nose in the loose tendrils of chestnut hair that curled on her nape. His words, like his emotions, were only for her. "I love you. I need you."

A tiny cry of pleasure escaped her lips and she wound her arms around his back.

He smiled. Dear God, it felt so good!

Then their lips met and they kissed deeply, oblivious to the world around them.

The blood-curdling battle cry that sounded from behind them rudely shattered the moment.

Eugenia's brain reacted slowly. In one instant, her body was melting into Steven's embrace, and in the next, he roughly pushed her away. A blur of roiling velvet on the other side of the room caught her attention. Then, from behind the curtains burst an unmasked blond man clad in medieval garb, a huge sword clutched in his hand.

Somewhere in the house, a clock chimed midnight and a great roar erupted in the ballroom. Applause, laughter, and shouting filtered down the hallway. As did an explosion of yapping. Stunned, Eugenia stared at Dashie galloping across the room to attack the blond invader.

The man, his sword glinting in the candlelight, surged toward Steven.

Unarmed, Steven made a quick step to the side, and the man plunged past him. Skidding to a stop just in front of the library doors, the man turned and faced Steven.

"You're a dead man, now, St. Charles," he growled, brandishing his sword. "You tried to ruin me, but you could not. I'll not have you trying again."

Steven's smile was transformed to a smirk. "So. You and Sir Nigel are compatriots. It all makes sense now, Fitzie. No wonder Nigel refused to accept my report when I discovered you were a French spy. He harbors French sympathies, too!"

"It is only a matter of time, now, St. Charles. Bonaparte will rule the world!"

"We shall see." Much to Eugenia's surprise, Steven calmly folded his arms across his chest. "There are just a few minor details that I do not understand. Why did Sir Nigel wish to plant a seed of suspicion in Prinny's mind about Bowlingbroke?"

"Bowlingbroke was growing too powerful in his influence with the Prince. Nigel meant to change all that."

"Ah, yes." Steven stroked his chin. "A good plan—Nigel would divert the Prince's suspicions from himself and direct them toward a totally innocent man. But why bring me into the picture? I was all but finished in the spy business."

The man Steven called Fitzie laughed cruelly. "Just so. But Nigel saw the opportunity to bring me back into the fold. You see, you did discredit me when you accused me of being a Bonapartist, St. Charles. You couldn't prove it, and everyone concluded that you made the charge out of bitterness and jealousy. Catherine loved me more than she ever loved you, after all. Everyone in Mayfair knew you'd been cuckolded."

Eugenia's gaze flew to Steven's. His expression was unreadable, but his body bespoke no tension. Given the weapon that Fitzie was waving at him, Eugenia couldn't comprehend Steven's equanimity. Then she looked back at Fitzie—and saw the hem of Mother Goose's red cap puddled just outside the library doors.

"So, Nigel thought to rehabilitate your reputation by ruining mine, is that it?"

Nodding, Fitzie turned the sword in his hand so that the sharp tip of his traced a pattern in the air. "Lady Catherine was to lure you into a compromising situation tonight. Prinny would catch you with her—"

"Did she even plan to cry rape, Lord Fitzhaven? How exceedingly clever," Steven said.

"Your credibility would be irreparably damaged, and the Prince would know that your previous report concerning me wasn't worth the paper it was written on. I was to return to Mayfair and the Crown's good graces without a hint of taint on my credentials. The Prince would henceforth never question my trustworthiness again."

"A fine plan!" Steven cried. "Except that it didn't work."

"And that is why I must kill you now." Fitzhaven hefted his sword, tightened his grip, and took a step forward.

Eugenia raised her hands to her mouth and stifled a scream.

Aunt Clarissa, straw basket hooked over her elbow, slipped over the threshold, and crept stealthily behind Fitzhaven.

Steven saw it all, shrugged, scooped Dashie from the floor, and said, "Well, old girl, I believe you have made a friend for life." The dog replied with a squirm and a wriggle and a sloppy lick to Steven's jaw.

Startled and confused by the merry laughter that burst from Steven's lips, Fitzhaven paused.

And never saw what hit him.

Aunt Clarissa swung hard, clanking the blond villain at the back of his head with a doorstop she later confessed was purloined from the Bowlingbrokes' fancy water closet.

ONE MONTH LATER
GRETNA GREEN, SCOTLAND

"You've won the bet, Genie." Taking Eugenia's arm, Lady Jane drew her aside.

The day was sunny and warm, a perfect day for a double wedding. Gazing at the small country chapel from which she'd just emerged, Eugenia smiled—sincerely and from her heart. There was no pretense in her smile now.

"I don't want to be away from my husband for very long, Jane. Steven and I are leaving in just a few minutes. We want to be alone."

"I understand, dear, so do we! But the wager! You have won."

Eugenia looked over her shoulder. Sir Steven stood on the church steps amid a path of rose petals strewn by Aunt Clarissa, the Terrebonnes, and the Bowling-brokes. Meeting her gaze, he smiled. Then Lord De-laroux touched him on the arm and spoke in hushed conspiratorial tones. Both men laughed heartily.

A flood of warmth flowed through Eugenia's veins. Turning to Jane, she said, "But the bet is not important now. Even though I must say I had the best time of my life trying to win it. I suppose I could extract my winnings from you, Jane, but I would only demand that you kiss the man you love, Lord Delaroux."

"Call him *Robert,*" Jane replied with a giggle. "And I shall kiss him anyway, no matter our wager."

"Where on earth did he get that purple waistcoat, Jane?"

"Oh, I don't know. Isn't it atrocious? Father nearly fainted!" Strolling back, Jane linked her arm through Eugenia's. "But do you know something, Genie? I wouldn't change a thing about him. Not a hair on his head—"

"He wouldn't let you."

"I love him exactly the way he is."

Eugenia understood completely. "And I love Steven," she said as the two rejoined the small gathering that spilled from the chapel and milled about the carriages. Their husbands approached them, each taking his own bride by the hand, both men looking vastly pleased and proud.

The Bowlingbrokes and the Terrebonnes hugged the happy couples, then waved them adieu as the carriages rumbled down the road, southward, toward London for a brief holiday before embarking on a three-month long honeymoon in the British West Indies. According to Sir

Steven St. Charles, the Continent was still far too dangerous a place to begin married life.

Sighing his relief, he settled on the leather squabs inside the carriage. Then he wrapped his arm around his wife's shoulder and drew her close to him.

Thinking of his love for her, he couldn't resist a chuckle.

She looked up, touched his lips, and whispered, "Why are you laughing, Steven?"

"Because I am so absurdly happy," he replied, kissing her. "And because now that I know you love me, it is finally safe to laugh."

AUTHOR'S NOTE

Although boxing and sparring matches were popular Regency past times, The Pugilistic Club was not actually in existence until 1814.

More Zebra Regency Romances

Put a Little Romance in Your Life With
Constance O'Day-Flannery

The Queen of Romance
Cassie Edwards